I0600485

THE TRUTHS THAT TETHER

BOOK THREE

a QZ Regency Mystery

SANDRA & TAYLOR PREISLER

Copyright © 2025 by Sandra & Taylor Preisler

ISBN (ebook): 979-8-9900489-9-7

ISBN (Paperback): 979-8-9929861-0-5

ISBN (Hardcover): 979-8-9929861-2-9

All rights reserved.

No part of this book may be reproduced in any form or by any electronic or mechanical means, including information storage and retrieval systems, without written permission from the author, except for the use of brief quotations in a book review.

Without limiting the author's exclusive rights, any unauthorized use of this publication to train generative artificial intelligence (AI) technologies is expressly prohibited.

This book is a work of fiction. Any references to historical events, real people, or real places are used fictitiously. Other names, characters, places, and events are products of the author's imagination, and any resemblance to actual events, places or persons, living or dead, is entirely coincidental.

First Edition.

Cover Design by Sandy Robson.

Library of Congress Control Number: 2025905979

For Ken, husband and father. Thank you for being the kind of man who believed wholeheartedly the women in your life could accomplish all that they dreamed. And so we did.

~

In memory of Gloria
Our inspiration for Brutus

London 1811

Chapter One

L ord Graham Coleville. Your father was Lord Graham Coleville, viscount-to-be and heir to the Coleville estate.

Theo's words echoed in Quinton Huxley's skull still, days after his visit with the dowager. Theodosia Bexley had proven helpful many times in Quinton's career as an inquiry agent, but with those words she had fundamentally changed his life. All without realizing the extent, because she didn't have the additional piece of key knowledge he had recently gained from a murderer's final confession.

Quinton stared off into the middle distance, his fingers drumming rhythmically against the surface of his desk as he allowed his thoughts to drift aimlessly. He couldn't remember how long he'd been sitting there—a few minutes? An hour? A day? Time seemed an abstract and faraway concept, as if he was disconnected from his physical body.

A loud knock at the door interrupted his musings, and he started, the shadows shrinking to the dark corners of his mind as he brought himself back to the present. A dull ache in his shoulders and a dryness in his throat made themselves acutely known. "Come in," he said, clearing his throat and rolling his shoulder in an attempt to loosen up.

The door opened with a cold blast of winter air to reveal Lady Zoe Demas, whom Quinton had been expecting, her massive dog Brutus clinging to her side like a shadow. Zoe's dark curls tumbled down as she removed her bonnet, her nose and cheeks pink from the cold and her blue eyes sparkling as her gaze met his. While those brilliant eyes usually captivated him in their light, Quinton couldn't help but glance towards her cheekbone, where an ugly bruise was beginning to fade from black to a dull yellow. His stomach churned at the unpleasant reminder of their recent ordeal. A glove covered a deep cut in her left hand, but Quinton was painfully aware of its presence.

"Good afternoon, Mr. Huxley."

"Good afternoon, Lady Demas."

Following close behind was her lady's companion, Mary Fletcher—a girl Quinton had known well in their childhood. He had been, and remained to this day, good friends with her older cousin John. Quinton could still picture little Mary running after them, determined not to be left behind. Now of course she was not a little child grasping at her cousin's shirtsleeves, but rather a young woman of nearly twenty.

At a glance, the two women did not look much alike. Mary's curls were much tighter than Zoe's, tied back into a tight bun, and her skin was considerably darker, the result of her distant African heritage. In their eyes Quinton saw the biggest difference—Mary's were a dark brown, deep and thoughtful, while Zoe's blue were generally full of light and mischief. However, despite these differences, Quinton had rarely seen two companions whose spirits were more in harmony.

Although today an almost imperceptible distance lingered in the space between them . . . as if a thin curtain hung there, separating their usual bond. But perhaps Quinton was imagining it, projecting his own troubles onto them. He shook his head, attempting to clear away any remaining cobwebs.

"How are you then, Quinton?" asked Mary. Her smile was

glib, but Quinton could see the genuine concern in her expression.

He didn't blame her. The past few weeks had been trying upon them all, but the past few months had taken a toll on his soul few would envy. Less than two days since, the man who had murdered his mother eighteen years earlier had been hung from the gallows, found guilty of the murders of at least four other women besides—not to mention the kidnapping and attempted murder of both Zoe and Mary.

In the months prior, Quinton had fallen into a deep depression of spirit and will, brought on by the thought that his mother's killer would never be caught or brought to justice—that he had failed her when it mattered most, again. The void of despair had nearly swallowed him whole, and in the process caused a divide in his friendship with Zoe. They had managed to repair that fragile friendship over the course of an investigation into a recent murder, but in the process Quinton had come to a very painful realization—that he was hopelessly in love with her. At least, it had been painful because such a love could never be more than a fantasy. She was a lady and he was just the illegitimate son of a dead actress. But since then, Quinton had learned something else . . . something that could change everything. A truth he did not know how to process, so it sat heavy on his mind, weighing him down until such time as he came to a decision.

All of this must have shown in his face in some way, to prompt Mary's question. And his delay in answering would certainly belie his response: "I am well, Mary." Quinton managed a slight smile, though he did not imagine it reached his eyes.

Zoe, normally so keenly observant, appeared to miss the silent communication between him and her lady's maid. "And what of your visit with Felix Fairfax?"

Quinton swallowed hard, avoiding her gaze. "He said many words without saying anything of meaning. I am not ready to speak of it."

A pause settled as the two women exchanged a small glance,

the imperceptible curtain suddenly lifted. They thought themselves very clever and discreet, but Quinton could tell when they were conspiring.

"Very well," said Zoe. Apparently they had come to the silent conclusion that they would leave it alone for now. "Perhaps we should discuss my cousin's case then, before he arrives."

As if the mention of him had summoned the devil, another knock echoed through the room.

Quinton briefly wondered if there was any way he could feign an illness to get out of this meeting—perhaps a headache or stomach cramps—but then dismissed the frivolous thought just as quickly. "Come in," he finally said with reluctance.

This time the door opened to reveal Alexander Dovefield, Zoe's stepcousin. The man was not one whose company Quinton sought out, but today he didn't have the luxury of choosing his companions. Alexander was there as a client, and more importantly, Zoe had asked him to do this favour for her. No matter his feelings for Alexander, Quinton would do anything for her.

"I see I'm the only one missing from my own meeting." What Alexander perhaps meant to be a glib icebreaker came across as snarky and insecure—or that could have just been Quinton's interpretation.

Raised with privilege and entitlement most would envy, Alexander was the first son of Baldwin Dovefield, Zoe's stepfather's oldest brother. Baldwin held the family title of baron, meaning Alexander was one day destined to inherit that title and all that came with it. He was the type of young man who drifted and charmed his way through life, knowing all the rules of society but having the freedom to break them as he chose.

Zoe had given Quinton a summary of her relationship with her cousin before. Her mother had married into the Dovefield family when Zoe was nine years old and Alexander was not much older. They were young enough to have potentially bonded as cousins, but temperaments and family discord had decided otherwise. Baldwin hadn't welcomed his brother's choice of French bride and stepdaughter into their family with open arms, and Alexander had followed suit. Quinton knew, from both personal experience and reputation, that Alexander was snobbish and pretentious and dismissive of his stepcousin, even after the rest of the family had accepted the situation.

Given how Alexander felt about Zoe, the fact that he had gone to her for help told Quinton the man was truly desperate. Whatever the obnoxious man was caught up in, it must be serious, though Quinton struggled to find any sympathy. He suspected that whatever problems the baron-to-be was facing were likely the result of Alexander's own actions.

Brutus seemed equally unimpressed, perhaps sensing Quinton's disdain, as he rose from his place at Zoe's side and turned his massive head towards Alexander. He made no sound, just stood and stared without blinking at the man.

His expression uneasy, Alexander took a step back. The dog was big as a small horse, his shaggy black hide covered in old scars hearkening back to his days as a bull-baiting dog. Quinton allowed that Brutus could make a braver man than Alexander stop in his tracks. That was why Quinton liked having the beast at Zoe's side.

"Call off your beast, Zoe," said Alexander, a slight tremor in his voice.

With an impatient sigh, Zoe reached out to pat Brutus on the back, murmuring a reassurance. At her touch the dog visibly relaxed, returning to lay down at her feet. As far as Quinton was concerned, Brutus could do as he pleased after his lifesaving actions in regard to Zoe during the recent incident in which she had received that fading bruise. But those thoughts didn't need to be voiced out loud at the moment.

"Take a seat, Mr. Dovefield," Quinton said with a sigh.

Clearing his throat while continuing to eye Brutus, Alexander did as he was told for once. "It's Lord Dovefield, actually."

Quinton snorted at that. The statement was an echo to the

past—maybe Alexander and Zoe had more in common than they thought. "Why don't you go ahead and tell me about this situation . . . Mr. Dovefield."

Alexander shifted in his seat, clearly annoyed at the deliberate word choice but apparently deciding to let it go for now. "Very well. I assume Zoe has filled you in on the basics?"

Quinton glanced at Zoe. "All she said is that you got yourself into some kind of trouble."

Avoiding his gaze, Zoe shrugged. "I thought you'd want to hear it direct from the source."

"Mm. How considerate." Quinton turned back to Alexander. "Well?"

Shifting once again, Alexander's cheeks began to turn red. "Are you familiar, Mr. Huxley, with the gambling hell on Bell Street?"

A rough start already. "It's not an establishment I frequent, but yes, I am familiar with it."

"Well, you see, I have been a regular patron for some time—"

"Yes, your reputation proceeds you." Quinton made a circular gesture. "Just get to the point."

Alexander cleared his throat as his red complexion darkened. "Very well. There's a girl who works there—a Miss Katie Shorn. She's only been there for a few months, but I could tell right away there was something different about her. She was very shy and gentle and polite, not like the usual girls who end up in places like that." Alexander cleared his throat again. "Eh, regardless, one day I saw her crying in the alley. Now, I don't make a habit of inserting myself into other people's business, but she just seemed so vulnerable, and she was always friendly with me, so I asked her what was wrong."

"Uh-huh." Quinton resisted the urge to roll his eyes. "And what did Miss Shorn say?"

"She said her father was in debt to the owner of the establishment and she was being forced to work off his debt. But a girl like that didn't belong in a place like that, so I offered her some financial assistance."

"Mm-hmm." Quinton leaned back in his chair, clarity dawning on him. "And I assume she adamantly refused your offer of assistance?"

"Well yes, but only out of concern for my own well-being—"

"Yes, yes, yes. But you, being a gentleman, naturally insisted on giving her the money anyway?"

Alexander squinted. "Yes, as a gentleman—"

Quinton held up his hand. "I see where this is going. You gave her the money, but then she came back to you later for more. You gave it to her again, and then again, and again, in an endless cycle because there's always one more payment she needs or interest that's accumulated, or her father just can't stay away from the tables. By now she's bled you dry and you can't ask your father for a larger allowance without admitting what you need it for."

"Well . . . I mean . . . first of all, bled dry isn't accurate. Katie—Miss Shorn—is in real danger. These are very dangerous people—"

"Mr. Dovefield, I'm going to stop you there." Quinton sighed, leaning back in his chair. "This isn't what you think it is. The owner of the establishment is using this so called 'Katie Shorn' to scam rich young noblemen out of their allowances. They played on your instinct to protect a damsel in distress, and you bought it. Fortunately, it doesn't seem like any real harm was done. I would advise you to cut ties and find a new gambling hell. Furthermore—"

"*Quinton.*" Zoe cut him off, her tone sharp. "There is a bit more to it, if perhaps you'd care to listen for more than ten seconds at a time."

He blinked, surprised at the reprimand. "I apologize, Zoe. Please, Mr. Dovefield, continue."

"Thank you." Leaning forward, Alexander pressed his hands together, his expression serious. "Mr. Huxley, I don't think you understand. I know it sounds a bit far-fetched, but the danger is real. I've seen Katie with bruises on her face and arms, and I know the fear was genuine. These goons have even threatened me."

Quinton sat up straighter. "What do you mean they've threatened you?"

"At White's, one of them showed up just last week. I thought he was going to kill me right there."

"Well, that is unusual." Quinton frowned. He himself had been at said gentlemen's club last week and had a vague memory of Alexander in a very intense conversation with someone. He hadn't paid much attention at the time, but if what Alexander was saying was true, Quinton wondered how such low-level criminals had gained access to the exclusive club. Quinton only had access thanks to . . . a patron.

Before his thoughts could wander too far down that trail again, Alexander spoke. "But all of that is beside the point. It's not why I am here."

A long silence stretched out before them until Quinton realized Alexander was waiting for him to ask the question. He let out a deep breath, struggling to hide his annoyance. "Very well, I'll bite." Quinton reminded himself he was doing this for Zoe. "Why are you here, then?"

"Because Katie is missing." Alexander slumped back in his chair, running his fingers through his hair. "She hasn't shown up to work in four days, and no one has seen her anywhere. I think they've done something to her, and I don't know what to do. I can you assure you, Mr. Huxley, I would not be here unless I had nowhere else to turn."

Quinton wasn't so easily convinced. "Well then it sounds like your problems are solved. Why do you care what happens to this girl . . . unless . . ." A ridiculous thought occurred to Quinton. "You're not actually under some delusion that you're in love with her, are you?"

Alexander scoffed, but avoided eye contact. "Of course not. Love has nothing to do with it. But that doesn't mean I'm indifferent to her plight. I don't want harm to come to her."

The words appeared to be said in earnest, much as Quinton had trouble believing them. He glanced at Zoe. Her feelings on the matter were hard to read, her expression neutral, but there was something in her eyes . . . like a dark cloud on the ocean's horizon. Quinton suspected she was thinking back to when they first met —to when a woman in her sphere had been in trouble. That time the danger had been realized by Zoe too late to alter the poor girl's fate. Whatever Quinton chose to do, he doubted Zoe would leave Katie Shorn's fate up to chance until she knew for certain where the truth lay.

"You said the gambling hell on Bell Street?" he asked with a sigh.

It appeared Quinton had little choice in the matter.

Chapter Two

Quinton was a man of his word. He did intend to investigate the so-called disappearance of Katie Shorn, but it would have to wait for the light of morning. He had another matter to attend to that night.

As he glanced down at the pocket watch in his hand, the light of the moon was bright enough to read the time. Just past midnight. Late for a social call, but discretion was key to Quinton's purposes for this visit. He slipped the watch back into his pocket. The familiar token had been with him his whole life, but the weight felt different now, heavier.

He needed to talk to someone about what he had learned, someone who could give him advice stemming from wisdom and objectivity rather than his own crushing anxiety. At the moment, his personal life was devoid of such an advisor. His friend Rory Stewart had often filled that role for him, but the resurrectionist wasn't currently in a fit state to offer support to someone else, having only recently been released from Newgate prison with physical and emotional wounds of his own to heal. The other choices in Quinton's life were his childhood friends John and

Charlie, but he wasn't ready to discuss this with them. Their opinions would only complicate the matter.

No, at the moment Quinton could only think of one man to trust with his newly discovered knowledge—barrister Hugh Dovefield.

Of course, Lord Dovefield brought a different set of complications to the table, considering his relation to Zoe. Even worse, Quinton suspected Hugh knew of his apparently poorly hidden feelings for Zoe. As progressive as Hugh was, the thought of the bastard son of an actress romantically pursuing his stepdaughter would surely not be well received, and understandably so. Not that Quinton would have pursued Zoe, whatever his feelings might be for her. In an irony wrapped in a conundrum, those very feelings for Zoe had prevented him from acting on them. He understood the firestorm that would rain down upon her should she became entangled with a man like himself.

Or, rather, the man Quinton had always thought himself to be. But now everything he thought he knew about himself had changed, and he needed Hugh to shed some light on the man he might soon become.

Taking a deep breath as he stood at the Dovefield manor entrance, Quinton raised the door knocker, then let it fall, listening to the sharp sound echo through the still night air. Moments later, Quaid, the Dovefield's loyal butler, opened the door and peered out at him. Quinton wondered briefly, as he had often done, if the impeccably dressed man ever slept.

"Is Lord Dovefield at home?" he asked, although he was fairly certain of the answer.

The terrible events of last year had brought a certain closeness between Lord Dovefield and Quinton—something akin to friendship—and Quinton had become acquainted with Hugh's evening routines. The lord usually spent the hour before midnight with his wife Simone, Zoe's mother. At this hour,

Quinton hoped he would be in his study preparing cases for court, as was his usual habit.

Quaid didn't appear surprised at Quinton's appearance. He simply nodded, stepping aside to allow Quinton entry and then led the way to the small alcove off the entry. "Please wait here," directed the butler.

Their relationship had certainly progressed. Quaid was part of the old brigade, believing in the strict boundaries between classes and the necessity of propriety. But recent happenings had changed a few perceptions, and apparently even Quaid had come around to the idea that present circumstances required a softening of those boundaries. Apparently one could teach old dogs new tricks. The butler was still a work in progress, but the progress was real.

Quaid reappeared before long, leading Quinton back to Hugh's study. The spacious room was comfortably furnished with a masculine feel to it, but functional. One thing Quinton had immediately respected about the lord was that the spines of the books which lined the wall were all cracked from use.

Upon seeing Quinton, Hugh set down his quill and smiled, motioning for Quinton to take a seat near the fire. He began the conversation in the usual way. "Whiskey?"

Quinton returned the smile and nodded, feeling himself start to relax. It was as much the comfort of the familiar custom as the alcohol, but he couldn't deny a glass of whiskey did a great deal to settle his nerves.

Once the drinks had been poured from the decanter, Hugh gestured for Quinton to take a seat in one of the armchairs by the fireplace. For a moment neither man spoke as they settled into their seats, staring into the flickering flames.

Hugh broke the silence first. "Fairfax?"

Grateful the subject was not danced around, Quinton took a fortifying sip before replying. "Yes. Fairfax. You know I spoke to him before the execution?"

"Indeed."

"I did not want to speak to him, but I knew there would be no second chances." Quinton paused, unsure how to continue.

Hugh spoke quietly. "But what he told you has shaken you?"

"Indeed." Quinton sighed, realizing there was no delicate way to say what he needed to say. "My father was a nobleman. I already suspected as much, but according to Fairfax, my father and mother were . . . married."

"Married?" Hugh coughed, nearly choking on his whiskey. "You believe him?"

Quinton turned back to the fire. "That's why he killed her." He took another sip of the fiery drink, the burning sensation warming his throat as it made its way down to his stomach, grounding him in the moment. "Fairfax said he had wanted to marry her—my mother. She wanted nothing to do with him and said she would never marry a noble. Fairfax went to sea for years, and when he returned, he saw me. Apparently my parentage is obvious." Quinton faltered slightly, but after a moment continued. "When he confronted my mother that night, she told him she had not just borne a nobleman's child, but had also married him. That's when Fairfax . . . killed her."

"My God." Hugh leaned back, absorbing the information. Quinton understood—it was a lot to swallow. Then he asked the question Quinton knew he would. "Assuming he's telling the truth, did he tell you who your father was?"

"He did not." Before Hugh could ask another question, Quinton continued, "But the dowager did."

"Theo?" Hugh laughed. "My sister does seem to know the threads of every tapestry out there, doesn't she?"

"Indeed she does."

"Hmm." Hugh took another sip. "So then I assume that's is why you're here? To seek legal counsel on your next steps?"

"I am at sixes and sevens about the whole thing, my lord. I'm not sure what my next steps even could be." Quinton sighed and downed the rest of his whiskey—this was the inevitable part of the conversation he had been dreading. "As it happens, I am the first son of a first son of a titled family. Not only am I legitimate, but I am heir of not an insignificant fortune."

Hugh stared at him, his mouth agape. He rose slowly, grabbing the decanter from the sideboard and refilling their glasses. This time he left the decanter on the table between them. His next words were uttered so quietly as he sunk back into the armchair, Quinton almost couldn't hear them. "This changes everything."

The understatement of the century, but it did encompass all of Quinton's feelings, both good and bad.

Hugh suddenly blinked, as if remembering where he was. "I apologize, Quinton. This comes as a shock to me, but I'm sure it must be even more so to you. I'm assuming if you're unsure of next steps, then you must have some concerns. Tell me about them."

As always, Hugh's insight had gone straight to the heart of it. Quinton took a moment to gather his thoughts, but once he started to speak, the words poured out. "I feel as though someone has opened me up, taken out all my insides, shaken then up in a bucket of broken glass, and then put them back." Quinton placed his glass on the table. "What if the people who have filled the role of family in my life feel somehow less now? Charlie's hatred of noblemen is no secret, and neither him nor John have quite got the look or the breeding the ton likes to have reflected back at them. Then of course there's the body snatcher recently on trial for murder who also happens to be one of my closest friends." Quinton sighed—just saying the next words was painful. "The people who mean the most to me cannot exist in the same world as an heir of a fortune. What if I gain everything, only to lose anything that actually matters? What if they think less of me, or too much of me? I don't think I could bear it." Quinton leaned back in his chair, running his fingers through his hair. He waited for Hugh to respond. He didn't have to wait long.

"You are a man of honour, Quinton." Hugh set his own glass down. "Many would happily throw away everything to embrace a life of luxury and prestige. But you know the truth—what you have now is worth more than any title or fortune. What you have now constitutes true riches."

Quinton said nothing in reply for a moment, but he felt the words make their way to his soul, warming his heart as they went. He was grateful Hugh understood. He could not trade what he had to gain what he was owed.

But the real question, the one which had been weighing on Quinton the most, pressing down on his rib cage like a vice until it felt like his bones might splinter was: could he have both?

Quinton took a deep breath. "In the spirit of honesty, my lord, I am not immune to the lure of wealth. To never have to worry about how to pay the rent or whether food is within one's means . . . of course there's an appeal. Not only that, but this could allow me to help the people I care about in tangible ways. And . . . if one day I choose to marry, it would change what I could offer that person as well. It would change the lives of my children and my children's children."

Hugh nodded slowly, and Quinton thought the keen barrister understood his meaning. "Those things are equally true." He hesitated. "Quinton, you know at this point that this is all supposition and we may be putting the cart a bit before the horse, but do you mind if I ask which family it is you're related to?"

"Of course." Quinton supposed there was no avoiding the reality. "The family is the Colevilles."

As Hugh gave a low whistle, he refilled their glasses again. "A well-off family, you're not wrong about that. If I recall correctly, the eldest son died in a riding accident some years ago—your father, apparently. He must not have told his family about his marriage, or your birth. Then when he died, your mother must have chosen to stay silent, for whatever reason. Then when she died, there was no one left to reveal the truth, either to you or to your relatives."

"I've come to the same conclusion." Quinton thought back to his childhood. "A great deal now makes sense to me. My mother used to insist I speak 'posh,' as we called it. Proper English. She taught me how to address the nobility, which fork to use at dinner, how to dance—and dance well, even at eleven. It makes sense if one day she planned to bring me to the attention of the Colevilles."

"Hmm." Hugh nodded. "She must have had a plan in mind. It's a shame we can't ask her."

Truer words had rarely been spoken. "She used to say I favoured my father in looks. Perhaps she was waiting for it to be undeniable, or perhaps she just wanted to keep me to herself for a little longer. She couldn't have known her days would be so short."

"Indeed." Hugh fell silent again, gazing into the fire, obviously deep in thought. As the flames began to die down, he stirred it alive with the poker, adding another two lumps of coal.

"I will tell you of the legalities," said Hugh after a few moments. "Should you choose to move forward and make a claim, you will require proof of the marriage. The present viscount and the second son, the surviving heir at this time, will naturally demand a marriage license. At this time you have none, I assume?"

Quinton shook his head. "I have a few trinkets from my mother I saved these years. And this watch she said was my fathers." He brought the watch from his pocket, staring at it and running his thumb across the engraved coat of arms. "But no legal documents."

Taking the watch from Quinton, Hugh held it up to the light, squinting to make out the worn engraving. "So that's how Theo traced your lineage."

"It took her some time," replied Quinton. "The watch must have been a family heirloom as the crest is not current. But she managed to track it down in some old book of hers."

There was something else—something he was holding back.

Of everything he had learned, this was the thing Quinton was having the hardest time reconciling. But the third glass of whiskey had done its job, loosening his thoughts and his tongue. "You want to know the strangest part of it all? I'm familiar with Lord Coleville—the heir, not the viscount. I rent my current home from him. In fact, he was one of my first clients." Quinton shook his head. "Now I can only assume he was aware all along I was the son of his dead brother, and having that knowledge . . . did nothing."

Hugh's response wasn't what Quinton had expected. "Well, I wouldn't say that's entirely true," said Hugh softly. "If your resemblance to your father was obvious to Fairfax, then you're correct that Coleville undoubtedly did the math as well. And then, having that knowledge, he then reached out to offer you employment as well as your residence. During your troubles in the previous year, as a landlord he was more than fair."

Heat crept up Quinton's neck at the reference to his particularly rough year, when he had wasted away in his own filth and drowned his sorrows in more alcohol than any human should consume in a lifetime. With the clarity of soberness, the whole thing was an embarrassment. But there was no denying the reality that his lack of work during that time had led to an unfortunate lack of funds, leading to an unfortunate amount of back rent being due to Coleville, which the lord in turn had been very patient about.

Hugh continued. "I'm not making excuses for the nobility. But in fairness to Coleville, any nobleman would be unlikely to acknowledge the bastard son of his brother in any official way. But he did try to care for you, in his own way, which is more than most."

Quinton sighed. Hugh wasn't wrong, though he was loath to admit it.

"His world will be shaken when this happens," Hugh added.

"If this happens." Quinton sighed again. "I am unsure of my next move, but you are correct about one thing. I can go back and forth as much as I please, but none of it matters without proof."

"Fancy a trip to Scotland, then?" Hugh hesitated. "It's likely what your . . . what your parents did."

Quinton could hardly blame him for the hesitation. He found it a struggle to view himself as a person with two parents, both of whom had an impact on his life. "Gretna Green?" he asked. "I've heard it mentioned, of course, but I don't know the details."

"The destination of choice for many a couple who want a quick and quiet ceremony." Hugh sat up straighter, a passionate light in his eye that Quinton had only ever seen when he was about to speak about legal matters. "Many people think the attraction of Gretna Green is that a couple does not need to be of legal age or have parental permission to marry. But Hardwicke's Marriage Act of 1753 did not simply make it impossible for young people under 21 to wed without permission of their parents. The act required the couple to wed in the parish of residence for one of them, and required the banns to be read or a license to be obtained. For people like your parents, well, they would have wanted to avoid those things. The public announcement of the banns alone would have allowed your father's family to raise objections to the marriage. But though England and Wales enforced the law, Scotland did not."

Quinton managed a laugh. "Sounds like Scotland. The only Scot I know is stubborn as can be."

"There is no arguing that," replied Hugh with his own chuckle. "Regardless, Gretna Green is a popular choice for these kind of things. If your parents were married there, it should be possible to find those records."

Quinton was silent for a few moments, staring into the fire, considering the information. Then he took the last of his whiskey in a single swallow. "Thank you, my lord." Quinton stood, straightening his waistcoat as he did. "I very much appreciate you taking the time to listen, and to offer me counsel. But I'm still coming to terms with this, and I don't think I'm ready to open up this particular box quite yet. Whatever answers are out there, I think I shall seek them later. Perhaps when I've had a bit less whiskey."

Hugh rose as well, extending a hand by way of goodbye. As Quinton grasped the lord's hand in his own, he reflected that he was indeed fortunate to have a personal barrister he could call on in the dead of night.

Chapter Three

Having opted for a simple woollen cloak as a barrier against the winter weather rather than her usual bonnet, Zoe pulled the hood lower, hoping no one would recognize her in the fading afternoon light. Not that she didn't have every right to be where she was. She just didn't want to deal with the consequences of having to explain herself if someone saw her prowling around on the edge of Whitechapel. Of course, said person would also have to explain what they were doing there . . .

Brutus walked by her side, his eyes watchful of their surroundings. Beside him strode Mary, and on Zoe's other side was Quinton. An odd group to the untrained eye, but to Zoe it felt . . . right. But they were not there simply for a turn about the slum—they had a particular destination in mind.

When they reached the doorway they were seeking, Quinton wasted no time in knocking loudly. Zoe was grateful when the door opened almost as quickly to reveal a pox-scarred boy, who in turn quickly ushered them inside out of the bitter cold and up the stairs. Along the way, Zoe inhaled the pleasant scent of curry and spices which always seemed to linger in the air here . . . not that she had been invited often.

At the top of the stairs was Charlie Modi, one of Quinton's oldest friends and a figure of substance in the criminal underworld of London. The gangster had been the most difficult of the inquiry agent's associates for Zoe to win over, as he had a deep and understandable distrust of toffs—his aristocratic British father had abandoned his two children and their Indian mother to the streets. Charlie hadn't taken an immediate shine to Zoe, nor she to him, for obvious reasons, but his icy regard seemed to have thawed some over the course of the recent events.

Despite his newfound tolerance, Charlie didn't seem overly pleased to see her there that afternoon. "What are they doing here?" he snapped at Quinton.

"They insisted," Quinton replied with a shrug.

Charlie scoffed and shook his head. "When a man can't control the women in his life—"

"What's this I hear about controlling women?" shouted a voice from the back room.

"Nothing, *maa!*" said Charlie quickly with a wince.

"That's what I thought." Emerging from the back room, the voice was revealed to belong to Katy Modi, Charlie's mother. At all of one-and-a-half meters, she was a force to be reckoned with. Even Charlie didn't talk back to her.

"Bad manners." Katy tsked and shook her head. "Bad manners to be so rude to our guests."

"Hello, Miss Modi." Zoe smiled, inclining her head in greeting.

"Hello, Miss Zoe. Now you and Mary make yourself at home, and don't you mind Charlie none." With a quick arm pat, Katy began to make her way to the kitchen. "I'll fix you some luncheon. Half-starved, you girls are . . ."

"I'll help you, Katy." Mary too disappeared into the kitchen, Brutus following closely behind, both likely hoping to get any extra treats Katy might have tucked away back there. Although Katy made no secret of her dislike for pets in general, Brutus was the exception. The beast would not be disappointed.

Quinton had been watching the whole exchange with an amused expression, but once Katy was out of the room, he took a seat in an oversize armchair. Zoe followed suit, while Charlie shook his head, still sighing and muttering under his breath.

Finally he too sat down, defeated by the majority. "Well, Quinton, why don't you tell me why you sent your deaf errand boy over here to arrange this meeting?"

Leaning back in his chair, Quinton gestured to Zoe. "She'll tell you."

Zoe was just as surprised as Charlie by this, but she wasn't going to let them know that. "Yes, of course." She cleared her throat. "My cousin has fallen into a bit of trouble, originating at a gambling hell over on Bell Street. We were wondering if you might be familiar with the establishment?"

"Mm." Charlie sized her up, an effect made more intimidating by the white scar which ran from his forehead down to his chin, blinding him in his left eye. "I know of it. What kind of trouble has the toff gotten himself into? He owe them?"

"Not in the traditional way," replied Zoe, avoiding the question. "Do you know the owner?"

Charlie grunted. "Miles O'Malley. I know him. He's not a man to cross, I'll tell you that."

"Do you think he's the kind of man who would force a daughter to work there to pay off a family member's debt?"

"I wouldn't say he's above nearly anything." Charlie squinted. "So a woman's involved in your cousin's trouble?"

Zoe took a few minutes to lay out Alexander's story, then Charlie leaned back, his expression thoughtful. "Well, I'm not saying Miles is above hurting a woman, but what you're describing sounds like a scheme. I'd wager this Katie is just fine— Miles probably moved her on to one of his other less reputable endeavours by now."

"That's what I told them," added Quinton, unhelpfully.

"Yes, well, for the sake of being thorough, I would still like to speak with this Mr. O'Malley." Zoe glared at Quinton, who was avoiding her gaze. "If the girl was being truthful, she could be in real danger."

Charlie shook his head. "Absolutely not. A gambling hell is no place for a respectable woman, and even if that weren't an issue, Miles is a nasty piece of work. If he even agreed to meet with you, he might as soon cut your throat as hear you out."

"Charlie—" began Quinton.

"No," he said more firmly. "When you're in my territory, you're afforded some protection. But I can't guarantee anything if you go wandering off on the other side of Whitechapel—mind you, your cousin had no business being there in the first place." Charlie ended his statement by pointing a finger at Zoe.

"Be that as it may, what's done is done." Zoe absentmindedly tugged at the glove covering her left hand, suddenly painfully aware of the stitches in her palm. "And I wasn't asking your permission."

Before Charlie could utter his no-doubt brutal retort, Quinton interjected. "Calm down, both of you. I agree, Charlie, this is likely a waste of time. But Alexander Dovefield has hired me to investigate, and that is what I intend to do. Can you set up a meeting with O'Malley, just for me?"

Zoe crossed her arms. "What about me?"

Quinton shook his head. "Charlie is right, you have no business associating with someone like Miles O'Malley. I will meet with him, and then I will tell you what he says."

It took all her years of noble training for Zoe not to snap back at him with one of several cruel responses that flashed through her mind. Instead, she kept her face still, uncrossed her arms, and sighed. "Very well. But I want a detailed report."

Inside, her blood boiled at the casual dismissal. Who was he to tell her what business she had? She once again quashed the desire to stand and give him a piece of her mind. But this wasn't the time. One thing was certain—Quinton had no authority over her, whatever he may think.

Chapter Four

On the way home, Zoe was still quite peevish over Quinton's dismissal. She walked quickly, with Mary and even Brutus hurrying to keep up.

After a number of blocks, Mary had finally had enough. "I don't know what has your drawers in a twist, my lady, but either you slow down or you walk alone," snapped her lady's companion as she pulled back on Brutus's leash. "Or perhaps we could hail a hackney—I don't know if you've heard of one before? It's a vehicle which takes one back and forth from a destination."

Mary's use of the term "my lady" told Zoe how peeved Mary herself was. Zoe reluctantly slowed down, taking a deep breath to cool her boiling blood, and let Mary and Brutus catch up.

Mary began to say something, but Zoe beat her to it. "You are right, Mary. Let us walk together."

"Ah. Thank you." Mary snapped her mouth shut, matching her pace to Zoe's. They carried on like that for a few minutes until Mary spoke again. "I was in the kitchen, Zoe, when whatever was decided was decided. What has you all in a tither?"

Zoe sighed. "Nothing raises my ire as much as a man deciding what I can and cannot do. Why is it that I can't go anywhere unchaperoned, and then even with you and Brutus by my side, I still can't go into most of the city without a man by my side? And yet the two of them can go where and when they please." Zoe gestured wildly in the general direction of the way they had come. "It drives me mad."

"Mm-hmm." Mary raised an eyebrow. "And, of course, your heart has nothing to do with this frustration?"

Zoe waved her hand dismissively. "I don't see the advantage of feelings of the heart, Mary. A married woman is owned by her husband. There can be no happiness down that road for me. I want my life to remain my own. So I do not put stock in my heart."

Mary didn't say anything, but as Zoe glanced over, she could see her companion roll her eyes. It should have added to Zoe's annoyance, but the truth was it made her feel a bit more normal to see Mary behaving as she used to.

They walked in silence after that, until the adrenaline wore off and Zoe finally broke down and hailed a hackney. This was how they seemed to be recently—everything was normal when they were out with others, with Zoe blazing ahead unabashedly and Mary being her usual cheeky self, but then when it was just the two of them, the energy shifted. As if the mask they wore around everyone else just slipped away.

Zoe flexed her left fingers; even though it was covered by her white glove, she was still acutely aware of the wound which ran from her palm up to her wrist. She could feel the stitches which bound the edges of the cut together, pulling her skin taut as it healed. Eventually the thread would be removed and all she would be left with was the scar.

Now, though, the wound was fresh, as were the memories of how Zoe got it. When the madman Felix Fairfax had kidnapped Zoe and Mary, she had used the hairpin knife Quinton had gifted her to cut the bindings from her wrists. But with her hands behind her back and fuelled by terror and desperation, she had little choice but to cut into her own flesh to sever the rope. In the moment it had hardly hurt—the only thing she could concentrate on was survival. Now the pain seemed a constant reminder, making sure that if she had even a moment of silence, her thoughts would drift back to that night.

That plus the fading bruise across Zoe's face, tender to the touch but not visible to her own eyes unless in front of a mirror. Sometimes she could even forget it was there.

Mary had escaped unscathed . . . physically. But since then it seemed to Zoe that she was different as well. Mary's soul had a heaviness, which Zoe felt in her own, and yet neither seemed able to voice it out loud.

In fairness, it had been less than two weeks since their brush with death. When Zoe had attempted to broach the subject with her mother, Simone had reassured her that time would heal all wounds. That was how it had been for them when they fled France. As time went on and they settled into their lives in England, the nightmares became less frequent, and all the terrible dread and trauma eventually faded into distant memory.

At least, that's what Zoe had thought. Now she wondered if perhaps that trauma had always been there, simmering just below the surface, waiting for an opportune moment to bubble up. She wondered if she was destined to be haunted by nightmares forever.

She wondered if Mary felt the same way, but she didn't know how to ask.

When they reached the Dovefield home, Mary headed for her own room and Zoe, still feeling unsettled, walked to the parlour to ring for tea. To her surprise, her mother was already there and tea was being served.

"Oh, hello, love." Simone smiled at seeing her. "Would you like me to pour you a cup?"

Zoe slumped down onto a chaise. "Yes, please."

"Rough day, *ma fille?*"

"It's been fine." As her mother poured the tea, Zoe briefly wondered if perhaps her poor attitude was an overreaction. She'd become more self-aware over the past year, and she knew she could be a bit selfish sometimes. When she found herself in a snit, she knew she could be difficult to be around. It wasn't her favourite quality when the people in her life walked on eggshells around her, fearing her temper. She was working on checking her anger but not always succeeding.

She had started this journey of self-reflection when her lady's maid, Lucy, was found murdered the year before. Zoe had surprised everyone, including herself, by how much she cared about the woman's death. If she was being honest, a great deal of her investment had come from guilt over how she had treated Lucy in life. So she'd found a group of people to help her find Lucy's killer, including both Quinton and Mary. The process was difficult and exhausting, but during and after that investigation, Zoe had changed—she hoped for the better. She liked to think she had become less entitled and selfish, and in the inverse become kinder and humbler. Now, these many months later, Zoe knew the names of all the servants who worked at her home, as well as all about the footman's sickly sister and the coachman's preference for chestnuts.

She wasn't perfect, but Zoe took pride in her efforts to better herself. However, upon further reflection of the incident with Quinton, she decided her reaction was perfectly appropriate, and she would continue plotting her revenge. But that decision didn't justify taking her negative emotions out on undeserving friends and family.

Her mother eyed her cautiously over the brim of her cup, clearly attempting to form the right words.

That made Zoe feel even guiltier. "You don't need to look at me as if I am a wild beast in a shop of glassware," she said before her mother could start. "I will make every attempt not to bite your head off."

"Your restraint is appreciated." Simone took a sip of her tea, looking as graceful as ever. "You have always had spirit, *ma fille*. It is a strength, not a weakness. But I still know enough to speak with care when your eyes flash brimstone."

"Well, you've always been wiser than me." Zoe sighed and settled in more comfortably, balancing her teacup as she drew her legs under her.

Her mother waited until Zoe was comfortable to ask her question. "What is on your mind, *mon chou?*"

Zoe was quiet a moment, considering the answer. She was frustrated at Quinton's dismissal of her, but Mary's statement about her heart was still turning over in Zoe's mind. Her peeved state was more complicated than perhaps she wanted to admit.

Finally she asked a question of her own. "When you were young, *Maman*, did you ever find yourself conflicted? As if the path before you simply could not hold the depth of what you needed?"

Simone smiled softly. "Here is the *difficulté*, Zoe. You see the path ahead, and you think its direction is clear. But you do not actually know what that path holds, where it truly leads. Each choice in life reveals itself as you go. Unpleasant surprises sometimes arise from the most mundane of choices, but the joy of other moments can be equally unexpected."

Oh, good . . . a riddle. Just what I'm in the mood for today. Zoe took another breath, reminding herself to stay calm. Her relationship with her mother had not always been so friendly. They had navigated some rocky waters over the years, and Zoe took care not to reignite the cold war between them.

Despite being mother and child, the two women bore little similarity. Where Zoe was tall and awkward, with dark curly hair that refused to be tamed, olive skin, and a fiery temperament, Simone was petite and poised, her temperament something more akin to icy steel than fire, with shiny blonde hair and skin the colour of porcelain. If she were sitting still enough, one might mistake her for a doll—beautiful still, even in her mid-forties. The only physical characteristic the two had in common were their eyes—blue as sapphire and deep as the ocean.

Simone had often told her that Zoe took after her father. Zoe had to take her word for it. She didn't remember the man enough to know either way.

"I assume you are speaking of matters of some permanence? Perhaps Mr. Huxley?"

Zoe started at her mother's surprisingly insightful words, cutting straight to the heart of Zoe's troubles, although she didn't know why she should be surprised. Simone was a highly intelligent woman, and she hadn't gotten to where she was by being blind to the feelings of others.

Despite this, she was not yet ready to discuss Quinton with her mother. She did not even know her own feelings for the man. The whole thing was complicated and messy with no easy answer, so Zoe chose not to answer the question directly. "I have reached five and twenty years, and since you married Hugh, my life has had an order," said Zoe. "I wasn't always happy with that order, but it was my life, and I did my best to accept it. Now, that order has changed—through my own doing, I know. I've added new people and found new purpose, which is what I always wanted. But still I find myself unsettled, even though my life is more of my own choosing than ever before." Zoe slowed for breath, then rephrased her earlier question. "Did you ever find yourself at sixes and sevens about where your life was headed?"

Simone raised her eyebrow, a quiet laugh escaping her perfect lips. "I escaped *la Terreur* with the clothes on my back and only my child at my side, Zoe. Those were uncertain times, to be sure."

"I know, Maman, about those times." Despite herself, Zoe found herself returning her mother's laugh. "What about after we were here, in England? What about Hugh? Was it really so clear what choice to make when he courted you?"

As she set her teacup down, a thoughtful expression came over Simone's face. "During those years after we made it to British shores, my focus was simply on survival. It was difficult. Marrying a nobleman seemed as impossible as riding a horse to the moon. I had resigned myself to the reality that we would likely never again live the life we'd had in France."

Those years had been hard—Zoe had still been quite young at the time, not yet having seen her tenth year, but she remembered the fear and uncertainty in the pit of her stomach. She remembered her mother, gone for long stretches of time as Simone worked for money for the first time in her life and then came home tired and with still not enough food. Life had improved when Simone found work as a French tutor, but even still it was not easy. Then Simone had met Hugh and everything had changed for the two French refugees.

"So when Hugh showed interest, there was no question as to what path to take?" asked Zoe.

Something flashed in her eyes and Simone hesitated before responding. "I prefer not speak ill of your father, Zoe, but I understood from an early age that marriage was a transactional arrangement, and he fit into that worldview well. Ours was no romantic love story, but we both understood our roles, and for the most part I was able to build a life within what I'd been given. That is how I viewed it in the beginning with Hugh. For him, though, it was different. With Hugh, *c'était un coup de foudre.*"

Love at first sight. Zoe believed it. Hugh was still smitten.

Simone continued, smiling softly. "I needed security, and a way for you to rise above. Hugh offered that. But to my great surprise, I found that as I built my new life there was room for something . . . more. As I came to know the man I married, I found him to be kind, and honourable, and gentle. In time, I came to love him." Simone paused, considering her next words. "I chose a path, thinking I knew what lay along it, but a truth you come to understand as you get older is that a great deal of life is beyond your control—despite my best efforts to prove otherwise." She took a moment to tuck a stray curl behind Zoe's ear. "Whatever path you choose, remember you are French. Much of life is . . . *un acte de foi.*"

A leap of faith. The corners of Zoe's lips twitched as she suppressed a smile, and she took a sip of her tea to hide her amusement at the irony. Who knew it would be her mother, of all people, encouraging her to take a leap of faith. Truly a day for the history books.

Chapter Five

The evening air chilled Quinton, even with his thick wool overcoat. As he suppressed a shiver, he glanced over at his companion. Charlie looked out over the city, his expression unreadable, seemingly indifferent to the winter chill.

"Your friend couldn't have chosen a meeting place indoors?" asked Quinton, his annoyance thinly veiled.

"He's not my friend," Charlie snapped in response. "I wouldn't share a pint under the same roof with him if my life depended on it."

"Charming," muttered Quinton.

Charlie glanced over, his eyes narrow. "What's bothering you? Just yesterday you were all sunshine and giggles to help your lady friend, and now you're in a worse mood than I am, which is saying quite a bit."

"Nothing is bothering me, you twat," retorted Quinton, feeling as if he were twelve years old again.

The feeling of being a child again was only increased by the fact that his words were a lie. Quinton had a great deal on his mind, but he couldn't share his thoughts with Charlie . . . not yet. Perhaps one day, once Quinton had decided what he would do.

But knowing his friend's feelings about nobility, Quinton could only imagine his reaction to finding out Quinton was actually one of them. Charlie would see Quinton's legitimacy as a betrayal of unforgivable proportions, and even if Charlie forgave him, their friendship would never be as it was. Quinton wasn't ready for that.

Finally he heard the scraping of leather against wood, bringing Quinton back to the moment at hand. The stairs creaked as the men they'd been waiting on made their way to the rooftop. As far as meeting places went, the roof of a gambling hell wasn't conventional, but it was private. The dark shadows of the approaching men stretched across floor, lending to the unsettling feeling already present.

Miles O'Malley showed his surprisingly ugly face first, a man of average height with blond hair sticking out from under a cap and beady eyes darting back and forth, followed by a large and brutish looking man, presumably a bodyguard of some kind. This second man stayed back at the entrance to the stairs while O'Malley approached Quinton and Charlie.

"Charlie." O'Malley nodded in acknowledgment. "Well, how can I help you lads, then?"

Quinton hadn't met the Irishman before. His very presence made Quinton's skin crawl, but Quinton held his tongue. He needed to play nice for now if he wanted his help.

"Miles, this is Quinton Huxley," said Charlie with a gesture. "He's an independent agent, and his services have been engaged with regard to one of your schemes."

Quinton winced. That wasn't quite the way Quinton would have phrased it. He should have known better than to let Charlie do the talking—he wasn't exactly known for his tact.

O'Malley narrowed his eyes and crossed his arms. "What are you on about, talkin' about schemes? Just what are you implyin'?"

"Mr. O'Malley, we don't mean any disrespect," interjected

Quinton, trying to salvage this meeting. "Do you have an employee by the name of Katie Shorn?"

"Katie Shorn?" O'Malley frowned, his shifty eyes darting back and forth. "No, I don't have any lasses workin' for me by that name."

Quinton found that unlikely, but he forged ahead. "Well, this is a young woman in your employ who claims she's being forced to work there to pay off her father's debt. She's been missing now for three days. Does that ring any bells?"

Something flashed in O'Malley's eyes—or at least, Quinton thought he saw something, but it was hard to be sure in the dark. The Irishman clenched his jaw as he shifted from side to side, clearly weighing his next words carefully. "I dunno know anyone by that name." O'Malley glanced at Charlie. "Don't be wastin' my time like this again, Charlie."

With those words, Miles turned on his heel and departed.

Quinton looked at Charlie. "Well, what did you make of that?"

Charlie squinted, staring off in the direction Miles had headed. "He's hiding something."

"The scheme?"

"Maybe." Charlie cocked his head, contemplating. "He wasn't as cocky as I expected. When you brought up the scheme, I thought he'd crow, but he didn't. He got defensive, aye?"

"He certainly didn't want to discuss it."

"If I didn't know better . . . I'd say he was scared."

"Of us?"

"No." As he began to walk toward the stairs, Charlie ground his teeth. "As much as I hate to admit it, your lady friend may be right. There may be more going on here than meets the eye."

"Hmm." Quinton agreed with him. "We need to get a look inside."

"Neither of us are getting within ten meters of this building again."

Quinton knew his friend was right. Now O'Malley would be

on guard, anticipating their return. But there was someone else . . . someone charming and in need of a distraction, who might be in the perfect frame of mind to spend an evening in mild debauchery . . .

"That's fine," replied Quinton. "I have another idea."

Chapter Six

A s she picked up her cup of chocolate, Simone inhaled the rich steam deeply. Tea was usually her beverage of choice each morning, as she enjoyed the English tradition despite her French bones. Hugh and Zoe preferred the bitter flavour of coffee, though for the life of her, Simone could not understand why. But the children enjoyed the sweet treat of a steamed chocolate, and every once in a while Simone indulged herself with one.

The children—Simone and Hugh's children together, namely Phoebe and Walter—generally received their treat before their tutor arrived. The young orphan Gwen, whom Zoe had hired to care for her beast of a dog, also occasionally partook. It was a bit of a stretch to give a servant such a treat, but she was a sweet girl and the cook had a soft spot for her. Gwen had often worked for several hours by the time Simone's own children arose, and Simone thought the girl deserved the little luxury.

The reason for Simone's indulgence this morning stemmed from lack of sleep. Old nightmares had plagued her sleep, mixed now with new terrors. Her desperate flight from France, Zoe in tow, would always be a part of her—she was used to being haunted by those memories—but nearly losing Zoe to a madman now took centre stage in her bad dreams.

When her nights were that restless, Simone often moved to her own bedroom so as not to disturb Hugh's slumber, but last night she had remained in their shared bed. Every time she awoke, the other side of the bed had still been empty. If he had come to bed at all, it must have been in the wee hours of the morning, there and risen again by the time Simone herself woke for the day.

As she took a lovely, sweet sip, Simone appraised her husband over her rim of her cup. Dark bags hung under Hugh's eyes, betraying his lack of rest. But even as he settled into his late fifties, Simone found him to be a handsome man. She wondered what had kept him up so late.

"Where were you last night, *mon amour*?" asked Simone. "I thought I heard a voice when I was going to bed. Was Quinton here?"

"You didn't hear the conversation, did you?"

Simone was surprised—Hugh rarely spoke to her with such a sharp tone. Quinton had been a frequent visitor to Hugh's study, and to their home. Generally Hugh's concern was for the young man, not for secrecy. Many times she and Hugh had discussed Quinton's concerns, about his mother, her death, the killer at large, even Zoe. But with that one sentence, Hugh became a closed book.

Which, of course, made him an open book to his astute wife. Something different was afoot. If Quinton had not come as a friend . . . then perhaps he had come as a client. Hugh had always been careful of his clients' privacy in regard to legal matters.

"Of course not." Simone took another sip. "I simply thought I heard his voice as I passed in the hallway. Is he in need of the services of a barrister?"

Hugh swallowed hard, avoiding her eye line. "He did come seeking legal advice, and I assured him the conversation would remain between him and me."

As Simone had suspected. Legal advice. Interesting, but that did not explain Hugh's obvious discomfort. Perhaps it had to do with Quinton's equally obvious interest in Zoe. "Darling, I have no interest in Quinton's legal needs. Unless, of course, they are tied in with Zoe somehow." Simone kept her watchful gaze on Hugh as she spoke, again appraising him over the brim of her cup.

Hugh took a slow sip from his cup of coffee, clearly delaying his answer while he thought on what to say. But the delay itself told Simone that she was on the right track. "This is a personal issue that Quinton sought my council on," said Hugh finally. "I will say no more."

So now it was a personal issue. But Quinton came seeking legal advice. Even more curious.

Simone considered what she knew of the agent—a man who had recently discovered truths about his own life. Now he was here, seeking Hugh's counsel—a man familiar with the complications of Quinton's life and his recent solving of his mother's murder.

Quinton's mother's murder. The monster who had taken her life had recently been executed. Had Quinton spoken with Fairfax, the killer himself? Could he have learned something else, something requiring the advice of a barrister?

"I say, Simone, stop gathering wool. The question was not difficult."

Starting at the sudden statement, Simone quickly smiled at her husband. "I'm sorry, Hugh. I was thinking of The Haven and what needs to be addressed there, and if the old drapes could be repurposed, but that led me to remember that today I am due at Theo's for tea."

Her intention had been to distract Hugh with her comment about her shelter for unwed pregnant girls, throwing in Theo in the art of confusion, but the effect was the opposite.

"Theo?" Hugh cleared his throat, sitting up straighter. "Why are you speaking with Theo?"

Well, that was unexpected, but still telling. Theo must have some knowledge of whatever this matter was with Quinton that might concern Zoe. And, fortunately for Simone, she knew Theo would be more forthcoming than her husband.

Perhaps it was time to play on a bit of guilt to throw him off the scent. "I speak with Theo regularly to continue to raise awareness for the Haven, Hugh. You know that." Simone stuck her lower lip out in a small pout. "Theo is quite influential among the ton. And I happen to also enjoy her company. The feeling is even mutual, which is more than can be said for the rest of your family."

The strategy worked, garnering the reaction Simone had wanted. "I'm sorry, Simone" said Hugh, his expression contrite. "Of course you and Theo take time to visit. As you're already aware, I didn't get much sleep last night and I'm afraid I am poor company this morning."

"It's already forgotten, *mon amour*." Simone took one last swallow of her chocolate before slipping around the table to seek and receive a genuine kiss.

Before she headed up the stairs, Simone took the time to speak briefly to Quaid on the stairs, asking him to send a note to Theo.

Time to see what all the subterfuge was about.

Chapter Seven

Rory Stewart had not imagined spending his evening this way. When the day started, he'd pictured it ending with a good book and a glass of scotch. Instead, he was in the depths of a gambling hell looking for "anything suspicious."

At least that's what Quinton had told him when he'd traipsed into the little shed in Rory's garden where Rory did most of his work. The directive didn't really narrow anything down much. Everything in a gambling hell was suspicious.

Of course, Rory was no stranger to gambling. He held membership at one of the smaller, less snobbish high-class clubs, and he would on occasion play cards with the other men there. But the hells in the lower-class neighbourhoods of London were a different beast altogether. Here, people of all classes and races and genders mingled—which wasn't the problem, just to be clear. The part that set Rory on edge was that there were no limits. Almost anything went. It wasn't the kind of place someone who enjoyed a good book in the evenings would frequent.

The main room was decorated ornately but without taste, with poorly dyed burgundy curtains and cheap golden-hued accents. In the middle of the room a game of hazards was surrounded by a thick wall of people shouting out bets and curses in equal measure. Rory moved along the edge of the room, quietly observing and sipping on the cheap whiskey provided.

A few girls moved in and out of the crowd, refilling glasses and taking orders. A smart business plan—the longer the patrons stayed playing the game without having to leave for more drinks or food, the more they would bet. It didn't hurt that the drunker they got, the looser they would be with their money as well.

When he caught the eye of one of the serving girls, she quickly came over.

"Ello sir, what can I get ya?" she asked with a smile.

"Good evening, miss." Rory flashed his own smile, which he happened to think was quite charming. "I was wondering if Katie was working tonight?"

The girl's brow furrowed as she thought. "Katie? I don't think anyone by that name works 'ere."

"Really? Katie Shorn doesn't work here?"

"Nah, I don't think so."

"Oh." Rory scrambled to backtrack. "I must be misremembering. Dinnae mind me."

She was still smiling. "Can I get ya a refill, sir?"

"Ah, yes. Thank you, miss."

In the blink of an eye she was gone, his glass in hand and his coin in her pocket. She was efficient—all the girls were. Quinton had mentioned this Katie Shorn was claiming to be coerced into working in the hell, but that didn't seem a sound strategy when it came to acquiring workers for front of house. No one wanted the maid serving them to be gloomy faced or dragging their feet.

"How do you do, Mr. Stewart?"

Rory jumped at the sound of his name amid the din. As he turned, he saw the last person he expected. "Zoe—Lady Demas?!" he exclaimed

The infernal woman grinned, unfazed by her surroundings. "Zoe is fine."

"What are you doing here?" Rory hissed.

"The same thing as you." She smoothed her light lavender gown as if she had not a care in the world. "Investigating on Quinton's behalf."

"Oh, is that so?" Rory placed his hands on his hips. "Does Quinton even know you're here?"

She sniffed, her aristocratic nose high in the air. "I hardly see how that's relevant."

Rory hadn't known Zoe Demas very long, but he had come to enjoy her company on the rare occasion they met under social circumstances. She was a clever woman from a unique background—a woman his dear friend Quinton had become infatuated with over the past year. Usually his friend was the one who had to deal with situations like this. *Better Quinton than himself...*

"Have you even considered your reputation if someone recognized you in a place such as this?" Rory hissed.

Zoe gave a long-suffering sigh. "It's a gambling hell, Rory, not a brothel. I'd hardly be the first noblewoman to grace these halls." Zoe gestured behind her. "Besides, I'm not unaccompanied."

In his flustered state, Rory hadn't even noticed Mary Fletcher standing behind Zoe. If Zoe was oil, Mary was the match.

"I would assume the noblewoman you're referring to were likely . . . married, which would give them more freedom in society." Rory pointed at both women. "Neither of you have any business being here."

"Rory, will you stop yammerin' on?" said Mary with an exasperated sigh. "We can spend all night arguing, or we can do what we came here to do. But you making a scene isn't helping."

As he opened his mouth to respond, the serving maid returned and handed him his refilled glass. She quickly turned to the new patrons. "Can I get you ladies anythin'?"

"Two whiskeys, please," responded Zoe.

As the girl darted off again, Rory sighed. He didn't have the energy for this fight. A month ago might have been a different story. But then again, a month ago he might not have cared how Zoe and Mary spent their time.

"Very well," said Rory. "But be careful. Quinton will kill me if anything were to happen to either of you."

"Excellent, I'm glad we could come to an understanding," said Zoe with another grin. "Have you learned anything?"

"Only that no one by the name of Katie Shorn is known to work here, at least according to the young maid."

"Do you believe her?"

"I don't think she has enough guile to lie." Rory sipped the bitter golden liquid, wincing at the poor quality. "Perhaps this 'Katie' didn't give your cousin her real name."

"Perhaps." Zoe accepted a whiskey from the reemerging serving girl, who just as quickly disappeared into the throng. "Do you see any other illicit activity, other than . . . all of this?"

"No, but I haven't been here long. I was going to head to the card rooms next. Care to join me?"

Zoe slipped her arm around his. "I thought you'd never ask, Mr. Stewart."

"I think I'll stay out here," said Mary, eyeing the food and drink table. "Maybe try to make friends with the staff."

Rory escorted Zoe toward the back rooms, where the quieter games such as cards would be played. Gentlemen like Alexander Dovefield, looking to bet and lose big, would likely congregate there.

They were admitted to one of the rooms quickly—the very fine cut of Rory's suit and the high quality of Zoe's gown no doubt moving them to the top of the list. The staff were likely trained to recognize the trappings of money and give preference accordingly.

The first few hands were played without incident, with Zoe showing herself to be as quick with cards as she was with her wit. In truth, it was not altogether unenjoyable for Rory to spend some time on mindless diversion instead of being elbows deep in a cadaver for once. He felt his shoulders begin to relax as he played the game and drank the cheap whiskey.

He did have a passion for his work, of course. The study of the body was one of the most fascinating and important scientific advancements of the century. The knowledge gained could be used both in the apprehension of murderers as well as discovering cures for illnesses whose causes and effects had long been a mystery. Not to mention his career as a resurrectionist and amateur anatomist had proven quite lucrative, allowing him the lifestyle of a gentleman without any of the expectations or responsibilities. The best of both worlds in many ways.

But the events of the past few weeks had cast a pall over his usual outlook. Certain things neither money nor passion could solve. Being falsely arrested for murder and spending more than his share of time in Newgate had taken its toll, but even that paled in comparison to the real cause of his melancholy.

The course of true love never did run smooth.

The bard could afford to be poetic when it came to heartbreak. The real thing hurt rather more than Rory wished to acknowledge.

But this was not the time for wallowing—Quinton had tasked Rory with a job and he needed to focus. As he turned his attention back to the game at hand, he took in his surroundings discreetly over the tops of his cards.

The serving maids were coming in and out of these back rooms as well, keeping the booze flowing. Some of the patrons seemed to recognize the girls, but for the most part they were focused on the cards in their own hands. The girls themselves were skilled at being friendly without being familiar. They seemed well trained and relatively pleased with their work.

But if Katie Shorn wasn't one of these girls, how had she passed herself off as one?

Rory signalled to one of the girls—older than the first, with a more experienced look about her.

"Would ya like another whiskey, sir?"

"Yes, ma'am. I dinnae suppose you have any scotch?" he asked hopefully.

"I can check in tha back," she replied with a wink.

"It would be most appreciated, dear." Rory hesitated, as if it were just an afterthought. "By the way, is Katie working tonight?"

"Ain't no one by that name who works here, love." The woman smiled. "I'll be right back with yer scotch."

As Rory sighed, frustrated at his lack of progress, Zoe leaned over. "She answered that far too quickly."

Rory raised an eyebrow. "You think?"

"She didn't have to ponder the question at all." Zoe cocked her head. "When I've lied to my mother about where I've been, it was a scripted answer like that. She's hiding something."

"Hmm." Rory considered this. Perhaps he'd been too accepting of the earlier serving girl's answer. He really wasn't cut out for this kind of investigative agent role. What would Quinton do? "Have you seen the owner about? If he's running a scam out on the floor, dinnae you think he'd want to supervise a bit?"

"We still don't know if it is a scam," pointed out Zoe. "It could be they're trying to cover up whatever happened to Katie."

"Possibly," replied Rory with scepticism.

"As to the owner, no, I haven't seen him." Zoe glanced toward the door. "Quinton claims he's quite ugly, so I think I would have noticed him."

"Yes, he mentioned that to me as well." Rory followed her gaze toward the door. "Let's see if I can't speed his arrival along."

By the time they had finished their brief conversation, the older serving woman was back. "There ya are, sir." As she handed him the scotch with a flourish, Rory noted a bandaged wrapped around her left hand.

"Thank ye, love." He pointed to the bandage. "Are you alright? I'm not a proper surgeon, but I do have some knowledge of wound care."

Something flashed in the woman's eyes but disappeared just as quickly—so quick Rory wondered if he had imagined it. "Oh, this?" She shrugged nonchalantly. "This is nothin'. Just cut myself on a broken glass. Hazard of the job, I'm afraid."

"Of course." Rory made a show of sipping the golden liquid —poor quality, but he smiled anyway. "That is lovely. Is there any possibility I could pay my compliments to the owner?"

She hesitated.

"The staff here is just so excellent, I'd love to show my appreciation," pressed Rory.

That got her—no one would turn down the opportunity for a customer to tell their employer how well they were doing. Plus he'd made a show of being a big spender, so keeping him happy was still important.

"I'll be right back," she finally said after a moment's consideration.

It didn't take long for her to reappear with the man in question in tow—as ugly as advertised. Rory wasn't a tall man, but he was at least a head taller than Miles O'Malley. The Irishman attempted a friendly smile when his eyes came to rest on Rory, but the gesture twisted his features into something unsettling, making Rory think it wasn't something he was used to doing.

"Hello there." His Irish accent was pronounced. "Lydia tells me ye'd like to have a chat with me."

"Indeed." Rory returned the smiled, relying on his natural charisma. "This is a high-quality establishment. Your staff have treated me very well, and I just wanted to let you know that."

"Ah, well . . ." O'Malley cleared his throat. "I'm glad you're enjoyin' your evenin'. Eh, your accent . . . you're a Scot?"

"Well placed, sir. I originally hail from the Highlands."

O'Malley grunted. "Well, it's not Irish but it's better 'n British. Let Lydia know if ye need anythin' else."

"Of course, of course."

As O'Malley turned to leave, Lydia gripped his forearm. Her expression was difficult to read, but as she leaned in to whisper something in O'Malley's ear, he saw the man's face go pale.

Rory waited for them to get out of earshot before glancing at Zoe. "Well?"

Zoe shrugged. "He's a nasty piece of work, but I didn't get the impression Lydia was afraid of him."

"Possibly." Rory rubbed his chin. "But she did have that bandage on her hand. There's something about her reaction . . . I got the feeling she dinnae want me to know the truth. I've seen that same look on a woman's face before—when they're covering for the person who hurt them, either out of fear or loyalty."

"Hmm." Zoe appeared to contemplate that. "I suppose you may be right. I wouldn't put it past him."

"Agreed. But I'm not sure how that helps us." Rory sighed. "It seems our evening may have been a waste of time."

Zoe smiled with a shrug. "Perhaps. We will have to confer with Mary before we know for certain."

It was a small blow to Rory's pride, but as he thought over the course of the evening, he reflected she wasn't wrong. She hadn't been wrong about much. Well, they each had their specialities. He'd like to see her dissect a human lung. As his thoughts drifted back to the book he wanted to read that evening by the warmth of his own hearth, Rory thought that perhaps her superiority at investigation wasn't such a blow after all. As the bard said, *to thine own self be true.*

Chapter Eight

As they journeyed back to the Dovefield residence, silence loomed in the space between Zoe and Mary. Zoe wished she could find a way to overcome it—to just say what needed to be said and let everything go back to the way it was before, but she couldn't seem to find the right words.

As the carriage turned the corner onto their street, Zoe finally spoke. "Did you learn anything from the staff?"

"Nothing of particular note," replied Mary with shrug. "A couple I thought might have recognized the name, but none of them admitted to knowing Katie Shorn."

"Same for me." Zoe flexed the fingers of her left hand, feeling the stitches pulling against skin. "What did you think of the way they interacted with the customers? Rory seemed to think they were all fairly well treated and well trained."

Mary snorted. "They were well trained, but I'm not sure if it's in the same way he's thinking. I saw them watering down the drinks, as well as picking pockets and skimming. Not to mention that game of risk was definitely rigged."

"Well I would say that is of note." Zoe crossed her arms, mildly annoyed she hadn't seen any of this herself. She made a mental note to check the contents of her pocketbook later. "So they are scamming the patrons."

"At least on a small scale." Mary hesitated.

Zoe squinted, clocking that there was something else on her mind. "What?"

"I also saw a few . . . pair off with some of the men with a little extra to burn, if you know what I mean."

"Hmm. So I was wrong when I told Rory it was just a gambling hell, not a brothel." Zoe frowned. "Alexander may have been holding back a few details. Perhaps we should pay him a visit without Quinton."

"Perhaps."

The two lapsed back into silence as the carriage finally came to a stop. As Mary stepped down onto the street, Zoe tried to think of something—anything—to say, but no words came out. She watched her dearest friend walk up to the front door, knowing she should find some way to comfort her but unable to comprehend how to do so. A great hollowness ached in her chest, growing with each moment spent in loneliness.

Now she had only the long night to look forward to as she counted the seconds until the light of dawn would peak through her window and Zoe could put her mask on again. She wondered if Mary felt the same way.

Chapter Nine

Lady Theodosia Bexley, Dowager Dutchess of Wentworth, greeted Simone in her library with the warm enthusiasm she had expected. Simone has spoken the truth when she said the two women enjoyed each other's company. Hugh's family hadn't exactly been welcoming to his French wife, with the exception of his older sister.

Until Simone had come onto the picture, Theo had been the most important woman in Hugh's life. She had raised him from the age of fourteen, offering him a home when their mother died and their father had quickly remarried. It was Theo who had encouraged Hugh's passion to be a barrister, as well as financially secured his schooling. Her approval had mattered the most to Hugh, and Simone was grateful to have received it.

Theo ordered the tea, waiting for it to be served before she asked the obvious. "What brings you by, my dear Simone? Not that I'm not happy to see you, but I know how busy you are these days with your charity. You must have a reason to drop by for an unplanned social visit."

Simone had to smile. Theo was still sharp as ever. Never underestimate a woman's intuition. The dowager, well into her sixties and long since widowed, was still a strikingly beautiful woman. Her once-straw-blonde hair had faded to a lovely silver colour, making her eyes seem even more green, though the small lines around them revealed her age. She still stood straight, having the carriage of a woman who knew her worth—the fact she was titled and wealthy and intelligent didn't hurt either.

"Theo, first of all, I am truly happy to be here." Simone decided a little flattery would be best to start. "Your friendship has always meant the world to me. And to Zoe."

"You are both precious to me as well, Simone." Theo took a sip of her tea, her clever eyes looking Simone over. "But I've employed enough flattery in my life to soften someone up to know when it's being done to me. So what's going on, dear?"

"Very well." Simone placed her teacup down on the table beside her chair. "I'll get straight to the point. Hugh and Quinton had a meeting last night. Hugh told Quinton the conversation would stay between the two of them, but I can tell it was no social visit. He admitted Quinton sought legal help. When I mentioned coming here, Hugh practically swooned with horror, leading me to realize you must know something about this whole thing. I also got the unspoken impression it somehow concerns Zoe." She paused to take a breath. "So, my dear Theo, let me ask you. What do you know of this affair?"

Theo grinned, practically bouncing up and down in her seat. "I am so glad you asked. I have been dying to tell someone. These revelations are only interesting when they are shared. Of course I assured the boy I would be discreet, so you must keep this between us."

Simone did briefly wonder if Quinton would agree with Theo's definition of discreet, but she wasn't going to say anything —not when it was working in her favour.

Theo continued, "The lad Quinton did come here and we had a long talk. He was ready to know who his father was; he knew I would have answers."

The tea was cold and plates empty by the time Theo finished her story. She drew out the telling with considerable detail and flair, while Simone listened intently, asking pertinent questions. When Theo said that Quinton was a Coleville, Simone couldn't help but gasp, much to Theo's clear delight. The Coleville family was not only titled, but well respected in general and very, very rich.

"So that is what I know," said Theo, leaning back with a satisfied expression. "It's something isn't it?"

Nodding slowly, Simone absorbed this new information, but she leaned forward. "It is indeed noteworthy that Quinton has relatives of nobility and wealth." She paused, frowning. "But what could be the legal questions surrounding that? What reason could he have had to seek out Hugh?"

Theo mirrored her frown, her expression considerably diminished. "That is a valid question, Simone. Perhaps . . . perhaps he wondered about approaching the current Lord Coleville?"

"Perhaps." Simone remained unconvinced. "But that's still personal, not legal, isn't it? Hugh said it was also a legal matter. What about this could be a legal matter? And how does it concern Zoe?"

The two women lapsed into silence, both of them considering the facts as they'd been presented, the only sound to be heard in the room the occasional clinking of porcelain and the quiet slurping of tea.

Simone sifted through her thoughts. Why did Quinton want to know more after speaking to his mother's killer? Simone knew that Fairfax and Quinton's mother had had a history before her death. Did he know Quinton's father as well? That would make sense—they would have been of a similar age at the time, both young lords of the same social status. What else might Fairfax have known, that he would then relay to Quinton after all these years?

A single, unbelievable thought occurred to Simone.

Could it be possible? No. It wasn't possible. Was it? Simone raised her eyes and saw the same thought reflected back from Theo's.

Finally Theo spoke. "As a by-blow, he has no legal standing, whatever his bloodline may be. But—"

"What if they had wed?" Simone finished the thought.

Theo shook her head in disbelief. "It happens, of course. But it's exceedingly rare. It would have been a most unsuitable match."

"Of course." Simone leaned back, equally stunned at the possibility. "Why marry a girl when the promise of a wedding will do the trick? But it makes sense, doesn't it?"

"That a lord fell in love with an actress and married her? No, it doesn't make sense, but in this context, very little does." Theo swirled her tea round in the cup, her gaze distant. "Quinton's father was the eldest son. If we are correct about this, that makes Quinton the heir. However unsuitable the match might have been between his parents, if the marriage was legal, then he can't be denied."

The words hung in the air, gaining weight and standing until Simone stood herself and joined them. "This would change everything. I must speak to Hugh."

Theo stood as well but headed for the oak sideboard instead of the door, gathering two crystal glasses. "It's a bit earlier in the day than I usually imbibe, but this next part will need some fortification," said Theo as she poured claret from the decanter into the glasses. "Let's think this through, my dear. Hugh is a stubborn man of his word. If he has said the conversation will go no farther, it will go no farther. You and I must untangle this puzzle ourselves, without the help of the men." Theo handed her the glass. "You and I need to arrange an adventure."

Simone hesitated—she rarely drank during the day, but Theo wasn't wrong. She needed some fortification. And it was an excellent vintage. "Where would we even start, Theo?" asked Simone as she accepted the glass. "We need to narrow down the field."

Sipping the claret, Theo nodded. "The way I see it, there are two ways forward. One is to speak to Quinton directly."

"Well, there is that," agreed Simone.

"The other, of course, is simply to take our best shot and start looking."

"There are many places to travel for an elopement." Simone shook her head. "Gretna Green is popular but certainly not the only choice."

"This is true, but indulge me for now, dear. Let's try imagining ourselves in their place." Rising suddenly, Theo pulled the bell on the wall. When a footman appeared she requested a light repast then continued, "Graham Coleville was not just some youth trying to avoid a parent's disapproval—he was a man of means. If he was going to marry his mistress, he had the funds to do so in the least difficult way possible. If we assume Quinton's mother was with child as well, then it would be important that travel was as comfortable as possible."

"It's possible, of course." Simone paused. "She may have been *enceinte*. Or perhaps they were simply impossibly in love."

"You know I love you, but your French is showing, my dear," said Theo with a light scoff. "In the real world, a noble of Lord Coleville's station would not marry for love. In this scenario, the only way I can reconcile him making this choice would be because he was a man of extraordinary honour who wanted to give his unborn child legitimacy. If there was love, it would be a secondary factor."

Theo's dismissal was more than a little condescending, but Simone held her tongue. She was the furthest thing on this earth from a hopeless romantic, but she didn't see what good it would do to correct Theo.

"Where was I? Oh, yes, travel. Gretna Green is four long days by carriage one way, then four long days back. The journey is uncomfortable at the best of times, not to mention one has to travel along the main road out of England. They both apparently went to great trouble to ensure the marriage was a secret, so I doubt they'd risk a lord being recognized on one of the most travelled roads in the country."

Theo took another sip. "I think it would make more sense to go south, or even to France. The journey is easier for those who have the means, and there could be no question as to the legitimacy of the marriage."

The mention of her motherland brought up unexpected emotions in Simone—she blamed the wine. She thought back to her childhood growing up on the west coast of France. They had lived a short carriage ride from the sea, and she spent many an Elysian afternoon playing in the waves. Those were happy times, when the difficult future that lay in store was still unknown to her.

Another memory suddenly occurred to her, but this one didn't belong to her. They'd hosted a gathering after Fairfax's arrest, and she remembered that after a few drafts of whiskey, Quinton had begun to share things he remembered about his mother. He told them of a trip by sea to an island, where Quinton and his mother relaxed in the sun and splashed in waves of their own. She had spoken fondly of his father and reminisced about times spent with him. Quinton cherished that memory, as Simone cherished hers—a happy time before his own difficult future arose.

But Quinton had mentioned one more detail—he said the people there spoke French and English.

Why not just go to the coast of England if she wanted to treat Quinton? Why go to this island to reminisce about times gone by with his father? Unless it had some meaning to her . . .

Simone set her glass down with a loud thunk. "I have an idea of where they might have gone."

She related Quinton's story, pausing as the maid delivered a tray of cheese, fruit, and bread. Several jams were included, and the ever-present scones completed the board. Normally Simone loved a scone, but she was too excited to eat at the moment.

As soon as the spread was laid and the maid out of earshot, Simone began again. "A day's carriage ride would take them to Southampton, where they could catch a boat to the Isle of

Guernsey. An easy trip by most standards. They could even travel separately to avoid scandal. Perhaps the poor woman took her son to a place of sentiment—the place she wed his father."

Theo furrowed her brow. "Isn't the Isle still British, with the marriage law in effect?"

Simone waved her hand dismissively. "Guernsey recognizes the crown but has its own legal system. My family visited once, between wars. It's a lovely place."

"Interesting, very interesting." Theo's eyes shined, possibly aided by the wine. "Well, that settles it. We must go to Guernsey."

It was Simone's turn to scoff. "Theo, we're not even sure that Quinton's parents were married. This is all complete supposition on our part. We know nothing for certain."

"Exactly! What a grand lark!" Theo leapt to her feet, a grin on her face. "If we are correct, we come back with legal proof that Quinton is the heir to a fortune—and more importantly, eligible to marry your daughter, who is smitten with him. And if we are wrong, you and I enjoy a holiday together on a beautiful island. I can see no downside."

Simone hesitated. This was all a bit outside her comfort zone. She preferred to leave the digging into other people's lives to her daughter. But on the other hand, Theo was right—if they proved Quinton was a titled noble, any union between him and Zoe would be much easier for society to swallow. And what Simone wanted more than anything else in the world was for Zoe to be as happy as possible.

"Very well." Simone sighed, then returned Theo's smile. "Why not give it a try?"

"Excellent." Theo rang the bell again. "I shall make all the arrangements."

If Theo was making the arrangements, Simone knew they would travel in style. Now all she had to do was break the news to Hugh . . .

Chapter Ten

"**W**ell, Alexander, what do you have to say for yourself?"

Zoe's stepcousin shifted in his seat, eyes downcast. "I think you're making rather a bigger fuss out of this than necessary."

When Zoe had invited Alexander to tea at Twinings she suspected he thought it was to get an update on the case—at the very least he probably hadn't expected to be interrogated. But the man had left things out of his story, and Zoe had not slept well and was in no mood to coddle him today. "I think you're making much too small a fuss." Zoe took a sip of her tea, wishing it had a little something extra in it. "I want the truth, Alexander, unfiltered."

"Where's your other half?" Alexander muttered grumpily, sidestepping the conversation.

Zoe raised an eyebrow. "Quinton? I wanted to get your side of things before getting him involved. He already has a fairly low opinion of you."

"I was actually referring to Miss Fletcher," replied Alexander. "Or your bloody dog."

"Oh." Zoe cleared her throat, her cheeks suddenly warm.

"Mary is taking tea with her own cousin. And Brutus is not quite welcome here—trust me, I've tried to reason with them."

"Well at least there is one saving grace to this day." With a deep sigh, Alexander leaned back in his chair. "I can't believe you're accusing me carrying on with a . . . a woman of the night."

"You mean a prostitute?"

Alexander sputtered his tea across the white table cloth. "There's no need to be so vulgar."

"I'm French, Alexander. I think I'll make it through without swooning," retorted Zoe with an eye roll. "What I'm accusing you of is leaving out certain key details in order to make yourself look better. Now tell me the truth. Were you paying her for her . . . services?"

"Keep your voice down!" he hissed, glancing around the room at the other patrons. "Do you want the whole of the ton to know our business?"

Zoe nearly laughed. "Alexander, hardly anyone is here. Could you for once just pretend to be a human being and answer the question!"

He blinked, clearly taken aback by her shortness with him. For a moment Zoe regretted her sharp tongue, but then she recalled what her dear cousin was spending his inheritance on and felt less bad.

"Very well." Alexander sniffed, playing the offended victim. "Since you insist on being impertinent, I will tell you. I was not paying Katie for her . . . services."

"But you were using her . . . services?" Zoe pressed.

The blush which had flushed across his face was now a deep shade of red. "I do not see how that is pertinent."

"For the love of—" She took a deep breath to stop herself from cursing, reminding herself to lower her voice. "Could you please be honest and then I will decide what is pertinent? You came to me for help, if you will recall."

"I know, and I appreciate the irony of it. I know I haven't always been very good to you, and I am grateful you've agreed to help me." Alexander sighed. "But this subject simply isn't something a gentleman speaks about with a lady."

Zoe scoffed. "Of all the times for you to decide to treat me like a lady, you pick now?"

A shadow fell over the table, interrupting Zoe's tirade. She held her tongue—the one thing Alexander was right about was that their family business did not need to be aired out in every parlour by every mama of the ton.

As she turned her head to greet the nosy member of society, Zoe forced a smile on her face. But when she caught sight of the interloper, her smile quickly turned genuine. "Mabel!" she exclaimed. "How good to see you! What are you doing here?"

Her friend returned her smile. "I just stopped in to confirm a reservation for dinner later, and then I saw you and couldn't resist saying hello."

If someone had told Zoe a year ago that she would count Mabel Anderson as one of the few genuine friends she had in society, she would've laughed in their face. But things had changed when Mabel's sister, poor young Margot, had been brutally murdered. Mabel had approached Zoe, seeking assistance in finding true justice, believing the man arrested and convicted for the crime to be innocent. At the time, Mabel had still been in deep mourning, wearing all black and refusing to leave the house. Now that she had closure and justice had been done, she was in lavender to signify half-mourning, showing her return to the land of the living—and by extension, society.

"It is good to see you," said Zoe, and she meant it. "Have you met my cousin, Lord Alexander Dovefield?"

"I'm sure we've met in passing," replied Mabel noncommittally.

Seeing the lack of recognition in his eyes, Zoe gestured between the two. "Alexander, this is Miss Mabel Fletcher."

"Of course." Alexander smiled, putting on his usual mask of charm. "A pleasure to see you again, Miss Fletcher."

She was not a natural beauty—that had been left to her sister.

Her auburn hair hung limply, emphasizing the paleness of her complexion, while her body type was neither petite nor curvy but could best be described as straight. It wasn't that she was ugly, she was just . . . average. Some might say unremarkable. But there was a light in her eyes which Zoe hadn't seen in years past—it seemed to make the golden flecks in the hazel shine with newfound passion.

"Likewise." Those eyes appeared thoughtful as Mabel turned her attention back to Zoe. "Well, I won't take up anymore of your time. I would love to have a longer conversation with you. Would it be amenable if I called on you for tea tomorrow?"

"That would be perfectly amenable." Zoe reached out and squeezed her friend's hand. "I'll see you tomorrow."

As Mabel walked away, Alexander watched her and shook his head. "Such a tragedy, what happened to that family. It must be difficult to reintegrate back into society after something like that."

"Indeed." Zoe turned back to him. "But don't think you're going to deflect from having this conversation by pretending to show empathy."

Alexander crossed his arms. "My God, I forget how stubborn you French are."

"Only as stubborn as degenerate British gamblers. Now tell me."

"Fine. Did I know some of the girls offered . . . other services? Yes. Did I ever use those services?" Alexander took a deep breath. "Yes. But Katie wasn't like that. She only worked the front. She had . . . an innocent quality to her. It didn't seem to me that she had very much experience with men."

Zoe squinted. "And did you help her gain experience?"

He squirmed. "Fine, yes. Is that what you want to hear?"

"What I want is for you to be honest." As Zoe leaned back, she popped the last bite of a cucumber sandwich in her mouth. "So it's a start. I still think you're holding something back, but it's a start. Which of you initiated the romance?"

"I did, of course," he replied with a sniff. "A man knows his own mind."

That seemed doubtful, but Zoe decided to hold her tongue on that one. She wasn't entirely certain what had transpired between the two, but Quinton was still convinced it was some kind of confidence scheme. Having seen the gambling hell for herself, Zoe was more inclined to agree with him than before. Something was certainly going on.

"If you say so." Zoe ate another sandwich, realizing for the first time how hungry she was. "I paid the hell a visit. No one there will admit to knowing anything about Katie."

"You went there yourself? What possessed you—actually, never mind." Alexander shook his head. "But you do understand then, what I'm talking about? She's just disappeared."

"Yes, but it's more than that. No one I spoke to would even admit to knowing her at all." Zoe winced—the next words seemed to be stuck in her throat. "As much as it pains me, I must admit you may be right. It seems as though they're covering something up."

Alexander scowled. "No need to be so dramatic. What's the next step?"

"I'll talk to Quinton and let you know." She said the words with confidence, but in truth Zoe wasn't sure what would be next. She was hoping Quinton would have some ideas.

Chapter Eleven

Mary slipped her arm comfortably through her cousin John's as they continued to stroll through the tea garden. Though much smaller than the other, more prominent tea houses, this tea garden had an excellent blend they both enjoyed, as well as a particularly tasty lemon cake.

They bought their treats and walked around the small pond to a more private alcove. Often these private areas were used by couples to engage in some harmless kissing, but the cousins simply wanted to speak without being overheard. They settled on a bench bathed in the weak sun and enjoyed a few moments drinking their tea and letting the sun warm them. They rarely had opportunity to catch up without their mutual friends or horde of family around, and both relaxed at the freedom.

John spoke first, asking Mary about their shared family. She was able to reply she was trying to mend fences with her mother, but that she and her family had a different relationship now that Mary was independently employed. Mary was content with where things were.

"Aunt Cherry does fill my ear from time to time, but it's your life to live," he allowed.

Mary turned the attention to John's personal life. "And how is Savi? Is there an engagement announcement soon?"

"Engagement? Hardly." John, even with his darker skin, coloured as he spoke. "We have barely begun to court." He sighed suddenly. "She's so beautiful, Mary. When we walk out, men just stare. I can't imagine what she sees in the likes of me."

Laughing out loud, Mary couldn't help but wonder at the stupidity of men. "That girl has been crazy about you since she was a mite, you fool. It's you who's finally come around to her way of thinking." She smacked his arm, hard enough John flinched and rubbed it. When John said nothing, Mary hit him harder, punching his arm as he yelped in pain.

"Stop it, Mary. That hurt!" he snapped.

"It has to hurt, you dolt, to get past your manly humility. John, you probably don't see it, but you are a man to be proud of. You have a handsome face, a job that agrees with you, and your eyes twinkle when you are happy. And all that pales in comparison to your cheerful ways. You are almost always happy—God only knows how with what life has thrown at you. In addition, you are enjoyable to be around and intelligent and loyal to a fault. I am frankly surprised a girl hasn't already managed to wrestle you to the altar." She eyed him up and down. "What of that girl that serves you coffee where you like to go? She would have you."

John laughed, his cheerful ways, as she'd said, easily rising. "She is sixteen if she is a day, but she does have most of her teeth and one hardly notices her limp. You do know how to cheer a man up. Thank you, Mary."

Mary smiled as well. "I am happy for you, John, I really am. You deserve every happiness."

"As do you." John turned back to his scone, a twinkle in his eye. "Let me know, please, if there is ever a toothless cripple you yourself would like to meet. I will put in a good word."

This time, expecting it, he avoided her blow, cackling all the while. Once she settled down, John returned to his seat and they ate in silence for a few minutes.

"There's no easy way to ask, so I'll just do it," John said suddenly. "How are you doing since the . . . incident . . . with Fairfax?"

The question caught Mary off guard. She shrugged. "Eh, well, fine. I'm doing fine. It was Zoe who walked away with scars."

"Hmm." John side eyed her. "Not all scars can be seen from the outside. Have you spoken to Zoe about it?"

"No." Mary suddenly became very interesting in the crumbs of lemon cake on her lap, brushing at them vigorously. "No, I haven't seen a reason to. I'm fine."

"Yes, you said that." John sighed. "It's your life, Mary, as I've already said. You can do as you please. But I would suggest you find a way to let out whatever it is you have bottled up inside, before it eats you alive. Trust me, I would know."

Mary squinted at that, wondering what secrets John had bottled up. But she wasn't in the mood to ask him anymore. She had too much on her own mind.

Chapter Twelve

"Stop it, ya bloody menace."

The words would have carried more weight if they weren't muttered under the breath of a thirteen-year-old girl pulling rather desperately on the far end of a rope. But they did do the trick, as the menace stopped his race for the offending bunny as it disappeared down a hole, and his end of the rope stopped long enough for her end to catch up. Brutus eyed Gwen with his soulful brown eyes, and she continued her comments, grabbing his muzzle and looking into those eyes. "You and I both know that swearin' ain't at all ladylike, but you don't listen to my nice talkin'," she said seriously.

Brutus waved his tail airily and nosed Gwen for good measure. Then, confident his apology was accepted, he gazed hopefully about for another rabbit to chase. But Gwen pulled him solidly to her side, spoke in a firm voice, and walked out of the park with Brutus under control. She had no time for his capers today.

Truth be told, she was very fond of Brutus. She hadn't been convinced she could handle him when she first set eyes on him, but he had proven to be quite manageable when bunnies were not involved. And if truths were being told, her job minding Brutus gave her a warm bed and food each day, and for that she was grateful. She certainly knew what it was like to have neither.

Gwen strode along the streets of London, as familiar to her as her own tiny room at the Dovefield home. She knew which alleys were shortcuts and which to avoid, which doorways offered shelter and which ones offered the back of a hand. She knew which vendor might toss an apple to a hungry child, and which would just as likely have one arrested and hung. In past years of her life, that hard-earned knowledge meant the difference between life and death.

The streets of London were a part of her, as if the map of those streets mirrored her own veins. Her heart pumped London air, sooty as it was.

Her pumping heart and legs took her easily to Mr. Quinton's door, and she pounded loudly. If her brother Ezra was there alone, he would feel the vibrations. But it was Mr. Quinton who threw open the door and waved her in. "Ezra is delivering a message for me, but he said you were coming. He'll be back shortly," Mr. Quinton said as he closed the door. He gestured at the huge dog. "You're still minding Brutus on your half day?"

Gwen shrugged. "He needed a walk, so I walked him here. Ezra can come with and we can walk him back."

Quinton nodded, already distracted, as he made his way back to the formidable desk taking up much of the space in the first room of the two-room residence and settled behind it.

Gwen looked around, taking in the cot pushed against one wall and the long thin pallet underneath it. She knew her brother Ezra slept on the pallet near the fire most nights, and the thought gave her comfort. She wandered over to the desk, keeping an eye on Brutus as she did so. The beast had made his own way to the fire, but Gwen reckoned if Quinton's cat Oscar put in an appearance, Brutus would need backup.

Oscar, small size aside, was ruler of this roost.

Mr. Quinton leaned back suddenly and sighed. "Once a month I balance my ledger, and every time I would rather be chasing a thief down a back alley with my hands tied behind my back rather than work these numbers."

Gwen sat up straighter, eager to help. "I'm right good with numbers, Mr. Quinton. Maybe I could help."

Mr. Quinton's reaction to her offer was laughter—not malicious, but it wounded Gwen just the same. "Come now, Gwen," he said. "I'm simply not in the mood to show you how the numbers work. Maybe another time."

Taking a deep breath to cool her temper, Gwen walked around to the other side of the desk, looking down at the ledger for a full minute. "Mr. Quinton, you have made a dog's dinner right 'ere with two addin' mistakes, and you did the wrong takeaway over yonder," she finally said with confidence. "If you correct those, I think you will come close to settin' it proper."

Mr. Quinton took a look at the errors she had pointed out, quickly correcting them. He looked up at her, his mouth slightly agape. "How in blazes do you know about maths?" he asked.

Gwen answered easily. "A bricklayer let us sleep in his shop most of one winter. He taught Ezra about plaster and mortar. Ezra could patch that crack above your bed, no problem." Gwen paused to gesture to the ceiling above his cot, and to her surprise Mr. Quinton looked embarrassed. There was no need, as she was just trying to help. "But the bricklayer worked on his ledger once a week. He showed me how the numbers worked a few times and it seemed real simple. He said I have a head for numbers. So I learned how to keep a ledger right, though he checked my numbers every time. It was fun."

"I see." Mr. Quinton scratched his head. "I suppose I've just always thought of maths as more masculine."

Gwen rolled her eyes, frustrated at his denseness. "Different things come easy for different people, Mr. Quinton, boy or girl. Being a girl don't make me dumb."

Mr. Quinton was quick to course correct. "I didn't mean to say you were not intelligent, Gwen."

"Mr. Quinton, beggin' your pardon, it's a mistake to think

people fit in a box," said Gwen after a moment's consideration. "People got skills, even if you don't know what they are. And if a lady needs to get something done, she figures out how. Just like a man."

Just then Ezra burst through the door, hands flying in greeting, interrupting Gwen's conversation. With one last dark look at Quinton, Gwen departed with her brother, Brutus by her side. She'd take a bunny-happy dog over a shortsighted man any day. How someone as smart as Lady Demas could have feelings for a fellow like Quinton was beyond her.

Chapter Thirteen

Quinton headed out to meet John three hours after receiving Ezra's message, so when the boy rematerialized at his side, Quinton wasn't entirely surprised. Quinton reckoned Ezra and Gwen had already enjoyed their time together and parted ways. He felt bad about his interaction with Gwen—she'd left miffed, and Quinton couldn't help but think he was at fault.

He would have to make it up to her, but for now Quinton was grateful for his companion. It gave him something else to think of besides offending thirteen-year-olds or his upcoming visit with John.

Quinton's thoughts drifted back to when he and Ezra had first met. Quinton had been once again conversing with the young Gwen, who was then perhaps eleven to Ezra's fifteen. He was just about to leave when Ezra saw the interaction and tackled him, shoving him into the filth of the street.

Now Quinton understood how Ezra's fierce protectiveness of his sister drove the boy. It was a quality Quinton respected more than he could say, making him fond of Ezra from that day onward.

Turning the corner onto his desired street, Quinton

continued walking briskly. But when he felt a tug on his arm, Quinton stopped, watching the gestures Ezra made with his hands to communicate.

Their close association for over a year had allowed Quinton to learn a few things. He concentrated on the gestures, translating the mimed language into English in his head.

What's wrong? asked Ezra.

"What do you mean?" Although Quinton did try to use his hands as he spoke to Ezra, he also knew he wasn't as skilled as he wanted to be, so he spoke aloud as well so Ezra could read his lips.

You have been upset, replied Ezra. *Your eyes, troubled.*

Taken aback that Ezra had seen his distress, Quinton sputtered, considering his answer. Perhaps the boy's lack of hearing made him observant in ways others were not.

"I learned something about my mother and father that unsettled me," said Quinton finally.

Ezra was quick to respond. *Your mother and father are dead. That is behind you. Why are you upset now?*

A practical if harsh question, but Quinton didn't take offense. He understood that was just Ezra's way.

"What I learned will change my life now," replied Quinton. "It will change my future."

Ezra squinted, looking at him intently. *And you like your life now, no change?*

Quinton gave that comment real thought. Did he like his life now, without change? Parts of it, yes. He liked the people he had cobbled from makeshift to a real family.

But that didn't mean he didn't want anything to change ever. To have the funds to enjoy a life of wealth? To be able to help those he cared about meet their own financial obligations? To have the freedom to pursue Zoe without fear of consequence? Those were all things Quinton wanted.

"I want to keep what I like. Change what I don't," replied Quinton. "But I don't know if I can choose what changes and what doesn't."

Ezra again looked at him long and hard, as if peering into his heart itself, before finally nodding sagely. *You can't change who you are. The outside, it can change. You, inside, you are Quinton. The people who love you, they love you no matter what.* Ezra punctuated his last word with a finger aimed at Quinton's heart, and Quinton had to admit the truth in his words. The people who loved him would still love him, even if some things changed.

Quinton smiled at Ezra, thankful he had the boy in his life to set him straight. Who knew the boy who spoke with his hands would have the words to settle his heart?

Chapter Fourteen

T he Black Dog Tavern had stood on this very spot for close to a hundred years. The classic stone floor and dark wood were familiar to John, soothing his nerves as he waited for Quinton. John was a few minutes late and had been surprised to find Quinton wasn't there yet. As John found a table and ordered two tall ales, he found himself wondering at that. Quinton, as tightly wound as his Aunt Cherry's clock, was never late. Something must be amiss with him. That made John nervous. Though being late was a small thing, the last time Quinton had been out of sorts had been very unfortunate for all involved. And John already had his latest conversation with Savi to be worried about.

When Quinton did stroll through the door, much to John's surprise no storm dragged behind him. Instead he seemed strangely at peace—smiling at the girl behind the bar and greeting the regular patrons as if he had not a care in the world.

That made John even more nervous.

After Quinton sat down, he took a long drink of the dark ale, seeming to be in no hurry to get into the reason he had called for this meeting.

John, on the other hand, wasted no time on pleasantries. "What's going on?" he asked.

Quinton hesitated, clearly turning something over in his mind. He took another fortifying sip of ale before finally speaking. "I've had news on my mother and father. I am of two minds on what to do and could use some input from a friend."

"Oh." John took a sip of his own ale. "Please, continue."

"You and I have seen our share of bad through the years, haven't we?" Quinton chuckled sadly. John tried not to feel whiplash at the change of topics as Quinton continued. "Tragedy and loss and barely scraping by. I think we both know how to make the best of the hand we are dealt. We're used to that."

John nodded, his stomach uneasy. "It's true, ours hasn't always been a smooth road."

Leaning forward, Quinton took a deep breath. "Right. But the struggle I now have is that my circumstances have an opportunity to improve, perhaps drastically, and I do not know if I'm prepared to play that hand through." Quinton suddenly paused, as if gathering his next thoughts. The easy assurance he'd entered the pub with seemed to have deserted him. He looked . . . frightened, which was an emotion John wasn't used to seeing on his friend's face.

"If there is good coming to you, my friend, you deserve it," said John without reservation. "What is it about this good news that has you so shaken up?"

Lowering his voice, Quinton told John of his conversation with Felix Fairfax, of the killer's shocking claim that Quinton's parents were married, as well as his conversation with Hugh Dovefield. The story was not long, but the telling of it felt heavy, making it feel longer.

When Quinton finally finished, his words run out, John responded with a low whistle. "So you will have a title and money if you can prove this claim. Tell me again, what about this turn of events has you so perturbed?" As Quinton shifted in his seat, the answer occurred to John. "Do you really think I care so little for you that this would change anything between us?" he asked, more than a little insulted.

A look of relief came over Quinton's face. "Of course not. I mean, I don't know. It's a lot. But I want you to understand you are my family, society be damned."

"I already know that, Quinton." John downed the rest of his ale, signalling for the bar maid to bring another round. "But it's not me you're really worried about, is it?"

A long pause ruled as the ales were delivered, and each man took a substantial drink.

"No," replied Quinton finally. "It's Charlie."

John nodded. "Hmm. He does present a problem; I'll give you that."

They both knew full well Charlie's reasons for his hatred of the upper class, and those reasons were not unwarranted. If not for Charlie's mother's skills as a midwife, his family would have all starved when his British father abandoned them. That wasn't the kind of casual cruelty one was likely to forget . . . or forgive.

Quinton's stared dejectedly into his ale. "He will cut me off. I just know it."

"Well, that's a bit melodramatic." John rubbed his chin thoughtfully. "Charlie is a stubborn sod, I'll give you that, but he's loyal to his core. He'd do anything for his friends—even move a dead body for Rory, which you might remember appals him."

"I know." Quinton sighed. "And I would do anything for him. But I can't help but think he'll see this as a betrayal."

"His history with you runs deep as a brother's. I think you might be selling our friend a bit short when it comes to who he will keep in his life and what he will do for his brother." John finished off his second pint. "Even put his own belief system aside."

Quinton remained silent, thinking it over. John smirked, ready to send it home. "Of course, the only way to know for sure is to talk to Charlie."

"I'm not ready for that." Quinton downed the rest of his pint as well, eyeing John. "I know I have been preoccupied, but you seem out of sorts. And you are rarely out of sorts, especially with Savi in the picture."

John groaned and ran a hand through his tight curls. "Savi and I have had a quarrel." He hesitated, then spoke with more conviction. "She goes off in the dead of night to deliver a baby with no thought to the real danger in the streets of London at night. As a Runner, I see this danger every day, and the havoc that can be wreaked. I tried mentioning this to her, but she was determined to make no changes. So I informed her that if we were to wed, she would need to stop working, for her own good. I will not allow her to be unsafe." He paused, and glanced at Quinton. Quinton looked rather astonished, and John groaned again.

Quinton spoke slowly, choosing his words. "I am genuinely surprised you carry no injury after such a poorly thought-out declaration."

John shook his head glumly. "From the rage in her eyes, I believe she considered bodily harm, but she was raised better." He sighed. "I will admit, I came across rather heavy-handed. But my concern for her is real and, I feel, warranted."

Quinton leaned back and regarded him. "I am no expert on women—"

"Who possibly could be?" John interrupted, scowling.

Quinton smiled. "I'll give you that. But it seems to me any person would want their feelings and thoughts to be valued. You and Savi are perfect together. You will need to fully accept, however, that she is a woman who knows her mind. Treat her as such. It is a bit of a conundrum that you are clearly wildly attracted to a woman of spirit and courage, and yet also want her to easily bow to all of your thoughts. Apologize, man."

"That irony doesn't fall far from the tree," John shot back. He saw Quinton wince and immediately regretted speaking. "But you are right. Savi and I will find our way, and an apology on my part will help." Quinton said nothing, so John continued. "And you, my friend, will find your way with Zoe. This title changes what you can give her, and that must be foremost in your thoughts."

Quinton nodded slowly. "I have work to do as well, John. But I think both of us know who we want by our side." Quinton stood as he spoke. "Unfortunately I have to be off—I need to figure out how someone got to Zoe's blasted cousin in White's before it gets too late in the day."

John frowned. "The gentleman's club? Do you need any help?"

"No, I think I've got it." As Quinton moved to leave, he placed a hand on John's shoulder. "But thank you for this. I needed it."

As the sound of Quinton's footsteps faded, John contemplated the two empty glasses on the table before him. He had meant what he said—very little could alter how he felt about his friend. But as the reality sank in, John also knew that this would change things, for all of them. Change was, after all, the only constant in life. While there hadn't been a storm cloud hovering over Quinton's head this time, John could now see one forming on the horizon. He would just have to have faith that the bond between his adopted brothers would be strong enough to survive the storm. And see whether the same could be said of the tenuous new bond between him and Savi . . .

Chapter Fifteen

Zoe held her breath as she waited for Quinton to respond. He rubbed his chin thoughtfully, leaning back in his armchair, his dark eyes distant as he pondered. "Well, I can't say I'm surprised to find out he bedded the girl," he finally said. "I'm not sure how it helps us either way though."

"Oh." Zoe cleared her throat. "I thought you would be more upset about me going to the gambling hell."

Quinton snorted, an unreadable glint in his eye. "Oh, I'm not thrilled, but arguing with you has rarely gotten me anywhere. Seeing as how you've already done it, let's move on."

That wasn't the reaction Zoe had been expecting. She supposed it was good he wasn't upset. It wasn't like she wanted to fight with him. And yet, a small part of her was almost . . . disappointed that he hadn't pressed the issue further—which of course was completely irrational.

"Very well." Zoe brushed those ridiculous thoughts to the back of her mind and carried on. "I agree, it's not surprising to find he was . . . intimate . . . with the girl. But I thought there would be more to it. I still think he's holding something back."

"Why would he do that when he's paying me for help?"

"I don't know. That's what worries me."

Quinton shook his head. As he took a sip of his whiskey, the firelight from his own hearth reflected against the glass, causing strange shadows to dance across his face. It gave him an ethereal look, like a character out of fiction.

No one could deny he was a handsome man—the thought had crossed her mind more often than Zoe cared to admit. His thick, wavy dark brown hair was just long enough to fall into his brooding brown eyes at the end of a long day. His jawline was sharp enough to cut a finger on, and his cheekbones weren't far behind.

On this particular evening, he was wearing a loose-fitting white shirt held tight to his chest by a well-tailored waistcoat. The top few buttons were undone, and Zoe tried not to let her gaze rest upon the exposed skin. Even as her mind wandered into impure territory, Zoe noted a kind of heaviness which seemed to cling to him, weighing his eyelids down and pressing his large frame into the armchair.

That wasn't surprising, given recent events. His grief at the loss of mother had been a constant companion over the years. When he had spiralled into hopelessness over dead ends in the investigation, Zoe had wondered if he would ever recover. Now justice had been served and his mother's killer was nothing but a corpse being consumed by worms, but he was still living with the consequences. A little exhaustion seemed like his prerogative.

But though it logically made sense to her, something about his demeanour still bothered Zoe. Ever since his conversation with Felix Fairfax before the hanging, something else had been preoccupying his mind—something he hadn't shared with her. That bothered her more than anything.

"I could use another pour." Mary's words interrupted Zoe's inward deductions, bringing her back to the present. Quinton reacted quickly, pouring another draft into her glass. Mary was also preoccupied, staring off into the firelight, but the source of her feelings was less mysterious. Zoe quickly glanced away, clearing her throat again. "Did you have any luck at White's?" she asked.

"No, not really." Quinton sighed. "If they bribed someone to get a goon inside, I couldn't find anyone who would admit to it. It's still odd though."

"How so?"

"It's unusually aggressive. High risk. Lots of ways for that to blow back in a bad way. Most of the schemes, once there's a risk of getting caught, the culprits disappear like smoke. But not this time . . ."

"Well, maybe it's not a real scheme. Maybe the threat to the girl is real."

"Maybe." Quinton took another sip, his eyes still distant. "But I'm not sure what to do next. Unless something else happens, we might be at a dead end."

That didn't sound like him. Quinton wasn't one to just give up. Zoe opened her mouth, about ready to say as much, but a quick glance at his face caused her to decide against it. "How are you doing?" she asked instead.

He blinked, as if startled by the question. "I'm doing well, thank you. Why do you ask?"

"It's been a rough couple of weeks. We haven't really . . . talked about it."

"That's not true. We had that little soiree at your parents' home. We talked about it then," he retorted.

Zoe shook her head. "Not really. This is a major event in your life—a major trauma—and we haven't discussed it. We've just jumped straight back to chasing down clues without any real conversation."

"Very well." Quinton shifted in his seat. "If you wish to have a real conversation, perhaps we should start with what happened to you—to both of you."

Mary glanced up at that. She looked over at Zoe, and as their eyes met, it felt as though the two of them were able to acknowledge the reality for the first time. For a moment, the silent communication which had always come so easily between the two was turned back on, and Zoe understood instantly what Mary was trying to say.

And so, though she desperately wanted to push Quinton for what was on his mind, Zoe took her lady's companion's silent plea seriously and said, "On the other hand, perhaps it is best to let it lie for now . . ."

Quinton shrugged. "If you insist."

Mary stood suddenly. "I am wearied. Perhaps it would be best to head home, and tomorrow we can reconvene on these matters?"

"Yes, of course." Zoe quickly downed the rest of her whiskey and stood. "A good night's sleep may provide a solution."

She knew the words were a lie, even as she said them, as none of them would be getting a good night's rest for quite some time.

Chapter Sixteen

Her prediction came true—Zoe slept very little that night. She finally gave up the pretence, well before the weak dawn light could finally make its way through her window.

Normally when she was like this, she would just lay in her bed a bit longer, or else go to the park and paint, even in the winter. That propensity had stressed Lucy to no end. At the time, Lucy's distress and scolding had annoyed Zoe constantly. Now she understood Lucy hadn't desired to annoy her but rather had been driven by a fear Zoe could never understand. If she could turn back the clock, she'd apologize, but now of course . . . she would never have that chance.

Her new maid Camille would go with her if Zoe asked, but today she wasn't in the mood for painting. Truth be told, she hadn't been in the mood for painting in quite a while. That part of herself seemed distant now, like she couldn't quite grab hold of it anymore.

Sometimes she would talk to her mother when Zoe felt like this, or perhaps Theo, but they were both off on a last-minute holiday. The timing was inconvenient, and she'd never known her mother to do things at the last minute, but Zoe was glad Theo had been able to talk Simone into taking some time for herself.

Regardless, today the family member she wanted go see was the only one eccentric enough to also be awake at this hour—her uncle Sebastian.

Slipping out of the house without waking her family was easy enough—the only ones awake in the house at this hour were the servants, and they tended to turn a blind eye to her odd comings and goings. After that she caught a hackney over to her uncle's current residence at the home of one of his many friends.

Zoe had to take advantage of his presence in London. It wouldn't be long before that itch he had took him away again, on another grand adventure. He lived quite an exciting life, their Sebastian.

The butler who answered the door didn't know her, but he didn't seem surprised to see her either. Sebastian tended to have eccentric friends too. Zoe was quickly escorted to the sitting room to wait for Sebastian with minimal questions.

Sebastian appeared shortly thereafter—fully dressed and eyes bright. As Zoe suspected, he had been awake.

"Zoe!" he said with surprise. "What are you doing here?"

"Oh, nothing." Zoe cleared her throat. "It's nothing important. Do you have other plans today? I could come back tomorrow if that would be better."

His eyes narrowed as Sebastian looked her up and down. "No, I don't have any plans." He glanced toward the window. "How about we go for a walk?"

"Yes, let's do that."

Sebastian quickly retrieved his overcoat and then they were on their way.

Even in his mid-forties, he was the most handsome of the Dovefields—not that Hugh and Theo weren't handsome in their own way. Even Baldwin had a certain symmetry and dignity about him. But there had always been something special about Sebastian.

Zoe could picture him as a young man, his golden curls falling into forest green eyes, with a quick smile followed by a loud laugh. Even though he was a third son and known to be a little odd in his habits, his good nature, charm, and wit had made him popular in nearly every social circle. Now the gold in his curls had faded to a bit greyer and a few lines ringed those green eyes, but the quick smile and charm still got him far in life.

"So what's on your mind?" he finally asked after they had walked some distance.

A good question. Zoe didn't have a good answer. Her mind felt jumbled and unsettled, like she couldn't find a straight line of thought through.

"We haven't really spoken since our return from the colonies." Zoe shrugged. "I suppose I've just missed your company."

"At this hour?" Sebastian raised his eyebrow. "I know you're an early riser, but this is a bit much even for you."

"Yes, I suppose you're right."

He glanced over at her, his expression pensive. "Although a number of events have transpired since our last meeting. That bruise across your cheek for one."

"Ah, yes." Zoe reached up instinctively to touch the tender spot on her face. Unless she was looking in a mirror, sometimes she forgot it was even there now. The colour had faded from black and blue to a ghastly yellowish. "Did you hear about—"

"Yes, Theo gave me a brief summary of events. How are you recovering?"

"Fine." Zoe forced a smile. "I'm doing just fine."

"Naturally."

After that they walked in silence for a while more. Of Hugh's siblings, Zoe had always been closest with Theo. The dowager had taken an interest in Zoe from the beginning and was like a proper aunt to her. But when it came to similarity of spirit, no one could quite match Sebastian and Zoe.

The resemblance wasn't in personality, exactly. Where Sebastian was sunshine, Zoe was a thunderstorm—where he was warm, she was usually perceived as cold. But neither could bear to be stifled by society's expectations. People just seemed to like him better for it than her.

"So how is your man—Huxley, is it?" said Sebastian, breaking the silence.

"He's not my man," grumbled Zoe. "Why do you ask about him?"

Sebastian chuckled. "Our little venture to America was not so long ago that I could forget the reason you joined me. You moped on the boat the whole way there, staring off into the middle distance like a tragic heroine in a tawdry novel."

A fair point. The trip had been precipitated by a rather nasty falling out with Quinton. While she hadn't told Sebastian everything, it didn't take a genius to put two and two together.

"He is also fine," she said reluctantly.

"Fine?" Sebastian shook his head, a slight smile on his face. "It seems like a great deal is fine in your life. Which in my experience means things are perhaps not so fine."

"Perhaps not." Zoe sighed, her stride slowing. "Something is still weighing on Quinton's soul. He is better, of course, than when we first returned. But I thought learning the truth of his past would bring him some peace. Now I worry he will never be at peace."

Nodding, Sebastian paused to examine a snow-covered hedge. "And what would you do if he was at peace? Would it change your dynamic?"

Caught off guard by his question, Zoe too paused, examining the hedge herself. "Well, I suppose it would be beneficial to our friendship—"

"Your friendship?" Sebastian snorted. "That's a load of horse crock."

"Well, maybe I don't know!" Zoe threw up her hands, resuming her previous stride. "How do you do it?"

Sebastian jogged to catch up to her. "Do what?"

"Live your life exactly how you want to with no

repercussions!" Zoe increased her pace. "You do what you want, go where you want, live with who you want, and no one bats an eye! How do you do it?"

"Zoe, it's not that simple." Sebastian grabbed her arm, pulling backward. "Will you slow down, please?"

Reluctantly Zoe did slow her pace. She wasn't even sure why she was so upset. Was it because Quinton refused to investigate Katie's disappearance further? Or because of the rift between her and Mary? Or was it about whatever secret Quinton was keeping from her?

If she was being honest, what had kept her up all night was something much deeper. A circumstance Zoe tried not to think about because there didn't seem to be any solution in sight.

"You ask how it is that I am able to live my life as I please." Sebastian ran his fingers through his hair, staring off into the distance. "The truth is that in exchange for this life I have curated, I gave up many things."

Zoe rolled her eyes. "Such as what? Social convention?"

"You mock, but do you know who I'm staying with currently? The Earl of Kenswick and his wife. Do you know where I'll be in a month?"

"No."

Sebastian shrugged. "Neither do I. You see, I have a great deal of freedom. But I don't have the security of a home of my own. Even when I go to Baldwin's, I'm just a guest. I don't have a wife or children, or a place I belong. These are choices I made, but it doesn't mean I don't wonder about the path not taken."

"But you still have freedom," Zoe countered.

"And is that what you want, Zoe?" asked Sebastian. "Freedom?"

"Yes." The answer came to her mind and lips immediately. "The freedom to do what I want without the eyes of society judging me. The freedom to marry who I wish without being rejected by my family and friends." Zoe hesitated, swallowing hard. "The freedom to get married at all without being the property of a man. I feel as though no matter what I do, I will be trading one prison for another."

That was hard to admit out loud. She had no easy choices set out before her. Whatever she did, Zoe would be trapped, in one way or another.

"I understand, Zoe." Sebastian shook his head. "But the truth is there is no such thing as freedom without cost. But I trust you will make the correct decision for yourself when the time is right."

As they turned back toward the house, Zoe realized that Sebastian was right. It would be her choice to make, but every choice came with a cost. Only time would tell which price she was willing to pay.

Chapter Seventeen

W hen Theo had said she would make all the
arrangements, she evidently meant with haste. The
day after their conversation, the two women had
taken their carriage ride to Southampton and boarded their boat
to the Isle of Guernsey. The following morning they were out and
about on their mission.

Simone would allow the task was harder than she had
anticipated. They had spent some time asking at their hotel about
churches before setting off to visit the nearest. Two of them were
simply not old enough to have performed a wedding some thirty
years ago. One was closed and small, and though it may have seen
better days, both ladies did not feel it was where a lord would
choose to be married. A fourth they never found. They returned
to the hotel tired, hungry, and frustrated.

Fortunately for their spirits, the hotel at least had excellent
food. Simone's guess would be a French chef. The English knew
what they were doing with tea and scones, but that was about it
when it came to food. That area was for the French to excel.

Over an excellent sea bass, Simone noticed the tiredness
around Theo's eyes. Sometimes Simone forgot that Theo was not
as young as she used to be—the constant motion must be wearing

at her age. The older woman had also consumed most of a bottle of wine as well, no doubt adding to her weariness. Perhaps they should go up to their rooms for a rest.

Simone opened her mouth to suggest it but realized Theo's attention wasn't on her. She followed Theo's eye line, to where Theo was watching a nursemaid with an infant. The child was cherubic, smiling and giggling as babies did. It was a happy sight, but Simone didn't see joy reflected in Theo's eyes—rather, the gaze was filled a sadness she hadn't seen before, deep and raw.

"Did I ever tell you about my daughter?" asked Theo suddenly.

Simone gasped, fumbling with her fork, the clanking echoing through the restaurant. Theo had never spoken of a child— Simone had always thought she was childless. "No, you've never mentioned it." Simone cleared her throat. "I think I would have remembered."

"Ah, well, it was a long time ago." Theo waved her hand dismissively, but Simone could see the mist gathering in her eyes. "I've learned not to speak of it. My daughter came early, and we knew she would not survive. She died in my arms only a few hours after birth."

Simone felt her own eyes begin to grow misty. "I am so sorry. That must have been devastating."

"It was early in our marriage, before Hugh lived with us. I named her Caroline. I always loved that name, and I wanted so desperately to give her something lasting." Theo paused for a moment, her countenance growing dark. "My husband refused to acknowledge her at all—wouldn't say her name, not once. She's not even recorded in the family records. It was as if she never lived at all. He thought she was buried with some poor fool who had the misfortune of dying at the right time. But I paid a man to bury an empty box there, and she has a grave I tend in a small graveyard."

The words were said matter-of-fact, but Simone could see the anger simmering beneath the surface. The Dovefield family were

88

all fully aware that Theo's marriage hadn't been a love match, but it was rarely spoken of out loud. Simone had only ever known Theo as she was now—widowed and free of entanglements.

"That must have been terribly difficult," said Simone, not know what else to say.

Theo's eyes shone with an emotion Simone couldn't place. "Well, I got my revenge, in my own small way. If my daughter wasn't allowed to have a name, then neither was he. I haven't spoken his name since he passed."

Simone reached out to take Theo's hand in her own. She didn't have any other sage or comforting words to say, but she could hold her hand.

"It's fine, dear, it's fine," said Theo, using her other hand to pat the top of Simone's. "We are women of steel you and I. We bear our pain silently and adapt to the world as it is, but that doesn't mean we are without feeling. Now if you will excuse me, I believe I need to go up for a lie down. This wine has gone to my head."

"Of course. I will see you for dinner."

As she watched Theo move gracefully across the floor toward the stairs, Simone contemplated their conversation. To survive as a woman required sacrifice—to thrive required equal parts luck and cleverness. Some of the things she herself had done to survive, only she knew. Some she was proud of. Some she hoped never saw the light of day.

Theo took dinner in her room that night, and when morning came around, Simone wondered if the woman regretted her discussion from the night before. But Theo emerged looking rested and unperturbed. "Thank you for letting me blather on yesterday, Simone," said Theo as she poured a cup of tea. "I have not spoken Caroline's name aloud for many years."

"You were hardly blathering, Theo," retorted Simone. "We

have been friends for many years. I'm honoured you shared that part of your life with me." Simone didn't say it out loud, but she wondered if Theo's history was part of the reason she had been so welcoming to Simone and Zoe. Perhaps they had helped to fill a void in her life left by the loss of her own daughter. There was something . . . pleasant in that idea to Simone.

They both companionably finished their breakfast, a new bond between them, and only belatedly did Simone notice that the girl clearing the dishes was French. When Simone spoke to her in her own language, she mentioned their quest. The girl was quick to tell her that the Town Church, on the southern edge of town was a beautiful church, exceedingly old, where many marriages were held and foreign weddings were welcome. She helped them arrange transport with a local carriage company and was rewarded with a healthy tip. The girl was beaming as she made her way back to the hotel, and Simone suspected there would be no shortage of assistance at the hotel in the days to come. Finally things were looking promising.

Until they reached the church. Men of the cloth generally made Simone uncomfortable, but this one seemed determined to confirm all her prejudices against the profession. Feeling her blood begin to boil, Simone was grateful when Theo stepped in with the stubborn vicar, explaining their quest once more and throwing in her title.

"And I will repeat meself, milady, as you clearly are not from these parts," said the shockingly annoying man. "In our neck of the woods, the womenfolk don't ask for official documents. It's best, really, if they remain at home and let the men handle matters of import."

Having been widowed quite young, Theo had spent the last couple of decades doing as she pleased, and Simone knew if it came to a battle of wills, the vicar would be on the losing end. The dowager began, "I am willing to give you a bit of grace, my good man, as you must be still unaware of my title. I will repeat it for your benefit—"

"I heard ya the first time, milady," the vicar interrupted. "It don't matter around here if you was the Queen herself. We don't cater to women."

Theo drew another breath to speak, steam practically coming out of her ears, but another voice called from behind them. "Thank you, Deacon Francis, for your fine defence of the church papers. But, please, allow me to handle this from here."

An elderly man strode up, his age evident in the lines on his face and the grey of his thick head of hair but not in his vibrant step. Without waiting for permission, the new man raised his arm to guide the ladies towards the rear of the church, carefully refraining from actually touching either of them. Grasping this as a possible solution, Simone and Theo easily allowed themselves to be herded to a small office in the corner, with books and papers comfortably scattered across the surface of the small desk. Two straight-back chairs rested in a corner, and the man pulled them forward, waiting for each woman to be seated before seating himself in the worn chair behind the desk.

"I did not hear your entire conversation," said the man. "But I can still spot a lord from five paces and a lady from ten. I am Bishop Bridger."

"You are quite the saviour, sir," said Theo with a dazzling smile. "We are deeply grateful to you. I hope you will be able to fulfil our, needs, if you will. I am Lady Theodosia Bexley, Dowager Dutchess of Wentworth."

Theo batted her lashes briefly and Simone was astonished to realize that she was flirting. Simone glanced at the bishop, and the twinkle in his eye was unmistakable.

"I may be old, milady, but I can still recognize feminine wiles. I appreciate the thought of swaying this grey horse. Perhaps you can tell me what your wishes, er, needs are, and I will see what I can do."

Her smile turning genuine, Theo leaned forward. "It is a matter of legality, as we were explaining to your colleague, sir. A close friend of the family, who always believed his mother to be unwed, has recently come across information leading him to believe she and his father were secretly married. My sister-in-law, Lady Dovefield, has accompanied me to ascertain if perhaps that secret wedding took place here, many years past."

Bishop Bridger nodded, his expression contemplative. "Our dear friend Deacon Francis has been leading this diocese for nearly three years. Before that, the privilege was mine. The adjustment has brought . . . challenges I did not anticipate. I've delayed my full retirement in the hopes of smoothing over some of the deacon's rougher edges." He sighed deeply. "You did not come here to listen to an old man's problems. If your friend's parents were married here, it would have been me who performed the ceremony. Do you have a date in mind?"

Almost an hour later, Simone and Theo emerged from the dark recesses of the church, blinking at the bright sunshine. They looked at each other for a moment and then Theo spoke. "Our passage home is in two days. That will give us time to prepare our minds for what comes."

"If there is to be a battle," Simone replied easily, "let it begin."

Chapter Eighteen

John did not enjoy starting his day this way. He rubbed his bleary eyes and suppressed a yawn, ignoring the siren song of returning to his soft—not to mention warm—bed. The icy winter wind cut right through his thick red woollen overcoat, causing him to shiver. But as cold as he was, it was nothing compared to the poor lass they were pulling out of the Thames.

The constable had rousted him before dawn, gibbering on about a body caught up in some tree roots in the river. It was sad, but not entirely uncommon. People drowned in the deep water on a regular basis—some were drunkards who slipped while passing by, others children who would bathe in the shallows, daring each other to go out farther and farther until the unexpectedly strong current pulled them under. But it was the wrong time of year for bathers, and even if it was a drunkard, someone still needed to confirm the death was accidental. So it fell to John to be dragged from the warmth of his hearth and down to the frozen riverbank at that ungodly hour.

The rivermen were using ropes and hooks to free the body from the roots, but even obscured, anyone could see it was a woman from the dress and the long hair. She was face down, bobbing in the current, with half her body under the thin sheet of ice which stretched from the bank out toward the centre but was unable to freeze fully due to the fast-moving water.

The sight of the ice caused John's mind to drift back to the last time the Thames had frozen over completely. There had been a frost fair that year, and his mother had taken him. From one side to the other, the ice was covered in tents and booths and the press of humanity in search of entertainment. The two of them mingled with the crowd, and she bought him a hot chocolate. They watched some of the couples dancing, and he tried ice skating for the first and last time. She laughed as he wobbled about, flailing his arms like a baby bird falling from the nest. His mother had had a beautiful laugh.

That was one of John's last distinct memories of her—a figure in the distance, arms wrapped around her chest to hold onto body heat, head thrown back in laughter. That little boy had no idea it would be less than a year before she was gone forever. He was just happy. It was a perfect moment, one of the few in his childhood. John was grateful to have it.

John wondered if there would ever be another frost fair where he took his own children. He could almost see it clearly happening in front of him—two boys racing across the ice, with a little girl toddling behind them, determined to keep up with her older brothers. A warm hand slipped into his own, and John glanced over to see the mother of his children. She was the most beautiful woman he had ever seen, with warm golden-brown skin and long, thick black hair framing her expressive dark eyes. She smiled at him, and John's heart skipped a beat.

Only recently had John perceived Savita Modi as anything other than Charlie's younger sister, but he already could hardly picture a life without her. Savita was not only beautiful but witty and kind, not to mention hardworking and talented in her occupation as a midwife. She was the love of his life, which some might find humorous considering they had only been courting for two weeks, but John knew—he knew she would be his wife, despite his contradictory words to Mary. Of course there was the recent quarrel. If he could just make her see reason on her own safety. His apology had not settled the stormy waters as much as he hoped.

"Got 'er!" shouted one of the rivermen, bringing John crashing back to reality.

"Good." John strode over, shaking his head to clear the cobwebs. "Turn her over, please."

The woman was turned with a wet squelching noise so she lay face up. John crouched down beside her, looking over the body, trying to avoid her pale, unseeing gaze. Despite her skin being swollen and wrinkled by the water, John could tell she was young, but not a child—perhaps closer to twenty. Her face would have been considered pretty if not for the cuts and scrapes which covered it. She was wearing a simple shift dress, but her arms, legs, and feet were bare. Any patch of exposed skin was scraped and raw, likely from being dragged along the bottom of the river bed.

John stood, turning to the shivering constable. "Fetch a wagon to take the body to Rory Stewart."

"Are ye sure, sir? She mighta just fallen in."

"I don't know about you constable, but I don't take many strolls in February without shoes."

"Maybe they were taken by the current."

"Along with her coat?" John shook his head. "Just go fetch the wagon."

Chapter Nineteen

"Well, Rory, you better have a good reason for dragging me here at this hour," growled Quinton as he stalked into the backyard shed where Rory did most of his work.

"The sun is well over the horizon." Rory waved a dismissive hand. "For the working class, this is a perfectly reasonable hour. Only members of society have the luxury of still being asleep now."

The words turned Quinton's stomach, but he quickly dismissed his guilty thoughts. "Just tell me what's so urgent."

Rory sighed, stepping to the side to reveal the body of a young woman on the table behind him. "I think John may have fished your missing young woman, Miss Katie, out of the Thames this morning."

"What makes you say that?"

"Well, I cannae be sure. But she matches the description you gave me—young, Anglo, blonde hair, blue eyes."

Another wave of guilt washed over Quinton. He had just been complaining to Zoe that there was little else to do in this case unless something new turned up. He had wished for it, and like some kind of twisted gift, the universe had answered him. He had been so preoccupied with his own internal conflict, only giving this case half his attention—less than half. Now the missing girl was dead and he would have to live with that.

"Can you tell how long she's been in the water?" Quinton asked, dreading the answer.

"It's hard to say for certain," replied Rory. "The Thames is frigid this time of year, and that slows down the body wasting away. But her skin is loose, meaning it's not attached to the muscle underneath, which in my experience usually happens after about a week."

"So she's been dead at least that long?"

"I'd say so."

A wave of relief swept over Quinton, easing his conscience. At least the girl had already been dead when he made his ill-thought-out wish.

He stepped around Rory to take in the body. She was naked, with several scrapes and cuts on her arms, legs, and face. Her chest down to her stomach had been cut open, but without the usual precise, clean lines that Rory made. This was a jagged wound with a series of even punctures along its edge. Off to the side was a pile of pieces of black thread.

"What happened here?" he asked, pointed to the mutilation.

"Take a look inside."

Swallowing hard to prevent the bile in his throat from coming up any farther, Quinton leaned over. It didn't take him long to perceive the bloody anomaly. "Are those . . . stones?"

"Aye. Someone cut the poor lass open and filled her body cavity with rocks, likely hoping to weigh her down, then sewed her back up." Rory pointed to wounds in the upper chest of the body. "Punctured her lungs too. Bloody smart. It's a miracle the lass was ever found."

Quinton shook his head. "How would someone know how to do that?"

"Experience."

The dark utterance sent a shiver down Quinton's spine. He

had treated this case like a nuisance—an inconvenience to a gentleman seeking entertainment outside of what society had dictated but nothing actually serious. Never had he expected it to veer in this direction, but veer it had. Whoever had done this was a creature beyond empathy or basic human decency—a monster in the truest sense of the word.

"My God," he muttered under his breath.

"It's quite nasty," agreed Rory.

"Can you tell if she was still . . . alive when any of this happened?"

"Again, there's more than a fair bit I can't be certain of due to the water. But I would say it's unlikely."

"Thank God for small mercies." Quinton crossed his arms, taking a step backwards. "Do you have any ideas on what did kill her?"

Rory nodded, taking the head in his hands and turning it to the side. "Her neck is broken, and there's damage to the back of her skull. It's possible this damage came from just being dragged along the riverbed, like the rest of these abrasions, but it's the only injury I've found so far that would have been fatal. All the organs seem to be in decent condition, which doesn't definitively rule out poison but does make it less likely."

For just a moment, Quinton could picture another person lying on the table, lifeless and cold, her blue eyes vacant but open and her neck bent at an unnatural angle. When Zoe had disappeared during their previous investigation . . . he'd been terrified of finding her like this. None of them wanted to admit how close it had been. Did it make him a bad person that as he looked down at this poor dead girl, he felt a sense of relief that it wasn't Zoe?

"Interesting." Absentmindedly, Quinton rubbed the back of his own neck. "Have you told John any of this?"

"Not yet. But this is an official matter now, so I'm obligated to share my findings with him. I suggest you loop him."

"Of course. I'll get in touch as soon as I leave here." Quinton started to walk to the door. "I'll get the cousin over here to confirm the identity."

"One more thing before you go . . ."

Quinton paused. "What?"

"Whoever did this dressed the lass after the mutilation."

"What of it?"

Rory cocked his head, his eyes thoughtful. "It's not necessary. They could have just thrown her into the river naked, or wrapped in a blanket. But they took the time to put her dress back on, fastening each button carefully, like they didn't want her to be exposed."

"I don't understand," said Quinton, his eyebrows furrowed.

"I think whoever did this might have genuinely cared for Katie."

Quinton scoffed. "You can't be serious."

"I know, it sounds mad, given the mutilation. But all of that likely happened after death, meant to conceal the crime. Even the fatal injury could've been accidental—maybe from an awkward fall or something of the like." Rory sighed. "I'm telling you, the dress means something. I'd bet money she knew whoever did this and that their relationship was friendly."

It didn't make sense to Quinton—how could someone do this to someone they cared for, to someone they called a friend? But he had learned to trust Rory over the years, especially when it came to minds of those who took the lives of others.

"Very well," he said after a moment's consideration. "I'll keep it in mind."

Quinton continued to contemplate the incongruity of someone caring for someone they tossed in the Thames, and after a moment he felt Rory's eyes upon him.

"Ya got something on your mind, lad? " The question was simple but took Quinton off guard. It reminded him that Rory was insightful in the ways of the living as well. Of all the people Quinton had agonized over telling about the change in his status, Rory was the one he worried about the least. Despite his rather unorthodox occupation, Rory already existed in a world surprisingly close to the nobility and had no particular feelings of animosity towards the upper class. Rory regularly attended scientific lectures, went to the theatre, and enjoyed the finer restaurants of London.

Might as well get it over with. "As a matter of fact, I do." With few details, Quinton explained to Rory his still-new change of understanding regarding his parents' marriage and what that meant.

The story still made him unsettled, but Rory smiled broadly and clapped him on the back. "Life is funny, lad. Sometimes it gives, and sometimes it takes. Embrace it when the odds fall to your winning side." He paused a moment, and came to the real heart of the matter. "Your feelings have been obvious for Miss Demas. Is this what you need to make them known?"

Quinton had come to regard Rory as a man of advice, so he answered easily. "My feelings I admit readily, Rory. But my understanding of that woman's mind on any level, therein lies my fear. She both confounds and mesmerizes me. I do not know if having a title will change that. I have come to wonder if I will ever fathom Zoe Demas."

Rory laughed. "Let me put your mind at ease, my friend. You most certainly never will. And that is part of the beauty of love. In fact, when love endures, the mystery never ends. That itself is a blessing, not a curse."

Quinton listened quietly and found himself agreeing. He smiled suddenly and spoke. "I see it was worth my early arrival after all, Rory, on several fronts. As usual, I have learned a great deal."

Chapter Twenty

Alexander didn't take the news well. Zoe attempted to comfort him, but they had spent most of their childhoods as antagonists, so it was a foreign concept for her. She patted his back awkwardly as he stood in shock outside the shed in Rory's garden, his mouth agape and eyes welling with tears.

Finally she managed to bundle him into a hackney, giving the driver instructions to take Alexander to her home rather than his own. He wasn't in any condition to be alone, and his father certainly wasn't the type to sympathize with him on this— Baldwin wasn't the type to sympathize on many things. With Theo still on holiday, it would have to fall to Hugh to take custody of his nephew until Zoe could return. It wasn't that she didn't feel bad for him, but Zoe needed to discuss the next moves with Quinton, and Alexander wasn't helpful for anything beyond identifying the body.

"I've told John the details we already know regarding poor Katie Shorn." Quinton sighed, running his fingers through his hair. "He's going to take a constable and go back to the gambling hell to investigate officially, but I don't think he'll get very far.

Whatever is going on here, the people involved are far cleverer than I thought."

He looked tired still, but less defeated than yesterday. Behind the exhaustion was a quiet determination. This pleased Zoe. Quinton needed a purpose in order to feel fulfilled, and now he had one.

"What makes you say that?" asked Mary.

"What they did to conceal the body. Cutting her up like that . . . it's ruthless, but smart. They've done this before and gotten away with it." Quinton hesitated before continuing. "Rory even thinks they may have cared for the girl, which is even more disturbing."

A chill ran up Zoe's spine. "Why?"

Shaking his head, Quinton stared off into the distance. "Because if you can do that to someone you care about, there's no limit to what you're capable of."

He wasn't wrong. Just hearing the basic details from Rory had been enough to turn Zoe's stomach. *That poor girl . . .*

Zoe shook off her disgust—this wasn't the time. "So what's next?"

Quinton met her gaze, his eyes intense. "I need to know more about Miles O'Malley—I need leverage to get him to talk. He must be the ringleader in this scheme. If Katie had a change of heart or tried to steal some of the profits, then he's likely her killer as well."

"I don't know about that." Zoe glanced over at Mary. "He's repulsive, certainly, but clever . . . I'm not so sure."

"I agree, he doesn't give the impression of a criminal mastermind," concurred Mary.

"Be that as it may, he's our only lead right now," Quinton countered. "Regardless, I think our time would be best spent having a conversation with Charlie."

Zoe's brow furrowed. "I thought they weren't on friendly terms?"

"They aren't. Which is why I'm sure Charlie knows what old Miles had for breakfast this morning."

Chapter Twenty-One

T he cold whiskey burned on its way down, but Charlie enjoyed the burn. It was a little early in the day for alcohol—and if you asked his mother, there was never a good time—but Charlie didn't care. He especially didn't care when his mother and sister were out of the house, delivering new life into an ugly world.

His mind drifted under the influence of the whiskey. His supervision was needed for three shipments of brandy coming in that afternoon, plus a visit to a brothel madam who had recently stopped paying protection. Then there were rumours about a new gambling hell popping up in his territory—an unauthorized one, which Charlie couldn't tolerate without a response. Once they thought you'd gone soft, in his line of work . . . that was a death knell.

A loud knock at his front door broke Charlie out of his musings. The young boy who worked for his family answered the door, and a few moments later he showed his guests up the stairs. It was Quinton, followed by Quinton's friend Zoe and John's niece Mary. A sigh escaped Charlie's lips—he would have to have a chat with the boy about allowing just anyone into the house.

"Whatever this is, I'm busy, so make it quick." Charlie downed another sip.

"I can see that." Quinton raised an eyebrow, the corner of his lip quirking up. "We'll try not to take up too much of your valuable time."

Charlie glared—if anyone else spoke to him like that . . . but Quinton wasn't just anyone. "Get to the point," Charlie growled.

Quinton took a seat in his usual armchair. "Did you hear about the dead girl who was fished out of the Thames this morning?"

"I might have heard something about it." Little that happened in London that Charlie was not aware of, but he preferred to keep his cards close to his chest. He didn't need everyone up in his business, even his friends.

"It was Katie Shorn," said Quinton in a matter-of-fact manner.

Charlie choked on the golden liquid he had just sipped, sputtering as he coughed. "Are you certain?"

"Yes. My cousin identified her," said Zoe.

"*Are baap re.*" Shaking his head, Charlie refilled his glass and then passed out glasses to the others. "That is a shame. How'd she go?"

"Broken neck, Rory reckons. Then cut open and filled with rocks," replied Quinton.

Charlie paused, a chill running up his spine. He set his glass down with a thud, trying to conceal the slight shake in his hand. Few things shocked him, and realistically, this wasn't one of them. What gave him such pause was that two days ago, when a man had beat a prostitute to death in one of the brothels under his protection, Charlie had arranged for the brute be taken care of in a very similar fashion.

"I know, it's quite shocking." Zoe sighed, daintily sipping her whiskey. "It's hard to believe such savagery exists in the world."

Charlie cleared his throat. "Yes. Quite."

This wasn't a part of his world he could share with them—

not even Quinton. Though they had grown up on the streets together, their dispositions had always been different. Quinton understood that violence and survival sometimes went hand in hand, but there was an innate sense of mercy and kindness in him which the harsh reality of poverty had never successfully stomped out. Some might call it weakness. Charlie didn't think of his friend as weak, but he had always understood that there were certain things for which only he had the stomach. It wasn't that he was cruel—at least, he didn't think of himself that way. But there was no warm, squishy centre to him. He had a sense of right and wrong and lived by a moral code of his own making, but that part of himself which might have drawn back in horror at such a thing was long since broken.

He avoided eye contact with Quinton and Zoe, though he couldn't pretend he didn't notice Mary's gaze upon him. Mary was no fool, and though she was a good person, she was also practical. Life experience didn't allow her to live with blinders over her eyes.

"I'm sorry the girl is dead, but why does it bring you to my door?" asked Charlie, shifting in his seat.

Quinton leaned forward. "I wanted to ask you what you know of O'Malley's character. Do you think this is something he is capable of?"

"Ah. O'Malley. Of course." Charlie picked his glass back up, swirling the whiskey around. "My estimation of his character is that he has none. Do I think he lacks the moral scruples necessary? Yes. Do I think he's smart enough to do such a thing . . . that would surprise me."

"There's another thing." Zoe hesitated. "Whoever . . . cut her open . . . put her clothes back on after. Rory thinks that means whoever did it cared for her."

That gave Charlie pause. "Then it can't have been O'Malley."

"What makes you say that?" asked Mary.

"Because the man doesn't have a shred of decency in his bones." Charlie downed the rest of his whiskey, pouring himself another draught. "And if he's capable of caring for someone, then that's news to me."

"Charlie, how can you be sure—"

"Quinton, stop," he snapped. "I know Miles, much better than you. I know what he's capable of. Isn't that why you came to me?" He swallowed hard, clenching his fists in an effort to control his temper. The rage inside him was always right beneath the surface—the slightest bump could send him over the edge, where all he'd see was red. Even with his friends, control was a struggle at times. But he was trying harder, on the counsel and scolding of his mother.

"I understand, Charlie. I don't mean to say you don't know what you're talking about." Quinton's tone was soft—like one would use to speak to a vicious stray dog. That somehow made Charlie angrier. "But maybe if you could tell us why you hate him so much, it would help me—us—understand better."

Charlie stood abruptly, slamming his glass down as he did, and stalked over to the fireplace. How could he possibly explain to them what a man like Miles O'Malley was capable of? This was his world, and they were just tourists in it. His fists clenching and unclenching, he took a deep breath to calm the rage boiling within him. The truth was he wasn't angry at Quinton, or Mary, or even Zoe. No, if he was being honest, he knew this anger was directed more inward than outward.

"There was a time when you and I had . . . grown apart," Charlie started. "It had been less than a year since I lost my eye." He absentmindedly reached up to touch the raised scar which had been his constant companion for over a decade, running his finger from the top of his head down over his cheekbone to the base of his jaw. Quinton was very familiar with this history, but he expounded on it for the sake of the ladies present. "The three of us boys were at that age when our paths were beginning to become clear, and ours were headed in separate directions. That barrister—Dovefield—had taken an interest in John, and he was on his way to becoming a constable, despite only having just passed his sixteenth birthday. You were making a name for yourself as something of a fixer in the neighbourhood; only a year John's senior, but that posh accent and the way you carry yourself made people take you seriously. That just left me."

He paused, considering his next words. "Miles O'Malley was the first man to take me under his wing. He taught me more than a bit about smuggling—how to grease the right palms and deal in goods that would turn a handsome profit without drawing undue attention. From him, I learned how to operate a gambling den and secure a share of the earnings from a brothel."

"So you were . . . close?" asked Zoe.

Charlie glared at her. "I was a boy who hated the father who had abandoned me. He was a man approaching middle age who took an interest in me. I don't know if I would say close, but he filled a void . . . for a while."

"What happened, then?" Zoe set her own glass down, leaning forward. "I mean, I met the man and he's distasteful to be sure, so I understand a separation after a period of time. But you don't just dislike him—you downright hate him."

As loath as he was to admit Zoe's perception, it was a fair assessment. As Charlie tried to organize his thoughts, he let his gaze wander across the room. He had worked hard for this home. They had a sitting room, a separate kitchen, and even two bedrooms. His mother and sister slept in one while he took the other. It wasn't anything grand or large, but compared to the tenements he had grown up in . . . It was a palace, as fine as any estate filled with toffs.

As much as it pained him, part of his success was due to O'Malley's instruction. Charlie had worked hard for everything he had—he'd fought for it, centimetre by centimetre and metre by metre with blood and sweat. For a half-Indian boy left without a cent, he had done pretty good. He was proud of every centimetre he had gained . . . except for the start.

Charlie sighed and tugged at the sleeves of his shirt. "John can't know."

The three guests exchanged glances.

"Very well, if that's your wish." Quinton crossed his arms. "Any particular reason why not?"

"Because he is a lawman, and I don't want to place him a difficult position." That was part of the reason, but Charlie also knew John was the best of them. He didn't want his friend to lower his opinion of him.

Quinton nodded. "Very well."

"Good." Charlie swallowed hard, avoiding his friend's eyes. "Miles had a nephew—Robbie. He was a little older than me and we did quite a few jobs together. Nice enough, for an O'Malley. But the kid couldn't get anything right. He didn't have the head or the heart for the business. One day, Miles asked me to pick Robbie up and take him to an empty warehouse by the docks. I knew Robbie pretty well, so he trusted me. I suppose I told myself Miles would just to talk to him, maybe rough him up to set him straight. But once I got him into the warehouse . . ."

Charlie paused, taking another swig of whiskey. "Miles told me to wait outside. Next thing I know, the building is on fire. I tried to go back in, but Miles stopped me. He said Robbie was bad for business, and we needed to send a message that bad business wouldn't be tolerated. To this day, I can still . . ." Charlie gritted his teeth, the words to describe the horror stuck in his throat.

Finally he shook his head. "That's the kind of man Miles O'Malley is. He burned his own nephew *alive* to make a point. He isn't capable of caring."

The room was silent following his admission. Charlie understood. What was there to say to such a thing? It was heinous. He regretted many things in his life, but that was the only one which woke him up in the middle of the night in a cold sweat. How could he describe it to them? How could he tell them that sometimes he swore he could still hear the screams and smell the smoke and burning flesh; that he could still feel Miles's hand on his shoulders, his fingers digging into his skin as Charlie struggled?

"My God," said Zoe quietly. "We should have him arrested."

Charlie shook himself out of his self-pity. "Miss Demas—Zoe —you're still new to this, so I'll explain how it works to you. O'Malley owns half the constables on the east side. It's my word against his. He'd never be convicted, and all you would do is ensure I hang in his place." He sighed again. "What's done is done. The only reason I'm telling you now is so you can understand what kind of a monster Miles is."

Quinton stood, moving closer to Charlie's side and placing a hand on his shoulder. "I know that wasn't easy to share."

"Don't be ridiculous." Charlie glanced away, suddenly feeling something irritating in his eye.

Another short silence fell, but fortunately Mary was quick to understand that the time had come for a change of subject. "Well, where does this leave us as far as Katie Shorn?"

Zoe rose to her feet as well. "Mr. O'Malley is still our best link. Perhaps he didn't kill her, but at the very least he knows more than he's saying."

"Agreed." Quinton gazed at Zoe with the eyes of a man devoted, and for a moment Charlie felt a distinct pang of jealousy. Whatever they wanted to call the relationship between them, it was obvious they cared for each other. Even John had found companionship, with Charlie's own sister Savita, a situation he was doing his best not to overreact to.

It wasn't that he was unhappy for them. Of course he wanted his friends to be content—to have a wife and children and a home to call their own. But Charlie's life was a lonely one. He had his friends, and he had his mother and sister—for now—so it wasn't that he was completely alone. But he wondered if he would ever have anything beyond that. It wasn't easy in a world lived in the shadows to find a woman who was willing to live there as well. He'd like to think he would be a better father to his own son than his was to him.

But it didn't matter regardless. Charlie quickly rid himself of those ridiculous musings—he had a full life already, and daydreaming about a woman and children wouldn't change anything.

"Let me know if you need any more help," he said as he refilled his glass. He was grateful when they declined and tromped out of his house, full of discussions on how to bring justice to Katie Shorn. Another downed whiskey snuffed the last of the remembered screams, and Charlie turned his attention back to the day at hand.

Chapter Twenty-Two

If someone had told Zoe a month ago she would be spending her evening in an underground gambling hell twice in the span of less than a week, she would have laughed in their face. Despite this, she did find that the proceedings weren't entirely unpleasant.

This time Quinton was by her side, and Zoe more often than not found her gaze drawn toward him rather than the raucous game of risk. But when his eyes found hers, he quickly glanced away, clearing his throat and sipping his whiskey. Zoe didn't know what it was, but she knew something was bothering him, even with his newfound peace. She wished he would confide in her, but this wasn't the time or the place for that conversation, so she forced her attention back toward the games.

"Shouldn't we ask to see Mr. O'Malley?" she asked.

"I don't think we'll have a problem getting his attention." Quinton took another sip. "He knows I'm a friend of Charlie's. It won't be long until he summons us."

Patience wasn't her strongest suit. Zoe sighed and nodded in acknowledgment, glancing over at her other companion. Mary was smiling again, chatting and flirting with the coat check boy. The two of them had always gotten on so well that sometimes

Zoe forgot how young she still was—her twentieth birthday had just passed them by. Old enough by society's standards to be considered a grown woman, but still four years Zoe's junior.

The world gave girls so little time to grow up. Zoe knew ladies Mary's age who were already married with their second child on the way, and that was just among the ton. Being twenty-four, Zoe was considered an old maid already. For girls of Mary's class . . . they were working from the time they could hold a broom in their hand. They too would marry as soon as possible, and after that their life would consist of the work of perpetual motherhood.

It wasn't that way for men. Working class men did work, of course, usually from an early age, but they still had more freedom than their female counterparts—the freedom to play the field as young men, and then to go out with their mates for a pint after work when they got older, leaving their wives at home to care for their hoard of children. As for men of the ton . . . they were incorrigible in comparison. No one expected a gentleman to marry in his late teens, or even his early twenties. Their early days were spent learning dead languages and playing in the garden until they were old enough to tour the continent. After that they filled the hours socializing with others of their ilk and doing their best to squander whatever family fortune they could get their hands on in brothels and gambling hells. A few might go to university, but even that was more about prestige than actually improving their person. They carried on like that until they became bored enough to deign to seek a wife, usually in their late twenties or early thirties, though no one would bat an eye if it was later.

For Zoe, the injustice in comparison was infuriating. But for all her protests, that was the way the world worked. Many girls were eager to start that next chapter of their lives, or if not quite eager, they were at least anxious to secure it. She wondered what Mary wished for her own future. Did she desire a husband and children? Was she content with her life with Zoe, or did she feel time slipping away? A pang of guilt made her realize she had never asked her friend these questions.

Even if Mary had been content before, the events of the past few weeks might've changed her mind. Nothing like a brush with death to make a person reevaluate their life. And now they might never find their way to deep conversations on topics like this again.

Finally one of the serving girls came over, saving Zoe from her continual melancholy musings. "Mr. O'Malley would like to see you, Mr. Huxley," the girl said demurely to Quinton.

He downed the rest of his whiskey before setting the glass down on a nearby table. "Let's go, then."

Zoe caught Mary's eye and the two of them moved to follow, but the girl frowned. "Just Mr. Huxley has been requested."

"Well, that's too bad, because we travel as a pack." Zoe gestured ahead. "Lead the way."

Quinton gripped her arm, pulling her slightly off to the side. "It might be for the best if you waited out here."

"For the love of God, Quinton, sometimes it's like you've never met me before." She scowled up at him. "We are coming, so I suggest you think before causing a scene out here."

He held her gaze for several heartbeats before releasing his grip and taking a step back. His expression was unreadable, but it didn't take a mind reader to know Quinton wasn't happy at her insistence.

The girl opened her mouth to say something more, but then closed it again, apparently thinking better of voicing further objections. She led them out of the loud chaos of the main room, down a hallway to the private rooms in the back. Zoe recognized the way from when she had played cards that evening with Rory. But they went past that room, down to the end of the hallway, then turned left down another long hallway. Finally the girl came to a stop in front of a seemingly random door and knocked.

"Come in."

She opened the door, then stepped off to the side. As Zoe

entered the room, the last of them to do so, she glanced back, but the girl was nowhere to be seen. It was as if she had faded into the wallpaper.

Miles O'Malley sat behind a desk, leaning back in his chair with one hand resting on the desktop, his fingers restlessly tapping away on the surface. As his beady eyes scanned the group, his faced soured even more than it already was. "I didn't realize you travelled with a female entourage, Huxley."

"And I didn't realize you were a spineless horse's arse, O'Malley." Quinton placed his hands flat on the desk and leaned forward, using his large frame to emphasize his point. "We're learning a great deal about each other, I'm afraid."

O'Malley swallowed hard, his fingers going still. Zoe didn't blame him for being intimidated. Sometimes she forgot what an imposing figure Quinton could be because that wasn't how she pictured him any longer. But when he wanted to put someone in their place, a switch flipped to make him truly threatening. His broad shoulders and height lent to that impression, and right now his face was like stone, his dark eyes hard and cold.

Fortunately for O'Malley, the crime boss wasn't alone. His hulking bodyguard stepped forward, causing Quinton to slowly straighten up in response.

"Before I have my man here gut the three of ye like fish, I'm curious what makes you think you can walk into my establishment and insult me."

Quinton snorted. "You're not going to kill us."

"Oh, and why's that?"

"Because we're friends of Charlie's. If you harm any one of us, Charlie will burn your businesses and kill your men. It will be war, and as nasty as you are, he's smarter. He won't stop until he's hunted you down, and I can promise, your death will not be quick." Quinton took a seat in one of the chairs across from the desk, for all appearances as cool as a cucumber. "I could be wrong, but I don't think it's possible for anyone to be as stupid as you look. If you have any business sense, much less a self-preservation instinct, you'll keep your dirty little hands to yourself."

The room was silent for what felt like an eternity. Zoe held her breath. Quinton was going out of his way to provoke the man. She hoped he knew what he was doing.

"Very well." O'Malley leaned back in his chair. "Then perhaps you can at least explain what you're doin' in my establishment tonight. I know it's not gamblin,' so ye must want somethin'."

"Katie Shorn."

"I already told you, I don't know—"

"Save it." Quinton crossed his arms. "We know she worked here and we know she was doing something illegal for you. Tell us what you know, and we'll leave peacefully. You'll never hear from me again."

O'Malley hesitated for a moment. "Look, even if there was a lass by that name who worked here, and I'm not sayin' there was, it doesn't mean I know anythin' 'bout her whereabouts—"

"We know her current whereabouts," interrupted Zoe. "She's on a slab in a resurrectionist's shed."

It took a few moments for the O'Malley to process the information. He blinked rapidly, his brow furrowed. "What? She's dead?"

Zoe exchanged a glance with Mary. Quinton had taken the seat across from O'Malley, so Zoe couldn't see the agent's expression fully, but she imagined it mirrored her own thoughts. O'Malley seemed genuinely surprised that Katie was dead. Unless he had a secret career at Covent Garden, Zoe was inclined to believe his reaction.

Her stomach dropped at the realization. If O'Malley really didn't do it or know something about Katie's death, then they were back to square one.

Quinton hadn't given up yet. "Yes. Killed at least a week ago. Gutted and filled with rocks, then thrown in the Thames. You're telling me you don't know anything about this?"

While Zoe was concentrating on O'Malley's reaction, she

heard what sounded like wood creaking in the hallway. She listened for anything else but heard only silence

O'Malley's face paled. "No, of course not. I don't know anythin' about dead girls in the Thames." He hesitated. "I'll tell ye this much—I did know the lass. Katie worked for me. She was right good at entertainin' a certain type of clientele."

"Rich young gentlemen with money burning a hole in their pocket?" asked Mary.

"Aye. She has—had—that sad doe-eyed look young men go mad for, and if they felt like bein' a bit generous wit her because of it, I didn't discourage it."

"I'm sure you didn't," said Quinton with a snort.

The wording was careful, but Zoe could read between the lines. Quinton was right—it was definitely a scam. She'd known that was the most likely scenario, but she still felt a bit sorry for Alexander—if only a bit.

"So if she was such a good worker, why weren't you concerned when she disappeared?" Zoe asked.

O'Malley scowled. "She didn't disappear. Katie had been grumblin' for a while about wantin' to leave. I just assumed she did."

Mary crossed her arms. "Did she turn in her notice?"

Something flashed in O'Malley's eyes. "Not to me."

"What does—"

"I'm done answerin' these questions," snapped O'Malley. "I've told ye what I know, now kindly leave."

Zoe opened her mouth to argue, but Quinton abruptly stood before she could speak. "Very well," he said. "But if I find out you're lying about any of this . . ."

"Don't threaten me," retorted O'Malley. "Now get out."

The three of them took their leave. Zoe was the first to step into the hallway, and as she did, she almost thought she saw the shadow of a figure slipping around the corner on the edge of her vision. But when she looked over, nothing was there.

As the three of them made their way back out into the frigid cold, Zoe was the first to speak. "What did you think?" Zoe shivered as the cool winter wind cut through straight to her bone, even with her cloak.

"I think no working-class woman would leave her job without references," replied Mary.

Quinton rubbed his chin. "So do you think he's lying?"

"Maybe." Mary shrugged. "I don't know."

Zoe shook her head. "Did you see his face when you asked him about turning in her notice? Something about that bothered him."

"Agreed." Quinton sighed as he hailed the hackney. "But I'm not sure what to do about it tonight. Now if you ladies will excuse me, I have an appointment. We'll regroup tomorrow to discuss our options."

Zoe opened her mouth to make a tart reply when suddenly she remembered that she had invited Mabel to tea, then completely forgotten to go home. Even worse, she had sent Alexander back to her house instead. Rubbing her head, Zoe could not think of a ruder thing to do to her friend and began to compose a letter of apology in her head. Delivery of such a letter would have to wait until tomorrow, but it was the best she could do. Quinton was gone before she could so much as say goodbye.

Glancing at Mary, she started walking. For once in her life she knew what to do.

It was time to go home.

Chapter Twenty-Three

With a deep sigh, Quinton closed his eyes and sank deeper into the welcoming depths of the comfortable chair. It was rare a chair in a public place so perfectly accommodated his large frame, but White's managed nicely. The gentlemen's club catered to the nobility, and no comfort was done half way. The colours of each room were muted and the lighting soft. Since snuff was the only tobacco permitted within the walls of the club, the air was free of cigar smoke, and the entire effect was restful. The staff padded softly about, refilling drinks and keeping the tab straight.

The evening had already grown late when Quinton had arrived, but the club was nearly at capacity. The nobles, not having gainful employment, tended to keep very late hours. Quinton didn't have the same luxury—yet—and he felt exhaustion clinging to him like a wet bed sheet. He hoped to finish this meeting quickly so he could retire.

Forcing his eyes open, Quinton regarded the man sitting across the low table from him. Lord Coleville was well into his third round, making him nowhere near in his cups but decidedly relaxed.

"I'm not sure how anyone of a questionable nature could even get into the club, Quinton," said the lord. "The staff check for membership if one is not known."

Quinton had requested the meeting under the pretence of asking if the lord knew of any workarounds to get undesirable elements into the club, but that wasn't the real reason for his interest in speaking to the lord—a man he now knew to be his uncle. Knowing they shared blood . . . it changed everything, and Quinton was curious to view the man through this new lens.

"I thought the same, my lord." Quinton eyed his uncle from the side. "But I appreciate you taking the time to speak in person."

During one of Quinton's many talks with Rory Stewart over the years, Rory had told him of a military tactic involving going ahead of the rest to quietly ascertain the risk. This scout would seek out how big the threat was, if the military against them was too powerful, or if there were physical vantage points to keep in mind, and then that report would determine his commanding officer's next move.

Reconnaissance.

He still was unsure of how he wanted to proceed, but if there was a possible battle to be fought with his blood relatives, Quinton wanted to get his own the lay of the land.

Lord Coleville, unaware of the conflict on the horizon, drank his whiskey and sighed. "It's fine, Quinton. You know I love any excuse for a night at the club."

"Of course, my lord. Who doesn't love a night at the club?" Quinton reckoned it was time. "Since we're here, I did want to thank you again for your patience with me last year. I have recovered fully and, as you can see, am working regularly, so I will have your rent on time from now on."

"Think nothing of it." Lord Coleville waved his hand. "We're square, lad."

Quinton paused, swirling the whiskey in his glass casually. "I have found myself curious about the building. Is my place of residence a family estate, or did you purchase it yourself?"

"Well, that's an odd thing to be thinking about." Lord Coleville rubbed his chin, clearly thinking back. "My brother purchased that building as a young man. We never knew why, as he died shortly after he bought it." The lord smiled sadly. "Graham had many modern ideas. He undoubtedly had a plan for the place, but we never knew what. It remained empty for some time, until you took residence."

Quinton nodded in acknowledgment but remained silent. He had found through his work that most people could not abide silence. They were compelled to fill it with words, and the employment of many words often led to saying something of use to Quinton. He waited patiently, hoping the atmosphere and the whiskey would have a reminiscing effect on the lord. He was not disappointed.

"Graham was a complicated man," Coleville said with a sigh. "As a boy looking up to his much older brother, I adored him, idealizing everything he did. But as a grown man, I can acknowledge he wasn't perfect. He made some very poor choices, about which he and my father fought to no end."

A spark of anger ignited in Quinton's chest at the idea of "poor choices." He knew his mother would no doubt fall under that category. He wondered what other "poor choices" his father had made.

But this wasn't the time for that conversation. "How old were you when he died?" asked Quinton, smothering the spark as best he could.

It was a risky question, bordering on impropriety. But the lord did not seem bothered. The late hour and generous amount of whiskey had loosened his tongue, just as Quinton had hoped it would.

"I was fourteen." Lord Coleville shook his head gloomily. "I remember coming in from the stables when I heard the two of them—Graham and our father—arguing. Nothing out of the ordinary about that. Like chalk and cheese, those two. But this time, it was angrier. I heard Graham shout at my father that his life was his own, then the door burst open and he stalked out of the study. He paused, just for a moment, to put his hand on my shoulder. I thought he was going to say something, but he didn't. Then he was gone, taking his horse and racing hell-bent over the hill."

Lord Coleville took a bracing slug from his glass, his gaze unfocused. "A neighbouring stable hand found him later that day. The fool broke his neck after being thrown from his horse." The lord's tone didn't change, but Quinton could see the grief hanging over him like a dark cloud. Despite the years gone past, Coleville still missed his beloved brother.

After giving him a moment to recover, Quinton spoke. "It must have been a difficult loss for you, my lord. There's nothing so cruel as a life taken too young. Who knows what he might have accomplished if not for that unfortunate accident."

Sitting up a bit straighter, Coleville glanced over at Quinton. Something different shone in his eyes, as if he was seeing Quinton for the first time. Quinton held his breath, wondering if he'd made a mistake. But after a few moments, Coleville leaned back, apparently satisfied in what he had seen.

"Indeed, Quinton. Indeed." Coleville cleared his throat. "My brother was a man of ideals—a good man, but not always a practical one. He was so busy seeing the world as it could be that he often dismissed the way it was in the present."

"Perhaps if more people saw the world as it could be, the world would change for the better," said Quinton quietly.

"You sound like him." Coleville gave him another glance. "But I'm cut from a different cloth—a less sentimental one. I know the rules of my world, whether I like them or not. I respect the traditions that keep our lives ordered. Without order, society would collapse."

As Lord Coleville paused to signal for another whiskey, Quinton contemplated his response. He could see how much Graham—his father—meant to Coleville. And for Quinton's complaints in how he had handled the matter, he could acknowledge now that Coleville had also attempted to help his nephew, in his own way. But Coleville had built his entire life on propping up a system that had no room in it for people like Quinton or his mother. It was hard to imagine he would take the truth of Quinton's circumstances well.

"Of course, my lord. Tradition is as British as the prince himself. It's interesting though, when tradition hinders a man, instead of helping, if it remains the unmovable pillar." Quinton stood, leaving his whiskey only partially consumed. "I thank you for your time and opinion on the other matter. As always, I value your input."

"It is no trouble at all, Quinton." As Quinton moved toward the door, Coleville suddenly reached out a hand, grasping his wrist. "I'll always make time for you. Don't ever hesitate to reach out if you need something."

Quinton nodded in response. Perhaps there was room for compromise after all.

Chapter Twenty-Four

The weather had turned decidedly colder. Quinton pulled his scarf tighter around his neck, grateful for his thick greatcoat as he walked back home from the privy. A smattering of dirty snow still coated the walkways, icy from the drop in temperature. He used to dread this kind of weather as a child, when he'd only had the hope of Katy Modi's hearth for warmth.

The memories of his time spent as an urchin turned Quinton's thoughts to Ezra and Gwen. They were no longer living on the streets, a feat Quinton took pride in. He had managed to procure a position for Gwen in the Dovefield's household, and Ezra was under his care. Their improvement in circumstances was already more than most children in their position could hope for, but Quinton couldn't help but imagine what he could do for them if he had real power, the kind that mattered in society.

A great deal could be accomplished with money and a title, beyond just Gwen and Ezra. He couldn't save them all, but Quinton could help some of the orphans who littered the streets of London—children discarded and forgotten, as he had once been.

But was he just trying to justify what he wanted, rationalizing his way into accepting a position he'd secretly always desired? And if he got that power, would he become like all the others? Would he become just another Coleville, trying to keep everything the same so he could hold on to power and status, at the cost of everything else?

Quinton's negative spiral was interrupted when he realized he had reached his intended destination—his own residence. Right on time, Charlie turned the corner.

"What other business could you have to conduct this early in the morning?" asked Charlie with a raised eyebrow.

"I just went for a stroll, if you must know." In no mood to share the private details of his stroll, Quinton unlocked the door. "Needed a bit of fresh air to clear my head."

They entered together, and Quinton quickly stoked the coals in the hearth to get the fire going again. Fortunately for them, the small space heated up quickly, and they were soon comfortable enough to remove their greatcoats and hang them on the hooks.

Quinton took a deep breath, bracing himself for what was to come. His discussion with Coleville had made him consider the bond between brothers and the regret one might have at not taking the time for a difficult conversation. If Quinton kept this secret from one of the men he considered to be his brother, he would regret it. Charlie deserved to know, even if he never forgave Quinton.

As they settled into the armchairs by the fire, Oscar quickly padded over, jumping up onto Charlie's lap immediately. The traitorous beast had always liked Charlie best.

"Would you like a cup of tea?" asked Quinton.

"Only if you put some whiskey in it."

Quinton quickly fixed the tea for them, pouring a splash of whiskey in Charlie's cup. After a moment's hesitation, he added some to his own as well.

"It's a bit early for spirits, isn't it, Charlie?" Quinton handed him his cup.

"It's a bit early for a great many things, Quinton, namely this conversation." Charlie took a sip of his tea. "Something's been on your mind for a while now, ever since Fairfax swung. And I think I know what you want to tell me so bad."

Quinton shifted in his seat, his eyes cast downward. "I sincerely doubt that."

"Oh, you doubt it?" Charlie chuckled. "Fine. I will wager you a bottle of that very expensive whiskey you like that I already know what you're about to tell me."

"Is that so?" Quinton leaned back in his chair. "Very well, I accept your wager. What do you think I'm going to tell you?"

"You plan to wed your French toffette, and you are worried that my known distaste for her kind will drive a wedge between us. How close am I?" Though his wager had been made with a spirit of amusement, Charlie's voice had now taken on an angry edge.

Closer than I expected...

Oscar uncurled herself and leapt to the floor, feeling Charlie's mood drop. Smart cat.

Quinton shook his head. "You've always been too clever for your own good, Charlie, but you're only half right."

"Really?" Charlie leaned back, clearly satisfied with himself. "What did I get wrong?"

"Well, it has nothing to do with Zoe—at least not directly, so put that out of your mind." Quinton hesitated, unsure how to say the next words. Finally, he decided there was no good way to say it, so he might as well just spit it out. "How would you feel if my station in life did rise, however that came to be?

Charlie's eyes narrowed. "How high would your station be rising?"

"Fairly high."

A long stretch of silence followed the exchange. Charlie stared at Quinton, his good eye unreadable. Quinton held his gaze and said nothing, bracing himself for the inevitable explosion.

Suddenly, Charlie leaned back, as if a decision had been made.

"You know how I feel about blue bloods with nothing but time on their hands and no thoughts in their heads."

Quinton's heart dropped into his stomach. "I know, Charlie. And I understand the source of your bitterness." This was the direction Quinton had thought the conversation would go. Charlie couldn't forgive his father for abandoning his family—and the truth was, Quinton wouldn't ask him to.

As Quinton began to stand, suddenly wanting more whiskey in his tea, Charlie reached over and put his hand on his arm. "I wasn't finished. Sit down." Charlie sighed, staring off into the fire. "You're right, there's no love lost between me and the upper class. But I have come to understand recently that things aren't always so simple. Your barrister is a good man, despite his breeding. Your French toff has grown on me as well."

Quinton didn't say anything, waiting for Charlie to finish. This wasn't a version of Charlie he was used to dealing with, and he had no idea what his friend was going to say.

"We can't control the circumstances of our birth—whether we come into the world as a nobleman or as a brick mason," said Charlie after a long pause. "The only thing you can judge a man for is what he does after, with whatever opportunities he's given —or takes. You are a good man, Quinton, and will continue to be, whatever station in life you occupy."

Stunned at this evolved and wise conclusion, Quinton felt his eyes grow misty. He had been dreading telling Charlie the truth, and now he felt embarrassed at how much he'd underestimated his friend.

Charlie glared at him. "Don't go getting soft on me now— that I won't tolerate. Now, get the whiskey and tell me. If it's not wedding bells about to change your fortunes, then what in the bloody hell is going on?"

Chapter Twenty-Five

"What are you contemplating so intensely out the window, dear?" asked Hugh.

Simone turned away from the window, smiling at her husband. "Nothing, dear. Just admiring the dreary British weather."

She had arrived late the night before, the carriage dropping Theo off first. The strain of the journey was felt keenly by both of them, but Theo had been completely spent. Simone hoped she was recovered enough by this morning to join her in battle.

But first Simone needed to share the news with Hugh, something she was strangely reluctant to do. She and Hugh had built their marriage on not having secrets, and Simone worried again at Hugh's reaction to the ladies' clear plan of already executed action—and her choice not to include him in that plan until now.

The voice of her first husband popped into Simone's head. *Mieux vaut demander pardon que la permission.* It was too late for permission. Time to put money on forgiveness.

"There's something I need to tell you, Hugh," she began.

"Oh?" Hugh looked up from his steaming cup of coffee and smiled. "Did you find what you and Theo were searching for?"

Simone choked on her tea. She coughed to clear her throat and set her tea down on the table.

"Are you quite alright, dear?" asked Hugh, an amused twinkle in his eye.

"Are you laughing at me?" retorted Simone as she wiped her face with a napkin.

"Of course not. I have nothing but admiration and respect for you, and for my dear sister." Hugh smiled. "But I am not quite as dense as you think I am, my love."

"I have never thought of you as dense." Simone wrapped her silk robe more tightly around herself, crossing her arms. "When did you realize?"

Hugh smiled wryly. "As soon as you mentioned The Isle of Guernsey. An odd choice for a holiday. The weather is far from perfect this time of year, and the journey is challenging. You've always been clever, cleverer than me, and I realized I must have given too much away in our conversation, and you had somehow deduced Quinton's quandary and made the choice to look for answers there."

She had underestimated Hugh, not for the first time. He was wrong when he said she thought he was dense, but Simone sometimes did forget how clever he was in his own way. She felt a pang of guilt at how she had treated him.

Simone returned his smile. "You revealed very little, Hugh, but I was able to fill in the blanks. I would have spoken to you further, but I didn't want to put you in a position to have to break your word to Quinton. So Theo and I decided to take matters into our own hands."

"Naturally. I would expect nothing else."

Pleased at how the conversation was going, Simone still had one last thing she needed say. "I would never deceive you on a matter between us, *mon amour*. I want you to know that, and I'm sorry if this crossed a line between us."

Rising quickly, Hugh moved across the room to her, wrapping his arms around Simone's petite frame. "There's nothing to apologize for. I've always known who I married, and I meant what I said, Simone. I have nothing but admiration for both you and Theo. And the need for respite was real, my love. I hear the nightmares plaguing you as well, and I know when you are ready to share your fears, it will lessen their power." He paused, but when Simone remained silent he continued, smiling wryly. "The truth is I also ignored Quinton's wishes and sent my own man to Gretna Green. A single man on horseback can get there and back quite quickly. I, however, came up empty-handed. It does stab at my male pride that I suspect you fared better."

As she leaned in her husband's familiar body, breathing in the scent of coffee beans and lemon soap, Simone couldn't help but feel like the most fortunate woman in the entire world.

Hugh stepped back, looking deeply into Simone's blue eyes. "The question now is, what did you discover?"

"Yes, of course." Simone wiped away the gathering tears in her eyes and gestured for him to take a seat. "Quinton's parents were indeed married on Guernsey. The man who officiated is still there, at the church. He copied the necessary documents and signed them himself with his seal. It is incontestable."

Blinking rapidly, Hugh stared at her, clearly trying to comprehend the explosive information. "I can't believe you found the church. The documents. The officiator himself. That is . . . incredible. This changes everything." He reached out to take her hand. "Well done, my love, well done."

"Thank you," replied Simone, feeling very pleased with herself. "Now send a boy with a note for Mr. Huxley. Theo is expecting us all at eleven o'clock."

Here Hugh hesitated. "He had reservations about the situation. I'm not sure he's ready for this."

Simone withdrew her hand, picking up her cup of tea and taking a pleasant sip. "*Mon amour*, Quinton will take what is his. He might just need a bit of convincing."

Chapter Twenty-Six

T he silence stretched uncomfortably as Mr. Huxley stared at Hugh. Theo wondered who would speak first, but as another lifetime seemed to pass, she decided it would be her. "Are you quite all right, young man?"

Mr. Huxley turned slowly to face her, as if seeing her for the first time. "Are you sure?" The young man spoke the words with a quiet desperation. "Are you completely sure?"

He was still looking at her, so Theo assumed the question was directed at her. "Absolutely, Mr. Huxley," she replied. "Those documents in your hand are proof positive that your mother and father were legally wed. It cannot be contested."

Hugh stepped forward, putting his hand gently on the younger man's shoulder. "There can be no doubt, Quinton. You are a Coleville."

"Not just any Coleville," Simone interjected. "You are the legitimate son of Lord Graham Coleville, who was the eldest son of the Viscount of Hereford. That makes you the legal heir to the Coleville title and fortune."

This information didn't seem to help Mr. Huxley's catatonic state. Hugh gently guided Mr. Huxley to the oversized chair farthest from the fire.

"I just . . . I just can't believe it's actually true," Mr. Huxley stared down at the documents in his hand, his eyes unfocused. "I can't believe you found proof."

Theo exchanged a glance with Simone. They'd considered the possibility that good news could somehow be as weighty as bad. But she hadn't expected Mr. Huxley to look quite so . . . lost.

Fortunately they were British—sans Simone—and the British had long since found the solution for all things troubling.

Theo rang for tea.

As they waited for the fortifying beverage to be brought up, Mr. Huxley continued to stare at the papers in his hand. After a few moments, he looked up, his expression shocked. "Are these dates accurate?" he asked, his tone urgent.

"They are," replied Theo. "The deacon who officiated the ceremony copied the original documents exactly."

Huxley looked back down. "My birthdate is the eighth of June. The date of the ceremony is almost a year before I was born."

That couldn't be right. Theo took the paper from him, scanning the carefully written ink herself. There it was, plain as day. She glanced at Simone, who was looking very pleased with herself. The infuriatingly clever Frenchwoman must have already figured out the discrepancies in the dates.

Theo assured herself that if she had known the boy's birthdate, she too would have made the connection. But the truth was she was tired—more tired than she'd been in a long time. She wondered if perhaps she was losing her edge in her old age. Or perhaps all she needed was a proper holiday.

"*Tout son cœur.*" Simone smiled. "He married her for love."

The room fell back into silence as they all absorbed this new information. Theo personally couldn't believe it. It was almost unheard of for a man of title and status to take an actress as his *wife*—not without an accidental pregnancy to explain the behaviour. Graham Coleville must have loved his actress deeply.

Simone broke the silence, looking at her husband. "It was not to the same degree, but I was a tutor when I met my Hugh, and he was a nobleman. Though he loved me from the beginning, it took me some time to feel the same. In the end love guided us, and I, for one, am not surprised your father did the same."

Finally Mr. Huxley looked up, his eyes clear for the first time since he had arrived. He seemed to relax finally into his chair as the footman arrived with the tea. "You are right, Lady Dovefield," he said quietly. "Love binds your family together. I am pleased to discover the same about mine."

Simone handed him a cup of tea. "True, Mr. Huxley. But I think you will find love is greatly aided by a bit of wealth."

He snorted at that, but accepted the tea.

Theo took a sip from her own before asking the obvious question. "So now that you have all the facts, what do you plan to do with this information?"

"I don't know." An expression of guilt settled on Huxley's face. "I suppose if I am to go through with it, I must tell Lord Coleville. I feel . . . guilty about taking his title simply due to an accident of birth."

"He'll get over it." Theo rolled her eyes when Hugh gave her a disapproving glance. "Don't look at me like that, brother. Montgomery understands the way society works—if he has any grit at all, he'll accept the facts with grace and dignity." She turned back to Huxley. "But the longer you delay in telling him, the more difficult it will be. He deserves to know the truth."

Huxley considered her words. Finally he nodded. "Very well. But I don't want to ambush him in a group. I owe him the respect of telling him one on one."

Hugh cleared his throat. "I understand the sentiment, but if you're amenable to it, I'd like to join you. There are legalities to discuss, and I am in the best position to explain it to him clearly so there can be no confusion. We can use my study."

"If you insist." Huxley nodded again. "In truth, I would very much appreciate the assistance."

"Very good, very good. I will contact Lord Coleville and see if he is free this afternoon." As Huxley turned a ghostly shade of white, Hugh patted him again on the shoulder. "My sister is right. It is best not to delay. Go about your day, and I will send word when an appointment is confirmed."

With that settled, Theo could lean back in her sofa and relax. As soon as her guests departed, she needed a lie down.

Chapter Twenty-Seven

he crack in the ceiling is getting worse...
The thought continued cycling through Quinton's mind as he lay in his cot with Oscar curled up on his chest, staring up at the ceiling he knew all too well. This was a roof which had sheltered him for nearly a decade, provided by Lord Coleville—his uncle. Quinton had spent countless nights staring up at it, memorizing the texture of the plaster and the way the light shining through the window cast shadows across it.

The crack had always been there, so small you could barely see it at first, but spreading slowly over the years. Now it was wide enough to see the wooden beams it covered. A few times Quinton had thought about patching it. It wouldn't be difficult, or even take much time. But somehow he'd never quite gotten around to it. Always a little too busy and a little too tired to deal with it. So he'd ignored it, and in the long term it hadn't done too much damage. But some things couldn't be so easily ignored.

The conversation he'd had with the Dovefields and Theo Bexley occupied the edges of his thoughts, seemingly filling up any space it could until it felt as though his head would explode. His emotions swirled like thunderclouds—a flash of anger at

Coleville for not telling him, followed by a heavy downpour of guilt at the thought of taking a title from that same man, and then a spark of love for a father he had never known but who had loved his mother enough to marry her. Quinton didn't know quite how he felt about Simone and Theo taking such an interest in his background. It was a kindness he'd never expected, especially not from Simone. The information they'd uncovered changed everything.

It was a lot to take in.

He absentmindedly stroked Oscar as his thoughts wandered. Oscar rewarded him with a surprisingly loud purr, considering she herself was a rather small cat. Quinton closed his eyes, letting the sound start to soothe him.

A loud knock at his door interrupted Quinton's musings. He cleared his throat, dismissing the storm clouds—for now.

"What is it?" he shouted as he pushed the cat to the side and strode toward the door. He assumed it was the messenger to confirm his appointment with Hugh.

"Just opened the door!" came the response, followed by more insistent knocking. Quinton recognized the voice as belonging to John—so not a messenger.

"I'm coming, I'm coming," Quinton grumbled. He unlocked the door and threw it open. "What is so urgent?"

John eyes were dark. "Get your coat, Quinton. We just found another body."

"What?" Quinton's stomach soured. "Who is it? Another one of O'Malley's girls?"

"No, not this time." John sighed. "This time it's the Irishman himself."

The hackney driver made good time to Rory's, and it wasn't long before Quinton and John were walking down the path to the old shed in the garden. As they approached the door, Quinton could hear familiar voices coming from within.

"Listen here you stubborn son of a—"

"Don't you dare finish that sentence you loud-mouthed, bloody—"

"What is going on in here?" asked Quinton loudly as he stepped over the threshold and Rory and Charlie came into view.

The two men were standing over the slab in the middle of the room, one on either side. On the slab was the body of the Irishman, though it was obscured from view by Charlie. Rory and Charlie were clearly bickering about something, but they went silent at the sight of John and Quinton.

"Charlie, how did you beat us here?" John put his hands on his hips. "How'd you even know we found the body?"

Quinton squinted at Charlie. "You didn't kill him . . . did you?"

"No, of course not," snapped Charlie. "News spreads quick in my part of the city, 'specially when it concerns the likes of 'im."

Charlie's cockney accent only slipped in when his emotions were running high. His face was stoic, but Quinton couldn't help but wonder what thoughts were going on behind those dark eyes. Did he feel only righteous relief to see the man lying there, or perhaps a pang of sadness stemming from better memories nearly faded by time?

"I don't know if he killed him or not, but I do know he's driving me mad," grumbled Rory. "I assume you're both also here to hear my findings. I don't have much yet—I've barely had time to do a preliminary examination, which has been made increasingly difficult by our friend Charlie breathing down my neck and hovering at my elbow."

"I hardly think asking a few questions qualifies as breathing down—"

"Gentlemen, let's take a break," interrupted John. "Charlie, how about you come over here with me and Quinton and give Rory some space, eh?"

With great and obvious reluctance, Charlie did move to stand on the other side of the room next to Quinton and John. He crossed his arms, his face twisted into a scowl that could melt lead.

"Finally," muttered Rory, turning back to the corpse.

"So, what have you discovered so far?" said Quinton quickly before Charlie could respond.

Rory glanced back at him. "I told you, I've only had a chance to do a preliminary—"

"I know, Rory, I know. But just tell us what you have."

The sigh Rory let out seemed a bit excessive to Quinton, but he chose not to comment. He didn't want to get on Rory's bad side like Charlie. The truth was he couldn't really blame his hotheaded friend. He too was eager to hear what the Irishman's fate had been.

"Well, I can tell you he was likely murdered," said Rory.

"What makes you say that?"

Rory stared back at him with a deadpan expression, then pointed at the dead man's neck. "I'm basing my suspicions off the fact his throat was slit ear to ear."

"Ah." Quinton cleared his own throat. "Well, that will do it."

With all the drama between Rory and Charlie, Quinton had only given the body on the table a passing glance. Now that he focused on it, he saw what Rory was referring to. Blood had seeped down the front of O'Malley's neck and shirt from the wound, though by now it had lost its bright red colour, having faded to a dull brown. A violent death for a violent man. There was a certain poetic justice in it, though Quinton didn't take particular pleasure in the death of any person, even one like O'Malley.

"The wound is deep and clean—no hesitation marks," continued Rory. "Whoever did this knew what they were doing. There's no marks on his arms or hands, so I'm guessing the attack came from behind. Poor bastard probably never saw it coming."

"Save your pity for someone who deserves it," snapped

Charlie as he whirled to face John. "Where did they find him? Not the Thames again?"

"No. One of his girls found him in the alley behind his gambling hell."

"Just out in the open?" Quinton shook his head. "Strange that they went to such extremes to try to hide Katie's body but just left O'Malley in an alley."

"You think it's the same killer?" asked John.

"There must be some connection." Quinton thought back to his conversation with O'Malley. When Katie's body being found was brought up, the Irishman had seemed genuinely surprised. Perhaps he had his own suspicions about who had taken her life, and when he confronted that person, they had finished him off as well. But then why leave his body out in the open? It didn't make any sense. Unless . . . unless the killer wanted the body to be discovered.

"O'Malley's a big deal in the underworld, right, Charlie?" asked Quinton as he rubbed his chin.

"I suppose." Charlie sniffed. "I surpassed his operations a long time ago, but in certain circles, he was still relatively important."

Quinton exchanged a glance with John. "So now that it's common knowledge he's dead, everyone is going to be expecting someone to fill those shoes . . . Charlie, is there anyone who would benefit from his death? A number two at the gambling hell, or something along those lines?"

Charlie opened his mouth to answer, but Rory beat him to it. "As fascinating as the conversation is, would you gentlemen please take it outside so I can concentrate on my work?" The Scotsman's voice was polite, but Quinton could hear the underlying strain. He also noted the bags under his friend's eyes and the sag in his shoulders. This wasn't the first time Quinton had noticed it, but with everything else going on in his life, he hadn't gotten around to checking in on his friend. Rory's recent ordeal had taken a toll on him. Quinton made a mental note to come back later for a chat.

The other three men exited the shed. Quinton squinted at the bright sunlight, holding up a hand to shield his eyes. He pulled his overcoat tighter around his body, shivering at the cold breeze.

"In answer to your question, it doesn't really work like that," said Charlie. He had taken some deep breathes to regain his composure. "At the most basic level, we're just businessmen—not all our business is legal, but it operates much the same. O'Malley had people who worked for him, but he would have handled most of the day-to-day operations himself. It's more likely that his businesses will just be absorbed by a competitor."

"Someone like yourself?" asked John with a twinkle in his eye.

Charlie scowled. "I didn't kill him."

"Very well then, what's your theory as to why they didn't hide the body?" Quinton tried to keep the annoyance out of his voice at having his own theory shot down so quickly.

"What makes you think there's a reason?"

"What do you mean?"

Shifting from foot to foot and rubbing his arms, Charlie responded. "Miles was a man. He wasn't a tall man, but he was stocky. That's a lot of dead weight to move. The girl would have been easier."

Quinton didn't ask him how he knew that. To be fair, it was common sense.

John's expression was doubtful. "I don't know. Katie being put into the river like that . . . not to sound too much like Rory—"

"I heard that!" came the angry Scottish shout from the shed.

Stifling a chuckle, John continued. "But it's almost like she was being laid to rest. It wasn't like that with O'Malley. He was literally thrown out with the rubbish. That has to mean something."

"Perhaps." Charlie's scowl deepened. "Look, can we finish this conversation at a pub? It's freezing out here."

"Unfortunately, I don't think I have time." Quinton checked

his pocket watch. "I'm waiting on word about an appointment. But the two of you go ahead. I'll catch up with you later."

As the three men walked back up the path, Quinton mused on the facts. It couldn't be a coincidence that O'Malley turned up dead so shortly after their conversation about Katie. Whatever was going on, it was a secret someone was willing to kill to protect.

Chapter Twenty-Eight

Hugh had run in the same social circles with Montgomery Coleville for years, but he was not overly familiar with the man. Still, a part of Hugh did pity him. His whole life would change today, and this was the last time Coleville would have the luxury of ignorance. As Lord Coleville was shown into the study, Hugh didn't blame him for pausing when he caught sight of Quinton. This was not an ordinary circumstance.

"Whiskey, Lord Coleville?" offered Hugh, hoping to soften the blow with a little good alcohol.

"Certainly." Coleville took the offered glass cautiously before seating himself opposite Quinton. "Let us cut to the chase, Lord Dovefield. What business do you have with both Mr. Huxley and myself?"

So much for softening the blow. Quinton glanced at him, and Hugh took it as permission to move forward.

"There is a legal matter between you and Mr. Huxley, and I am here to mediate," replied Hugh, taking a decent swig from his own glass.

"A legal matter? Is this about the property you lease, Huxley?"

scoffed Coleville. "Didn't we speak quite recently? You could have approached me privately if there is a problem."

"This is no rental dispute, Lord Coleville," said Quinton quickly. "You have been nothing but generous with me regarding that agreement."

Hugh had rarely seen the young man so out of his element—he looked as if he wanted to peel up the floorboards and bury himself underneath the house.

The young man swallowed drily and continued. "However . . . some new information has recently come to light regarding our relationship that goes beyond just business."

Coleville became still, his gazed locked onto Quinton, clearly understanding his meaning. This was the point of no return—Hugh didn't know which way the rest of the conversation would go.

After a few moments' consideration, Coleville downed his whiskey in one go. "I thought there was something deeper in our last conversation at White's, but I wasn't sure if I was just imagining it . . . seeing ghosts where there were none." The lord paused, his eyes surprisingly soft. "You look so much like him. It stopped me in my tracks when I first saw you, the spitting image of Graham. Your eyes are different—darker, spaced wider. But it could not have been more obvious who your father was."

It was good the lord had admitted the family ties so quickly—that would make the next part easier. Hugh glanced back and forth between the two of them, waiting to see what they would say next.

Coleville rose and walked to the sidebar to refill his glass without asking. "I hired you to find that missing necklace just as an excuse to talk to you. It felt like the universe was giving me a gift, seeing a part of my brother live on. I didn't know the circumstances of your birth at the time, but I knew there could be no acknowledgment of you. Nevertheless I kept tabs on you after that, helping where I could. I know from your position that may not seem like much, but I did what I thought I could."

"It did help." Quinton took a deep breath. "I'll admit, at first I didn't know how I felt about your involvement in my life. But I know you did what you thought was right, and I want to say, whatever happens, that you did help me at a time in my life when I very much needed it."

"Of course." Coleville cocked his head, expression pensive. "So then I assume this conversation is about furthering your relationship with our family? I'm sure you know any formal acknowledgment is out of the question, but I could see about establishing a small allowance for you. My father could not be involved, he's not a tolerant man—"

"There is more you need to know, Lord Coleville," interrupted Hugh, handing the papers over to the lord.

"What is this?"

Neither Quinton nor Hugh answered, instead letting the lord come to his own conclusions. It didn't take long.

"This cannot be true." Coleville looked up, his face pale. "Graham was headstrong, but he would not have married an actress. It's enough he had a child with one, but he would never have dishonoured my father by wedding one."

Hugh glanced at Quinton, wondering how he would respond to that. Something about the statement bothered Hugh as well, beyond the obvious condescension. He couldn't quite place what it was, so Hugh dismissed the thought for now.

Something dark had flashed in Quinton's eyes at the reference to his mother, but when he spoke his voice was even. "And yet, he did."

There was little else to say to that. Coleville turned back to the papers again, reading through them again. He finally looked up, his eyes hard. "We will of course, fight this. It cannot hold up in a court of law."

Hugh sighed—this was the reaction he had expected. "Do as you see fit, Lord Coleville. But the man who performed the ceremony made the copy himself. The validity of the marriage is incontestable. I suggest you find a way to come to terms with it."

Shaking his head, Coleville began to stalk toward the door. "I need to see my solicitor. I will show him these documents and we will make our own decision on what to do next. But mark my words, this will not stand." With that, Lord Coleville swept out of the room.

After his footfalls had faded away, Quinton slumped back in his chair. "That went well," he said bitterly. "What if he destroys the papers?"

"I think it went better than expected." Hugh smiled. "And I'm not a fool, Quinton. Those are copies I made myself."

Quinton returned his smile. "Very clever. So, what now? What does this really mean, for Lord Coleville, for me, for everyone?"

There were few things Hugh enjoyed as much as explaining a legal matter. He settled back in his chair, considering how best to explain the situation. "In this case, Quinton, it is all about entailment. I too sought outside counsel, and Garrow and I spent a bit of time looking into the entailment of the Coleville estate, to make sure we understood the legal ramifications."

Raising his hands, Quinton shook his head. "You'll have to forgive me, my lord. I have only the loosest understanding of what an entailment even is. Doesn't it have something to do with inheritance?"

"Indeed, but there's more to it. An entailment itself is simply a clause in a will that extends beyond the person who makes the will, usually for three or four generations. It can be entailed to whomever the original person wishes."

Quinton's brow furrowed. "Doesn't the oldest son just inherit everything when it comes to these things?"

"Well . . ." Hugh bobbed his head from side to side. "That is the way these things are often structured, but the only thing that an eldest son must inherit in a noble family is the title itself. The entailment designates what else comes with that title—the estate, money, artwork, properties. The reason they are most often entailed together is that a title without an estate or fortune is virtually worthless."

"Interesting, I was unaware of that." Quinton nodded. "So then entailment is just a posh word for will?"

Hugh laughed. "Not quite. Once an entailment is established, it cannot be changed by future generations. Often the estates themselves are entailed with the title—as is the case with the Colevilles—but specific things, such as additional properties or jewellery, can be willed to other individuals."

"So once the entailment is established, it can't be changed ever?" asked Quinton.

"Not necessarily. In the Colevilles' case, the entailment was established for three generations, and started by the present viscount's grandfather."

Quinton sat up straighter. "So the entailment is no longer in force?"

Hugh sipped his whiskey. "Upon the death of the present viscount, the entailment is satisfied. Since you will be the fourth generation, you can act as you wish. You are under no legal obligation to do anything you don't want to do."

"I see."

As excited as Hugh had been to discuss the legalities, he could see Quinton was reaching his limit of understanding. All of this was a lot to take in in one setting.

"Garrow had some ideas that may appeal to you," amended Hugh. "For now, I suggest we let everyone chew on what they now know.

"Indeed, I believe that is best for now." Quinton stood, gratitude shining in his eyes. "Thank you, my lord, for your assistance in this matter. It has been a relief to have your support."

Gasping his hand in a firm handshake, Hugh nodded. "Of course. We'll speak again soon."

After Quinton had departed, Hugh sat back down, nursing the last of his whiskey. This was a prickly conundrum, but one thing was certain—it wasn't boring.

Chapter Twenty-Nine

"Quinton, what are you doing here?" Zoe was surprised to see him exiting her home. "Is something the matter?"

The man jumped at the sound of her voice but quickly recovered when he laid eyes on her walking down the path. He cleared his throat, running his fingers through his hair. "No, nothing is the matter." Quinton smiled, but Zoe noted it didn't quite seem to reach his eyes. "I just had a legal matter to discuss with your father."

"I see." Zoe glanced at Mary. "And was that Lord Coleville I saw getting into his carriage as we were arriving?"

"Eh, yes. The legal matter involves him, but I'm afraid it's private . . . for now." Quinton cleared his throat again.

Zoe suppressed a sigh. There he was, being secretive again. She knew he was keeping something from her, but she didn't feel like fighting about it now. Let him keep his secrets.

"Oh, have you heard about Miles O'Malley?" he asked, abruptly changing the subject.

"No, what about the old bastard?" replied Mary.

"He's dead." Quinton made a gesture, dragging his finger across his neck. "Throat slit."

"My God." Now that was a surprise. A queasy feeling churned in Zoe's stomach. They had just spoken with him the previous evening. It couldn't be a coincidence. She absentmindedly flexed her hand, flinching as the stitches pulled at edges of the wound. "Has anyone been arrested?" she asked.

"No. The body is with Rory, and John is speaking to the girls who were working at the hell last night."

The memory of that figure in the hallway popped into Zoe's mind. At the time she'd assumed she was imagining things, but now . . . Zoe pulled her cloak tighter around herself. "What do you think happened?"

"I don't know." Quinton sighed. "It can't be a coincidence that he was killed right after we asked him about your cousin's girl. When it comes to this case, I feel as though I have all the pieces of a puzzle in front of me, but I still can't seem to form a clear picture."

Exchanging another glance with Mary, Zoe considered her next words. It wasn't out of the ordinary for Quinton's brooding mood to make an appearance, but he seemed particularly unsettled at the moment.

"I'm certain things will become apparent." An idea occurred to Zoe. "Perhaps Mary and I should go to the gambling hell to assist John. The girls might be more willing to open up if—"

"No," snapped Quinton. "I don't want either of you going back there. It's too dangerous."

A familiar anger rose in Zoe's chest at his words.

"I don't recall asking your permission, Quinton," she snapped back. "I can take care of myself. My life is my own."

Taking a step forward, Quinton locked eyes with her. As much as Zoe wanted to move away, she found herself rooted to the ground. Craning her neck to look up at him, Zoe swallowed hard, uncertain why she was so uncomfortable.

As he looked down at her, Quinton spoke with absolute confidence. "I have never met anyone who is more capable of making their own choices, Zoe Demas. I would never take that from you. But your safety will continue to be my concern. I'm not giving or retaining permission. I'm explaining my position."

Zoe couldn't make herself look away. She wanted to slap Quinton across his stupid, confident face, but at the same time, she also wanted to grab him by the lapels of his coat and pull him down in a kiss that would make him see stars. It was a very confusing feeling.

Finally Quinton stepped back and Zoe let out a breath she hadn't realized she'd been holding in.

Mary cleared her throat, breaking the crackling tension in the air. "Perhaps it's time to get the group together to compare notes . . . on the case."

Quinton cocked his head, as if nothing had happened. "Perhaps you are right. Do you ladies have plans this evening?"

Shaking her head, Zoe managed to respond. "No."

"Good. I'll send Ezra to inform Charlie and John." Quinton inclined his head as a way of dismissing himself.

As Zoe watched him walk assuredly away, she couldn't help the feeling that, in that moment, everything had changed.

John sighed, pinching the bridge of his nose. "So you didn't see anything unusual last night?"

The young girl shifted from foot to foot, her eyes darting around the room. "I wasn't workin' last night. Can I go, mister?"

"Yeah, fine." Another sigh escaped his lips.

This was not going well. John had questioned most of the staff, and they all claimed to either have not been working or to have seen nothing. The whole endeavour was proving to be a waste of time.

"Hello there, officer."

As John turned toward the voice, he saw a woman casually

leaning against the counter—older than the girl he had just been talking to, but still young enough to be considered in her prime. She wasn't unattractive, but there was a plain quality about her, as if she might blend into the wallpaper if you weren't looking directly at her.

Where the other girls had kept their heads down and avoided his gaze, this one held it evenly, her head cocked as if she were considering him. "Heard you were askin' about what happened last night . . . in regard to Mr. O'Malley," she said.

"That's correct, Miss . . . ?" replied John.

"Lydia." She smiled. "Just Lydia."

John raised an eyebrow but didn't comment. "A pleasure, Miss Lydia. I don't suppose you happened to have seen anything unusual that happened last night?"

"Well, I didn't see the actual act itself, of course." Lydia shook her head, tutting. "Poor Mr. O'Malley. I can't believe he's really gone."

John cleared his throat—not quite the sentiment he would have expressed. "Yes, er, quite. Was he a good boss then?"

She shrugged. "He wasn't the worst I've had. Kept food on the table. Ye want a drink, Officer?"

"Er, no. Thank you."

With another shrug she reached behind the counter and poured herself a generous draught. John couldn't really blame her. While the cat was away—or dead—the mice would play. As she put the bottle back, he noted a bandage wrapped around her left palm.

As she took a sip, John carried on. "So what else can you tell me about Mr. O'Malley? Did he have any enemies you knew of?"

She laughed. "Well, Mr. O'Malley wasn't known for makin' friends. But I wasn't privy to those aspects of his life."

"Of course, of course." He circled back around to his original question. "Were there any disturbances last night?"

"Well, there's always a few disturbances." Lydia winked. "This being a gamblin' hell and all. But I remember Mr. O'Malley did get into it with one of the young gents in his office. Could hear the shouting all the way out 'ere."

John's ears perked up at that. "Oh? I don't suppose you happened to catch the gent's name?"

"Aye, I did. 'Twas that young Dovefield—Alexander."

Chapter Thirty

As she sipped the whiskey in her hand, Mary glanced around the room that constituted Quinton's lodgings as well as his office. The ragtag band would often gather here when they needed to discuss things as a group. It wasn't a very large room, but everyone somehow managed to find a place around the hearth, dragging over chairs from the dining table and finding space on the floor. Quinton sat in one of the armchairs, chatting with a pacing Charlie, and this time Zoe and Mary shared the other.

It was a tight squeeze for the two women, but the close proximity didn't feel uncomfortable. She had rarely felt such affinity for another person as she did for Zoe. The two were like twin flames—as it they had always been meant to be in each other's lives, connected by an invisible thread until they finally found each other. Whether they were brought together by chance or fate didn't matter to Mary. She was just grateful to have found a friend—a true friend—who made her life so much more than it had been.

No, it wasn't the proximity that felt strange—it was the lack of it. She was still terribly fond of her friend, but ever since that night . . . a wall stood between them. They had gone through something horrific and terrifying, and though they were probably the only two people who could truly understand that experience, they couldn't seem to discuss it. Sometimes when they were with the others, it almost felt the same as it did before. But then Mary would look over and see the fading bruise across Zoe's cheek and the stitches along her wrist and it would all come rushing back. Now, sitting in the chair with her, looking out at the others, Mary could almost completely put it from her mind—almost as if it had never happened.

Mary's eye line drifted over to Rory. She'd always been good at reading the energies of people, as far back as she could remember. A gift of intuition she'd inherited from her mother, and her mother before that, and her mother before that. And something was wrong with Rory's energy.

There was a time not too long ago when his larger-than-life personality would have filled the room with Shakespeare quotes and words of wisdom. But recent events had taken a toll. It wasn't just his appearance. Physically he was thinner and bit paler, but he was already beginning to fill out again. His hair was neatly trimmed and his bruises either faded or covered by clothing. No, the effect which still lingered seemed deeper than that. A sadness to him manifested in the slouch of his shoulders and lack of light in his eyes. Mary had little reason to think so, but she suspected the darkness around him went beyond just his false arrest and imprisonment. An air of grief hung over him like a dark cloud, as if he had lost something deeply precious to him.

Though she was fond of Rory, Mary wouldn't consider the two of them particularly close. Of all the group, Quinton was the one most bonded to him. Normally she would expect the inquiry agent to talk to his friend, but Quinton had his own secret troubles on his mind. He was distant and unsettled whenever she saw him recently. She might have to take on the responsibility of helping Rory herself.

She didn't really mind. Anything to avoid her own problems.

"Where is John?" snapped Charlie, his arms crossed.

"I'm sure he'll be along presently." Quinton sighed. "We might as well begin without him."

"Hmm." Charlie slowed his pacing and moved to stand in front of the flickering flames. "Very well. What do we know?"

Mary considered the man standing before them. He had done this before, when Rory was in trouble not very long ago—taking charge of the discussion and directing the flow of conversation. It wasn't a role she was used to seeing Charlie in, but she was surprised at how well it suited him. Perhaps she had just never seen this side of him, given the less-than-legal nature of his comings and goings.

Zoe started them off. "We know O'Malley was running a scam on the young degenerates who frequented his establishment—my cousin included—and that Katie was a part of it."

"Then poor Katie is killed and laid to rest in the Thames," added Mary as she reached down to pat Brutus on his massive head.

"Right." Charlie frowned. "Then the sod himself got his own throat slit."

"And Charlie, you still don't believe the sod killed Katie?" asked Quinton.

Charlie gave a sharp jerk of his head. "No. If what Rory says is true about the killer caring for her, I stand by the fact that O'Malley wasn't capable of it."

Charlie's reference to him had sparked a reaction in Rory, the first Mary had seen this evening. The Scotsman started, as if he hadn't really been paying attention up to then.

"Uh, aye, that's true." Rory cleared his throat. "I've seen bodies pulled up from the Thames before who were sunk in a similar manner. With this poor lass there were no cuts in the dress from where the lungs had been pierced. It would have been easy enough to just do it through the clothes, but whoever did this took the time take the dress off and put it back on. The only reason I can think to do that is if they cared—cared deeply—

about the lass's physical appearance—the way one might at a funeral."

His reasoning made sense, in a roundabout sort of way, though it still seemed a stretch to Mary.

"What about the—er—" Quinton swallowed hard. "The incisions themselves? Anything unique about them?"

Mary winced herself at the mention of the cuts in the poor woman's body. It was a gruesome thing, to imagine someone cutting her stomach open, filling it with stones, and then sewing her back up.

"Now that you mention it . . ." Rory paused, his expression thoughtful. "There was one thing. The sewing to close the middle incision was very precise. It was a pattern I've never seen before on a person."

Another thought occurred to Mary. "What kind of sewing? You mean like stitching?"

He shrugged. "I suppose."

"Quinton, go get a piece of paper," she said, reaching over and smacking his knee.

"Why?"

"Just do it."

With great and obvious reluctance, Quinton heaved himself upward, clomping over to the desk and returning with a single piece of paper.

"And a quill and ink, you moron."

With a dramatic amount of silent protest, the quill was also retrieved.

"Thank you, Quinton." Mary rolled her eyes, muttering under her breath, "Acting like a spoiled child . . ."

He frowned as he fell back into his chair. "What did you say?"

"You heard me," she snapped before handing the paper and ink to Rory. "Can you draw the pattern for me?"

"Aye, I can." He looked confused, but took the supplies agreeably.

Suddenly the door slammed open as the last of their group

arrived—her cousin John. He strode into the room with the energy of a man on a mission. Snatching the whiskey bottle from on top of the mantle, he took a quick swig, his expression dark.

"What's the matter?" asked Charlie, his one dark eye and one white eye tracking John's movements closely. Oscar perched atop the back of his armchair, her gaze mirroring Charlie's.

John leaned against the wall and sighed. "Zoe's bloody cousin is the matter."

Zoe's body tensed next to Mary. "What about Alexander?"

"The fool was there last night." John took another swig. "At O'Malley's. Apparently he got into it with the man in front of quite a few people."

"Are you sure?" Quinton suddenly leaned forward. "I didn't see him when I was there."

John shrugged. "It must have been after you left, but one of the girls—Lydia, I think—was quite sure he was there. She remembered him by name."

An uneasy silence settled over the room like a heavy blanket. No one seemed to want to say the next words, so Mary took it upon herself. "Surely Alexander isn't capable of such violence?" she asked.

"Of course not," replied Zoe, shaking her head as if trying to clear cobwebs. "He's annoying, certainly, but I can't believe he would kill a man. Besides which, even if Alexander wished to, Miles had a bodyguard. There's no way he could have overpowered him as well."

Quinton nodded slowly. "That is a fair point. How did anyone get past the bodyguard?"

"I don't know," grumbled John. "The goon hasn't been seen since."

"Well there you go! Perhaps he is the killer then!" exclaimed Zoe.

"Perhaps, but that doesn't change the fact your cousin was seen arguing with O'Malley the same night as the murder," said John. "I'll need to talk to him."

Sitting up straighter, suddenly engaged in the conversation, Rory cleared his throat. "Will you arrest the lad?"

"Not without further evidence." John shifted from foot to foot. "He isn't like you, Rory. He's a gentleman from a well-respected family—you can't just arrest someone like that. But I do need to speak with him."

Mary held her breath, waiting for Rory's reaction, but instead of being angry he seemed more relieved than anything. He slumped back in his chair with a deep sigh. "Good, good. Wouldn't wish that hell on anyone. No, not anyone . . ." Rory mumbled under his breath.

Truth rang in those words. Mary had briefly visited the infamous Newgate prison alongside Zoe, and it wasn't an experience she would care to repeat. Something about the cold, damp stone walls made a person believe a building could remember the horrors committed within—as if the years of desperation could be preserved in the cracks themselves. If she believed any place was haunted—by memories, if nothing else—it was Newgate.

"I haven't met the snob myself, but from what I've heard, he's an arrogant twat." Charlie was speaking. "Do you think he'd even agree to speak with a runner, or be truthful if he did?"

"Charlie makes a fair point." Quinton glanced over at Zoe before quickly looking away. "Alexander and I have some history. I wouldn't say we're friends, but he did hire me to look into the girl's disappearance. He might be more inclined to tell me what happened if I approach him alone."

As he glanced away, Zoe shifted in the seat and Mary suppressed a sigh. Even though she was quite fond of her friend, she would never completely understand the upper-class mentality. Zoe was better than most—she claimed her independent thinking came from her French heritage—but she was still a nob. It was clear to anyone with two eyes that she was in love with Quinton, but she refused to do anything about it. The threat of scandal, both her own and that of her family by association, was enough to give her pause. Mary thought it was a strange world indeed were such an abstract thing could carry so much weight.

In Zoe's defence, Quinton was not a part of that world and yet seemed to have no intention of admitting his feelings either. Too honourable or too stupid for his own good—perhaps both. At first it had been amusing to watch the two of them dancing around each other, close, but never quite close enough. Now it was getting wearisome.

But Mary couldn't solve everyone's problems. One broken member of this group at a time . . .

"Very well. But keep me informed." John's face was passive, but Mary knew her cousin well enough to recognize he was frustrated. He might understand the logic of Quinton's suggestion, but John was a diligent man and a hard worker, and he didn't like not being able to do his job.

"Agreed. I would also be interested to hear what the nob has to say," added Charlie.

Zoe sighed. "I would offer to go with you, but I think you have more of a chance of him being honest with you if I am also absent. Alexander is prideful man—he always was, even as a child. He won't take kindly to being challenged."

Quinton nodded gratefully, perhaps remembering, as Mary was, the moment of tension between him and Zoe earlier that afternoon. "Prideful perhaps, but I don't think he's genuinely stupid. If it comes down to a choice between me or a Bow Street cell, I'm confident he'll pick me." Quinton chuckled, probably enjoying the mental image of Alexander spending a night in such a place.

Rory's brow furrowed. "But I thought—"

"Yes, but he doesn't know that," Quinton countered with a wink. "I have another appointment tomorrow in the early afternoon, but I'll call on him immediately after."

There was little else to say after that. The group finished their drinks, making some casual small talk before slowly filtering out into the cold.

As she pulled her thick woollen cloak tightly around her shoulders, Mary felt a presence appear at her side. She turned her head to see Rory.

He held out the piece of paper Quinton had fetched for him to draw the stitching pattern on. "Sorry. In all the excitement I almost forgot to give ye this."

"Right, of course." Mary had also nearly forgotten. "Thank you, Rory."

Folding it in half, she slipped it into her pocket. She would examine it later when the light was a bit better and her head was bit clearer. Suddenly she felt very tired. Her eyes fell on Charlie as he hailed a hackney. Perhaps she would pass the Rory issue on to him.

Chapter Thirty-One

The candlelight from her bedside table danced across the back of the drawing as Mary lay in her bed. Rory had drawn the stitching from Katie's body in short exact strokes, and the image teased Mary, doing cartwheels on the very edge of her memory. She knew she had seen the stitch before. She closed her eyes, letting her mind drift.

She arrived in her thoughts to a time when she was working as a maid, at her post before she met Zoe. It was late at night—later than even servants were expected to work—when Mary came across one of the lady's maids at the servants dining hall. The poor woman was working by candlelight of her own, desperately stitching embroidery to the base of a gown in the dim light. The eldest daughter of the house had decided on impulse she wanted the embroidery added before a ball the next day, without a thought as to who would have to stay up all night stitching it on.

What was her name? Eleanor—that's right. She wasn't the warmest of women, but Mary had felt sorry for her that night, so she'd stayed up with Eleanor, and in exchange Eleanor had taught her the delicate, neat stitch she used.

Mary suddenly opened her eyes, staring at Rory's drawing. The stitches were the same pattern. Small, neat, precise, crossed in a unique pattern at the bottom. A stitch no man would ever know.

She sat upright in bed, her hair still loose, not yet bound up in the silk cloth she typically used to fix it for bed, and reached for her dressing gown to throw over her nightclothes. Knotting it about her middle, Mary extinguished the candle, grabbed the drawing, then hurried through the door of her room, turning right to quickly run down the servants' stairs.

Within moments, Mary burst into Zoe's room without knocking and slid to a stop at Zoe's bed, finding it empty.

"Mary, what's wrong?" Mary jumped, whirling around to see Zoe curled up on her small sofa, book in hand, oil lamp lit.

"Rory's drawing! I know where I've seen that stitch!" Mary raced over, shaking the paper in front of her. "It's a herringbone stitch. A lady's maid at my previous posting taught me." With that she thrust the paper into Zoe's hand and collapsed alongside her on the sofa.

Zoe took the drawing, examining it closely in the lamplight. "Are you sure?"

"Yes, I'm sure. The slant is a little different at the end, but it's the same pattern." Mary snatched the drawing back, looking at it again. "Aren't you a lady of refinement? Haven't you ever done embroidery before?"

"Not my strongest suit—pianoforte on the other hand . . ." Zoe sat up straighter. "What are you saying, Mary? Our killer is a woman?"

"I don't think the men we have our sights on would know how to do this stitch," replied Mary. "Not Miles O'Malley, and certainly not his bodyguard. I doubt even Quinton knows anything beyond a basic backstitch."

The two of them sat in silence for a moment, processing the implications.

Zoe took a deep breath and brought up the obvious. "But the brutality. The cutting up of the body, the rocks . . . is a woman capable?"

"Asks the woman who stabbed a man and would have killed him given the chance." Mary shook her head, trying to dispel the image in her mind of Zoe standing there with blood dripping from her hands. "Women do what needs to be done. We always have."

Mary closed her eyes, taking a deep breath. Suddenly she felt Zoe's hand taking her own. When she opened her eyes, much to her surprise, she saw silent tears streaming down Zoe's cheeks.

For the first time since that terrible night, the words which had been stuck in Mary's throat finally broke free. "It wasn't your fault." It felt freeing to finally say the words out loud, as if a weight had been lifted from Mary's shoulders.

Zoe shook her head, sniffing in a most unladylike fashion. "It was. I am the one who wanted to go see Lady Fairfax. Because of me, you almost died. Because of me, you have to carry the burden of the whole sordid thing."

"Very well, you're right, it's a horrible thing." Mary sighed quietly. "We almost died, and we will carry the weight of what happened in that room with us for the rest of our lives. But that's not what wakes me up in a cold sweat in the middle of the night."

Zoe blinked. "Then what does?"

"You do." Mary turned away, feeling tears well in her own eyes. "I can see you get up, knife in hand. I see you walk toward that devil, and I know in my heart that he will kill you. You are going to die and there's not a single thing I can do about it. I'm completely helpless. That's when I wake up screaming."

Zoe squeezed her hand tighter. "We beat him, Mary. We won."

Mary shook her head. "Did we? I'm not so sure. It feels as though that bastard is still here, haunting us from beyond the grave, punishing us for surviving." Saying that out loud wasn't easy. Mary didn't want to give Fairfax anything more—he'd already taken so much—but maybe that's what made it so hard to admit she was struggling.

"I have nightmares too," said Zoe quietly. "Why do you think

I'm sitting here reading by lamplight that strains my eyes until I have a headache, rather than seeking the comfort of my bed?"

They sat there in silence for another moment. It was . . . freeing to finally admit that neither of them was fine after what had happened. The wall had finally crumbled.

Mary spoke slowly. "I thought I could come back here and just start living again. If that day crossed my mind, I just thought of something else. I wanted to pretend it didn't happen."

"As did I," said Zoe.

Mary turned to face Zoe. "Maybe that's the problem. Maybe we have to face the fear, and the hurt, and the memories. Maybe we need to wear the whole experience on the outside, not bury it within."

Zoe smiled sadly. "Perhaps. Easier to say than to do."

"True." Mary returned her smile. "But speaking of this together, it's a fine start. From now on, honesty between the two of us."

"Agreed." Zoe brushed the tears from her face. "We will get through this, Mary, together."

"I know." Mary brushed away her own tears.

Zoe held up the drawing, changing the subject. "Back to this stitch. Even if we allow the killer may be a woman, how do we narrow it down from half of London?"

"Most women who don't have servants do know how to mend, but embroidery is a different beast." Mary looked at the drawing again. "In this scenario, herringbone is an embroidery stitch. Since it's unlikely a lady such as yourself is involved, I would put down a significant wager that whoever did this was a lady's maid."

Zoe nodded, a light of excitement glowing in her eyes. "Then we need to talk to Quinton tomorrow. He needs to see this."

There it was—the emphasis that Zoe only put on Quinton's name. Mary sighed, shaking her head. "Didn't we just promise honesty? When are you going to quit pretending you aren't in love with him?"

The dumbfounded look on Zoe's face was highly satisfying.

"I don't, er, what?" Zoe scoffed, clearly trying to come up with something to refute Mary's statement. But after a moment she sighed and leaned back in the sofa. "Fine. Quinton is equal parts confounding, infuriating, and . . . irresistible." She sighed again. "Have I taken leave of every sense God gave me?"

Mary laughed softly. "I believe you have found something, Zoe, not lost something. You have found love, you silly, stubborn girl. Even better, he's in love with you as well."

"Ugh." Zoe threw her hands up. "It's inconvenient is what it is. And how is it you always know my feelings before I do? He drives me absolutely mad, but I can think of nothing else. I remember each and every time we have touched. I feel as if I have lost my mind."

"Sounds like love to me." Mary crossed her arms. "I suggest you come to terms with the situation."

Zoe sighed. "And how exactly would you suggest you I do that?"

As much as she loved the woman, Mary couldn't help but sigh. Zoe really could be as dense as a man sometimes.

"I would suggest you talk to Quinton," said Mary. "This is a conversation that needs to be had between the two of you."

"And what if we have this conversation and can come to no solution?" Zoe sat back up, leaning forward. "Besides which, shouldn't he be the one to approach me?"

Mary raised her eyebrow. "Quinton would rather stab his own eyeballs out with a hot poker than do something dishonourable. He won't approach you as long as he's afraid of bringing scandal down on you. As for finding a solution, I have faith that two intelligent people such as yourselves can find a way through."

Zoe said nothing in response to that. Instead she just leaned her head on Mary's shoulder. Mary understood. They didn't need words anymore.

Chapter Thirty-Two

Mid-morning had arrived by the time Mary and Zoe disembarked from the carriage into the cold winter air. Zoe pulled her heavy cloak around her and shoved her hands further into the muff of sheep's fur. Velvet hats had long replaced her summer bonnet, and this one was a lovely red, matching the red velvet trim on her cloak. The air was cold, and she heard Mary mutter as much with more colourful language.

She immediately spotted Quinton near his office, stomping his feet as he spoke quietly to John. Both men looked up as the ladies approached, though neither appeared pleased to see them.

Quinton spoke first. "John and I both have other places to be, ladies. What was so important it could not wait a day or two?"

Someone was in a rude mood. Quinton had been distracted for days, but today, impatience had come along for the journey.

Zoe opened her mouth but Mary beat her to it. "We found out an important piece of information," she snapped. "Sorry if we made you leave your warm beds to hear it. I didn't realize you men were so fragile."

Zoe wasn't surprised at Mary's irritation. Being out in the bitter cold always made her peevish, as did men dismissing her.

"Just get on with it, Mary," said John, clearly not intimidated by his cousin's short tongue. "What do you have to tell us?"

Pulling Rory's drawing from the warm depths of her muff, Zoe handed it to Quinton. "Mary recognized these stitches from when she worked as a maid. A lady's maid would know how to do this kind of sewing. We think the killer is a woman and at one time she worked as a lady's maid."

Saying his glance at the drawing was cursory would be generous. Quinton quickly handed it over to John and looked incredulously at Zoe. "This is what you wanted to tell us?" Quinton shook his head, as if he couldn't believe their stupidity. "There is no way a woman would have the savagery to commit this murder. The body was cut open, Zoe, filled with rocks, sewn back up. And there is no way a woman would have been able to move the body to dispose of it in the river."

Anger rose in Zoe's chest. Why did she have to be in love with the stupidest man alive?

Fortunately for Quinton, Mary spoke next. "And there is no way a man would know this stitching pattern. Maybe she had help to move the body."

The men exchanged a glance, clearly unimpressed with Mary's theory.

Zoe's jaw clenched—she'd had just about enough of this conversation. "You will not even consider the possibility that a woman is our killer?" she asked, her voice cold but controlled.

John shook his head. "I'm sorry, but it's simply impossible." He turned to Quinton. "I'm wanted at Bow Street. I'll speak with you later."

With that he stalked away, leaving Quinton with the infuriated women.

"I also am needed elsewhere," he said nervously.

Coward.

His eyes met hers and then immediately looked away. He swallowed. "I know you mean well, and you have good ideas, both of you. But you did not see the body. It just could not be a woman." Quinton took off his hat, running his fingers through his hair. "I will see you both another time."

And then he too was gone, leaving Mary and Zoe standing in the cold with their mouths hanging open. Zoe said nothing until Mary turned to her, her eyes flashing with anger. To forestall a string of invectives, Zoe said, "Let us find a coffee shop and get out of this bloody cold. We will find this woman killer without the help of the men."

Chapter Thirty-Three

L ord and Lady Coleville showed no signs of nervousness when Quinton entered their parlour. Quinton wondered if one day he would carry himself like the lord in front of him—with such easy confidence, knowing his worth. At this moment, he felt like a boy again, uncertain and backed into a corner.

They had asked him to come without Lord Dovefield, and though Quinton had hesitated, in the end he had honoured their request. But now he was reconsidering his decision.

The Lady Coleville, blonde and petite, smiled at him and gestured to a chair. "Please, Mr. Huxley, have a seat."

Lord Coleville stood across from him near a settee, waiting for his wife to sit before seating himself.

The parlour was decorated in the latest fashion. The furniture was heavy and dark, the end tables and serving table ornately carved from mahogany. The room was painted a deep blue, with equally dark curtains hung in the window. Quinton found the overall air draining, like an actual weight was attached somehow. Still, he sat in the offered chair, perching carefully on the edge.

No one sent for tea.

He waited for one of the couple to speak, using his tactic of silence to allow the other party to show their hand. After a moment it worked.

"My husband did not exaggerate. You do indeed look like Graham," said Lady Coleville.

"You knew him, my lady?" Quinton hadn't known that.

"Indeed." Lady Coleville smiled. "Our families were well acquainted. I was young when he died, but he's not the type of man one forgets. Besides, his portrait still hangs on the wall at the Coleville estate."

Quinton inclined his head. "Of course. I would like to one day see that portrait."

The couple shifted in their seats at the reminder of the reason for the meeting.

After a few moments of awkward silence, Lord Coleville cleared his throat. "As to that, my visit to my solicitor ended much as Dovefield assumed it would. We've sent a man to Guernsey to be sure, but it appears your documents are genuine. You are my brother's . . . legal son."

Quinton could tell it pained the lord to say the words out loud, but now they were spoken, so the worst was behind them.

"Our question is, what do you plan to do now?" asked Lord Coleville.

Lady Coleville watched him carefully, and Quinton recognized the fear in her carefully masked eyes. He didn't blame her. Their whole future was in the hands of a man they considered simple and common.

He said nothing for a long moment, considering his answer.

Finally he sighed, deciding honesty would be best. "I have not made any firm decisions about this matter. For now, Lord Dovefield has counselled me to simply establish my legitimacy." Quinton hesitated, considering his next words carefully. "Do you mind if I ask you a question?"

"Very well." Lord Coleville sighed, gesturing for Quinton to hurry up.

"Where does it stand with the viscount?" asked Quinton. "Is he aware of the situation?"

There was no missing the glance Lady Coleville threw her husband, and the pained look that crossed his face. This was certainly not the first time this had been discussed.

"We have decided to wait on discussing this with my father until things are more certain," replied the lord. "That being said, my wife came up with a possible solution that may benefit us all, should the legality be firmly established."

That was interesting, but it did explain why Lady Coleville was present. Generally legal matters were handled exclusively by men. Quinton was surprised his uncle had included his wife in the proceedings, but it raised Quinton's opinion of him.

Lady Coleville met his eyes. "I don't believe you have met our daughters, Mr. Huxley. Our oldest, Ivy, had her first season last year." She paused, allowing Quinton to work through why she brought up her daughter. "She is considered a diamond, sir. Her beauty is well known."

Quinton usually considered himself fairly quick-witted, but it took him a moment to understand her meaning. He stood abruptly, astonished. "You are offering your daughter—my cousin—to me in marriage? Have you lost your senses?" Quinton gaped at them. "She has never even met me, nor I her!"

"Calm down, Quinton." Coleville stood as well. "If you are to be a member of society, then you must come to the understanding that marriage is a practical institution. Please, sit for a moment and consider the benefits." He gestured again to the chair Quinton had vacated.

His emotions were conflicted, but after a brief hesitation, Quinton returned to his seat.

Lady Coleville spoke. "You are correct that Ivy and you have not formally met. But arranged marriages are common among families of our status. Our daughters are prepared for that reality. Ensuring the union between the two of you will keep the title and the estate within the family, and make your entry into society much easier."

This wasn't the direction Quinton had thought this conversation would go. A marriage proposal? If this was Ivy's first season, the girl couldn't be older than nineteen, at most, while Quinton was approaching his thirtieth birthday. It wasn't that he couldn't understand the logic behind the Coleville's argument, and he also understood this was a way for them to save as much face as possible. But Quinton didn't want to be married to a nineteen-year-old he hardly knew. Besides, he was in love with someone else.

"That is not my way, Lady Coleville," replied Quinton. "I understand your reasoning, but whatever people of my status may do, I have no desire to marry for convenience."

Lord Coleville sighed. "We mean no offense, Quinton. But I have observed you from afar for years. My brother's blood runs in your veins. I know you to be an honourable man. We are simply giving you an opportunity to do the right thing here."

Quinton did pity the couple sitting across from him. This wasn't an easy situation for them to navigate. But he had had enough. "With all the respect you deserve, your brother's blood didn't matter to you until now. I never knew the man." Quinton stood again. "I did know my mother, whose blood also runs through me. She is the person who taught me decency and honour, and she would want me to stay true to myself. I have very little interest in marrying your daughter simply because it is convenient."

Both the lord and the lady were silent for a moment, exchanging another glance.

"You were right again, Montgomery," said Lady Coleville softly. "He does sound like Graham."

Lord Coleville stood as well, still standing with dignity, but his shoulders sagging a bit more than when Quinton had entered. "I understand your reluctance, Quinton," he said. "If your concern has to do with your limited knowledge of Ivy, time with her can be arranged. But I urge you not to make a hasty decision while your emotions are running high. Take some time now for yourself to consider it and give us an answer later."

As tempted as Quinton was to simply tell them to shove off, he controlled himself and gave a brief nod before taking his leave. He knew their offer did have merit. In many ways, it was the perfect solution.

But then he thought of the blue-eyed French girl that already held his heart and knew it was not so simple.

Chapter Thirty-Four

Zoe was actually angrier when she arrived at her mother's charitable home, the Haven. The three cups of coffee she'd consumed at the coffeehouse had done little to soothe her rage. Having opted for hot chocolate, Mary seemed in slightly calmer spirits, but Zoe knew she was just as angry.

At the coffeehouse they had come up with their plan. Zoe could admit it wasn't a particularly good one, but at least they were doing something, since Quinton and John refused to help them. What did Quinton have to do today that was so much more important than her?

The young girl who answered the door recognized them immediately, quickly showing them into the sitting room. Simone didn't take long to make her appearance.

"What's wrong?" she asked, the concern apparent in her eyes. "Has something happened?"

"No, nothing is wrong," Zoe replied. "Why would you assume something is wrong?"

Simone frowned. "Well, you hardly make a habit of stopping by in the middle of the afternoon. I assume this isn't a social call?"

She made a fair point. The Haven was Simone's charity for

housing and training unwed mothers. The work here had consumed a fair amount of her time since she established it last year. Helping these young women had become her passion, one that Zoe respected, but Simone was right that Zoe didn't make a habit of stopping by socially. Not that she didn't care, but this was her mother's project, not hers.

"Well, no." Even though Simone was right, it still grated for Zoe to admit it—especially when she was in an ill temper such as this. Taking a deep breath, Zoe forced herself to rein in the snippy retort on the tip of her tongue. "We were actually hoping to consult with a few of your girls."

"About what?"

Zoe exchanged a glance with Mary. How much should they tell Simone? They hadn't discussed this at the coffeehouse, though in retrospect they probably should have.

She decided the truth would be necessary—with a few carefully omitted details. She explained Quinton was looking into the disappearance of girl who had recently turned up dead. Zoe did not mention the connection to Alexander, or her own escapades to gambling hells and the like. She also left out a few of the gorier details when it came to the stitching.

"So this stitching . . . was found on the body of the poor girl?" asked Simone.

"Yes. It's a herringbone stitch. We think it might have been done by a lady's maid—or someone who used to be a lady's maid." Zoe paused. "Since you happen to know quite a few of those, we were thinking we might consult with them about it."

"Mm-hmm." Simone turned to Mary. "And you have a drawing of this 'unique' stitching? Could I see it, please?"

"Of course," replied Mary as she handed the piece of paper over.

Simone studied the sketch for a few moments, her expression pensive. Finally she handed it back to Mary. "Well, you're correct that it's used for embroidery. There's something odd about it . . ."

Mary nodded, tucking the paper back into her pocket. "We agree. But we'd like to get a professional's opinion."

"Very well. I'll have Claudia gather the lady's maids who are in residence." Simone summoned the young girl who had allowed them admittance, sending her off on her errand with a quick whisper.

Simone turned back to them. "You realize this is a bit of a stretch?"

Zoe swallowed the irritated sigh brewing in her chest. "Yes, we realize that, Maman. But it can't do any harm to ask."

"Perhaps." Simone studied her, clearly deciding whether or not she should say the next words. In the end she did. "What did Mr. Huxley have to say on the matter? Have you spoken to him recently?"

The mention of the man's name fanned the flames of rage which Zoe had been attempting to dampen. Her cheeks flushed with colour and her nostrils flared as she huffed. "I don't need Quinton's permission, or his approval, to pursue my own line of reasoning," she snapped.

"Quinton and John think it's a load of . . . malarkey," said Mary, seemingly censoring herself from using a more colourful word. "They don't believe a woman could carry out some of the more . . . unsettling aspects of the crime."

"Hmm. So the stitching was found in such a way as to make you think the killer left it, not a witness?"

Zoe and Mary exchanged another look. Seeing this, Simone raised her hand. "I don't need to know more details—in fact, I'd prefer not to. But you do believe the killer to be a woman? And Quinton does not?"

"That is the short version," admitted Zoe grudgingly. "Quinton does not believe a delicate flower such as the feminine form could ever be responsible for such a heinous thing as hands-on murder—maybe a poisoning—but nothing that would involve her using her gentle fingers." She huffed again. "Even worse, he left us for some inconsequential appointment."

"In fairness," Mary began, "that isn't exactly what he said—"

"It's close enough," Zoe snapped.

Simone's lip twitched—if Zoe didn't know better, she would think her mother was suppressing a smile. "Well, while I don't entirely agree with his sentiment, I do know Mr. Huxley is a busy man. Perhaps the appointment was less inconsequential than you might think," suggested Simone.

Why is she defending him? Zoe started to reply, but Simone kept speaking before she could.

"Nevertheless, busy or not, he is still just a man." Simone gestured for them to take a seat, placing herself in a plush but small armchair suited to her petite size. "Men are often limited in their thinking. Even with the best of them, their minds can become rigid. It is a failing on their part, one which we as women must unfortunately make up for at times."

Zoe blinked, surprised at her mother's frank words. "So you don't agree that a woman isn't capable of murder?"

Simone met her gaze evenly. "I think, given the right circumstances, a woman can be every bit as vicious and violent as a man."

Thinking back on her childhood, Zoe couldn't help but agree. When the two of them had fled France . . . some memories from that time Zoe couldn't bear to look at for too long, lest she become lost in the blood lust and brutality. But one thing she did remember was that in the crowd screaming for the guillotine to come down were just as many female voices as male.

A knock at the door was followed by a line of women entering —Zoe counted five in all. She and Mary rose to their feet so as to be on the same level.

"Thank you, Claudia, that will be all," said Simone, dismissing the girl and then closing the door firmly behind her. She clearly didn't want any eavesdropping among the other women.

Simone turned to the five women. "My daughter and Miss Fletcher have some questions for you in regard to your previous professional experience. No one is in trouble—they would just like to consult you in regard to a sewing pattern."

Mary stood, pulling the sketch back out of her pocket. "Do any of you recognize this pattern?"

One of the women took it—about six months pregnant by the look of her stomach—examined it, then passed it down the line. "Aye, I recognize it. It's a herringbone stitch. I've used it to repair embroidery for my missus."

"That's what I thought." Mary nodded. "So it's not likely a man would know this stitch?"

She laughed. "No, it's not likely. A backstitch a footman or valet might pick up to do his own mending. But a herringbone? It's decorative—you'd only use it for embroidery or knitting, or repairing fine fabric. It's not particularly complicated or fancy, but I doubt a man would know it."

The next woman hesitated, her gaze thoughtful.

"What is it?" asked Zoe, feeling vindicated by the former maid's confirmation.

"Well, there's something strange about it." She handed it to another woman. "Martha, what do you think?"

Martha held the paper out squinting. "Hmm, yer right. It's the slant."

"Well, are ya sure yar holding it the right way?" asked the next girl, snatching it away.

"Yes," snapped Martha, snatching it back. "Look at the tie off. It has to start over here to end up on that side."

The last woman leaned over, straining to look. "Aye. The sewer uses her left hand."

"Don't be ridiculous," scoffed the first woman. "No housekeeper would let a maid sew with her left hand. It ain't natural."

"I knew a lady's maid that did."

"Really?" Zoe stepped forward, her heart beating a bit faster. "Who was that?"

This last woman was older than the others—not old, by any

means, but certainly in her early thirties—with an experienced look about her. She leaned toward plain-looking, but not ugly. She was the kind of maid who blended into the background, not drawing any attention to herself. The only thing that disrupted that impression was the swell of her stomach, just beginning to show the signs of pregnancy.

She continued, "She didn't work in my house, but she was on the same street, a few doors down. I didn't know her real well, but I remember the other maids whispering about her being left-handed. It was unusual enough to be compelling gossip."

"And her mistress didn't mind?"

She shrugged. "Not that I know of. She was a talented seamstress. Despite the wagging tongues, we all took our most difficult mending to her. At least, until . . ."

"Until what?" Zoe asked.

"She was dismissed. No references. The household was tight-lipped about why, but the rumour was she'd been caught stealing."

The girl was interrupted by a knock at the door. Zoe could have screamed as the door opened, but she swallowed her ire when she saw who it was. Savita, Charlie's younger sister. Simone employed her and her mother as midwifes for the pregnant women in the home.

"Pardon me, my lady, but Penny is getting close. She's asking for you." Savita's long hair was tied back, but a few wisps had fallen forward onto her sweaty forehead. Even clearly exhausted and dishevelled, she was still one of the most beautiful women Zoe had ever seen.

"Of course." Simone nodded to the girls. "If you'll excuse me."

As her mother glided across the room, Zoe turned back to the maid. "I don't suppose you happen to remember this maid's name?"

Her nose scrunched as she thought. "It was a long time

ago . . . Lily, maybe? Or Lillian? I'm not sure, I think it started with an L."

Zoe's heart suddenly stopped beating, her mind drifting back to the gambling hell and the serving woman who had fetched O'Malley that first time.

Mary beat her to it. "Could it have been . . . Lydia?"

Chapter Thirty-Five

L eaning against the outside wall of the house, Savita sighed and closed her eyes, letting her head rest against the cold brick surface. Her knees ached from kneeling next to the poor birthing girl, and exhaustion weighed on her shoulders, hanging on her body like a water-drenched cloak. The cold bit at her exposed skin, but the cup of tea in her hands warmed her fingers, grounding her in the moment.

Savita liked it out here in the garden. In the spring and summer it was particularly nice, with the one small tree covered in green foliage and the flowers in bloom, as well as the lush ivy which crept up the outside of the house. But even in the winter the snow-covered branches held their own charm. This was a place of peace, where one could take a moment away from everyone else and just breathe.

She wondered if she would ever have a garden like this for herself. She could picture such a life in her mind's eye—her children running around, laughing and playing in the snow while the man she had loved since childhood shouted for them to come inside before they caught a cold. Savita sighed, her frustration with said man ruining her daydream. John had been particularly difficult since they started courting, and she wondered if they could find a way to reconcile their two drastically different ideas of what the future would look like.

"Savita, what are you doing out here in the blasted cold?"

She opened her eyes to see the source of the question but didn't need to. She would recognize her brother's voice anywhere.

"I am taking a momentary break," responded Savita. "It's been a particularly difficult labour. Mother is with the girl now."

"So naturally you chose to come outside in the frigid air to take your tea." Charlie shook his head. "You'll catch your death out here, Savi."

"I just needed a minute to breathe." Savita suddenly realized something. "What are you doing here anyway? I've never seen you within fifteen yards of this house."

He shrugged. "I was in the neighbourhood."

The words were nonchalant, but Savita knew her brother well enough to know that something was on his mind. Once Charlie set his teeth into something, he was like a dog worrying a bone— he couldn't let it go. But Savita also knew better than to push him. He would tell her when he was ready, and she had better things to do than pull answers from his psyche like teeth.

"Do you want a cup of tea?" she asked. "The water is probably still warm."

"No, thank you. I'm on my way somewhere." Charlie hesitated. "You said mother is busy at the moment?"

"Yes. But I could go relieve her if it's important."

Charlie shook his head. "No, no, it's not important."

He'd been this way for as long as Savita could remember. Where John was late afternoon sunshine and Quinton the early morning fog, Charlie was the brooding thunderstorm hovering on the horizon. Sometimes she thought he enjoyed keeping secrets.

His gaze was distant, as if he was considering something far away. He'd been disfigured for so long, sometimes Savita forgot about his blinded eye. Maybe not quite forgot, but when she saw the scar, it just seemed a part of him, rather than a disfigurement.

She had been so young when it happened that she barely remembered him without it.

"Do you ever think about father?" he asked suddenly.

The question caught her so off guard that Savita choked on her tea, sputtering brown liquid across the white snow. Charlie never spoke of their father. Her brother's bitter, boiling rage over their father's abandonment always hung in the air surrounding their family, but it was never spoken about.

The truth was she could barely recall the man. A presence stood in her memories where she assumed he had been, but the details were hazy at best. She didn't even really recall India. What she did remember was the deep wound he left behind, in both her brother and her mother. There were times she wondered what they might be like if he had stayed . . .

"No, I don't think about him," she finally replied. "Why do you ask?"

"I've been thinking about that time quite a bit lately. How hard those early years were in this country—how hard Mother had to work to take care of us."

Savita squinted, but said nothing, letting Charlie say what he wanted to say in his own time.

"I keep thinking about that day—the day he told Mother he was leaving. They didn't know I was listening at the top of the stairs. He said his family was never going to accept us and he'd been foolish to try." Charlie paused, his expression pensive. "For so many years I thought he was being cruel. Now . . . now I realize he was actually just weak."

"Is there a difference?" Savita retorted with a snort.

That got a chuckle out of him. "No, I suppose not. But Mother was never weak, was she?"

"No. I would describe Mother as many things, but weak isn't one of them."

"Our whole life, everyone underestimated her—looked right through her as if she wasn't even there—but she never complained. She just did what she had to do. Now people look at me as if I'm the strong one in our family, but she was always the one in the background, propping me up." He turned his gaze to her. "The two of you, you're made of steel, Savi."

"And you're just now realizing this?" Savi punched him lightly in the arm. "What has gotten into you?"

He laughed again. "I may be a bit thick, but I'm not a complete idiot."

"No, of course not." Savita shook her head. "You are many things, brother, but a fool is not one of them."

Charlie cocked his head, with that intelligent glint in his eye that Savita found so annoying. "So, what are you doing out in the cold then? It can't be just a difficult labour that had you looking so forlorn when I arrived."

Savita sighed. "It's nothing. John and I have been fighting is all."

"Hmm." Charlie nodded. "I had noted his absence the last few days, but I assumed it was just because he was busy. What has he done wrong?"

"Why do you assume he is the one who is wrong?"

Charlie snorted. "Because you are my sister, and therefore I will always take your side over any suitor's, even if it is John. So what did he do?"

She couldn't help but laugh at that. "You have never taken my side on one thing, not even as children. But fine, if you must know, John is concerned about my safety. He has informed me that once we are married, I will discontinue my work as a midwife. As you can imagine, his declaration went over poorly." Savita sighed again. "He did attempt to apologize a few days ago for his manner, but he hasn't changed his mind. And I won't give up my vocation, not even for him. I do not know if there is a way for us to come to a compromise in this." The heavy sadness she had been trying to avoid settled into the pit of her stomach. "I suppose I just thought he was . . . better . . . than other men. I thought he understood how important this is to me. But John's attitude in this issue has given me pause."

Charlie was silent for a moment as he contemplated her words. Savita wondered what was going through that thick skull of his.

Finally he spoke. "If you don't wish to continue the courtship, then you are under no obligation. You must do what you think is right. But I will say in John's defence that he is better than many men—better certainly than me. He cares for you and wishes to protect you, and I cannot fault him for that. However, he is foolish if he thinks your safety means so little to me. I've had a man follow you and Mother on all your midwife-related excursions for years. No harm would ever come to you while you're under my protection."

Conflicting emotions competed for dominance in Savita's heart—anger that her brother would assign someone to follow her and Mother without informing them, surprise that Charlie had managed to keep the secret from her all these years, and love for the fool that he cared so much for his family.

"Are you angry?" he asked after a few moments of silence.

"Yes," replied Savita. "But I am also thankful to have you as a brother . . . even when you are infuriating."

Charlie shook his head. "No need to get sentimental. But I will speak to John and explain that he has no need to fear for your safety. Then the two of you can work out the rest."

Savita smiled. "Very well. Thank you, Charlie. But in the future, I would appreciate it if you would include me in decisions that affect me." She raised an eyebrow, a thought suddenly occurring to her. "Where did you say you were going, again?"

He smirked. "I didn't. But speaking of, I should probably be off."

"Fine." Savita suddenly realized how cold her fingers were. "I should go inside anyway. Who knew we'd have so many unlikely visitors today?"

Stopping mid-stride, Charlie furrowed his brow. "What other visitors?"

"Mary and Zoe. They were chatting up the lady's maids in residence about some stitch or another they had a drawing of."

"Really?" Charlie crossed his arms, his smirk replaced by something more genuine. "It seems I've underestimated the French lass yet again. Did they come up with anything?"

Savita shrugged. "I didn't hear everything. One of the maids was saying something about using the left hand. I guess she knew a girl who used to sew that way. Lydia, I think?"

"Hmm. Thanks, Savi."

With that, Charlie stalked off, continuing on whatever mission he was currently engaged in. Savita watched him walk for a moment, contemplating her strange brother. He was difficult at times, and she was vexed that he had made decisions on her behalf without consulting her. But despite her words to the contrary, Charlie was right about one thing. John was a good man. This was their first disagreement, and it would hardly be their last, but Savi had loved him since she was a child, and she knew his feelings for her were genuine. They would find a way to compromise— that's what people who truly loved each other did.

As she stepped back into the warmth of the home, Savi's thoughts drifted back to her musings before, picturing her future children playing in their own garden and John standing by her side where he belonged.

Chapter Thirty-Six

Charlie slipped into the shadows of the modest houses that lined this neighbourhood. It wasn't exactly his territory, this area, but he wasn't unfamiliar with it either. Years ago he had acquired his own modest home a number of streets away, far from the eyes of his sister and mother. That house had been useful to hide Rory when Rory was wanted for murder, before his subsequent arrest.

A person had to be clever about opportunities that presented themselves, knowing that such opportunities could prove to be useful in unexpected ways. And no one who knew Charlie judged him any less than devilishly clever.

Rory, however, was not smart in the same way. He was an intellectual man, but he sometimes had the self-preservation instinct of a blind cat. He had thrown away his freedom for the sake of a woman he wanted to shield from gossip and had all but hung because of that decision. A person had to put that kind of sentimentality aside to survive in Charlie's world.

Fortunately for Rory, he had friends on both sides of the law. Because of that friendship, Charlie found himself ambling up the back path, past a rock shed with an antiseptic smell which he took care to give a wide berth, to the back door of the small house where his Scotsman lived.

Well, friendship and the urging of John's cousin. Mary had called Charlie aside as the group scattered after the session at Quinton's and asked him to look in on Rory. Charlie wasn't blind—he'd seen the signs as well. The hollow smiles and the lack of light in Rory's eyes. Most concerning, not a single Shakespearean quote had been heard from Rory's lips since his freedom had been obtained. Hopefully Charlie could do something today to change that.

Charlie knocked on the heavy wooden door, then light from the room poured out to the stone landing, illuminating him as Rory opened the door.

"Is a man not safe anywhere?" snapped Rory, holding a glass of what Charlie could only assume was very fine scotch.

"Safe from what, Rory, people who care?" Charlie brushed past him. "Then no. For you, nowhere is safe."

A fire lit the main room of the house, and several large textbooks lay open on the table next to a comfortable chair. A small plate held a wedge of cheese and a thick slice of bread. Setting his own glass down with a grumble, Rory busied himself finding a glass for Charlie.

Charlie took the offered glass and chair near the fire and sipped appreciatively. He had come to understand and even enjoy the smoky depth of good scotch, and Rory always had good scotch.

If Quinton or John had come, they likely would have worked their way up to the reason for their visit, softening the blow. Charlie didn't have the patience for preamble.

"You look like the backside of mange-ridden dog, Rory," said Charlie. "I assume this has something to do with your stay in prison, so I've come to offer a listening ear, if that's what you want. If it's not what you want, then too bad. Start talking."

Rory stared at him for a few long seconds, then burst out laughing. It was surprisingly refreshing to hear him laugh.

"Don't hold back then, Charlie. Tell me how you really feel." Rory swirled the amber liquid in his glass, the tiny wave nearly reaching the rim of the glass. "Despite your lack of tact, however, I will accommodate you. You're correct that the time in Newgate was quite awful. I had better accommodations than most, thanks to Lord Dovefield, but . . . by the end, the noose was preferable to the cell, if my imprisonment were to continue." Rory took a sip, staring at Charlie over the rim of his glass. "But as unpleasant as the experience was, I have been through unpleasantness before. That is not the reason for the melancholy you've so aptly observed."

Charlie frowned. "Then what is?"

"I'm afraid it's much more mundane than my imprisonment and near-death experience." Rory sighed heavily, then downed the rest of his scotch in one go with a weak smile. "As my favourite playwright muses, 'To weep is to make less the depth of grief.' Would you believe the source of my misery is a broken heart? How pathetic is that?"

Huh. Romantic attachment wasn't exactly what Charlie had thought they'd be discussing that evening, but he was already here. He might as well hear what the man had to say. "Pathetic or not, I'm listening, Rory."

A moment of silence fell while Rory stared off into the fire. Charlie wondered if he was gathering his thoughts or just thinking of her.

"You already know the first part," began Rory.

"That you were shagging a married noblewoman?" Charlie shook his head, still annoyed about the circumstances around which he had found out about the affair. "Yes, I recall, since that was the reason you wouldn't provide an alibi. Your pride in the matter nearly saw you hang."

Rory sighed, resting his head on his fingertips. "It wasn't pride, Charlie. My feelings for her went far beyond the bedroom. She and I had developed a friendship well before the arrangement with Miss Amato. We talked of philosophy, of medical advancement, of changes in the world, as well as our hopes and aspirations. In short I . . . well, I fell in love with her."

Charlie still felt an element of pride was involved, but he refrained from saying so. The truth was, he'd never felt that way about any woman, so he wasn't exactly in a position to judge. Instead he stayed silent, waiting for Rory to say what he needed to say.

"She broke it off after I was released," said the Scot, his voice so low Charlie could barely hear him.

"After you nearly swung for her?" Charlie sucked in air through his teeth. "That's bloody cold, mate."

Rory glared at him. "It's not so simple. She was heartbroken I was forced to stay silent about my whereabouts because I was with her. She chose to protect me, as I had chosen to protect her."

Grabbing the bottle off the mantle, Charlie refilled both their glasses. "Then she has more sense than you."

"Aye," replied Rory, staring dejectedly into his glass. "But I still miss her company profoundly."

"I'm sorry." It was all Charlie could think to say. This wasn't his area of expertise. Turned out Rory would have been better served by John or Quinton or Mary, or even the French toff. But tonight he would just have to make do with Charlie.

After a few moments, Rory spoke again. "I still take note of her. I do not travel in the same circles, but I am close enough to watch the race. I learned recently she is with child."

Choking on his scotch, Charlie sat up straighter. "Is it yours?"

Rory shrugged, his eyes still downcast. "It's a third marriage for him, and neither of the others produced children. My money is on my seed. Not that it matters. The bairn will be born in wedlock and love and raised in the arms of wealth. What do I have to offer that compares with that?"

"But what if the child is born with red hair and his first words are Shakespeare quotes? Won't someone suspect?"

Rory laughed out loud for the second time. There was still a sad edge to it, but Charlie was pleased to see him laughing regardless.

"Fortunately her mother has reddish hair as well, so that winnaebe out of place. As for the first words, we will just have to see how strong my blood runs in its veins."

Fatherhood was not likely in the cards for Charlie, but the conversation made him thoughtful on the subject. How would he feel if a child of his was raised by another man? The thought angered him for a moment, as it felt close to abandonment and he had no use for men who abandoned their children. But that wasn't the case in Rory's situation. His child, if it was indeed his, would not be abandoned but rather welcomed and loved and raised as their own. A child who was wanted and cared for had more than many in London.

"Well, I wish I had some words of wisdom to help soothe your heartbreak, but words are more your strength than mine," said Charlie. "Is there anything your friend the bard has to say about time helping to heal?"

Rory gave a wry smile. "Not exactly. But Lady Macbeth did have some wise words to her husband after he murdered the king. 'What's done is done.' I cannae change if the bairn is mine or not, and I cannae have a woman who's bound to another. I've come to terms with this."

"Perhaps your head has come to terms with it, but I think your heart is a little behind," said Charlie, returning his friend's smile.

"You may be on to something there." Rory sighed, placing his glass on the table beside him. "But my heart will get there. Sometimes a man just needs to grieve. I'll heal, but in my own time." He paused. "Tell the rest of them to call back the cavalry."

"A fair request, Rory." Charlie nodded. "I'll pass the message along."

Now that they'd discussed Rory's problem, Charlie had to admit he wasn't there wholly out of the goodness of his heart. He needed some advice as well.

Rory seemed to sense his hesitation. "Is something else on your mind? Much as I've enjoyed our conversation, you aren't usually one to make house calls."

The Scotsman was too intuitive for his own good. Charlie laughed softly. "I was concerned about your welfare, but I'll admit I did have an ulterior motive to my visit."

"I thought so." Rory gestured for Charlie to speak.

"I had a question about your time in Miles O'Malley's gaming hell. What did you make of the women who worked for him? Did any of them stand out to you as different from the others?"

Rocking his head from side to side, Rory contemplated the question. "I do remember one lass. She and O'Malley had something between them besides her working for him—there was a tension there."

Charlie nodded. "I suspected as much."

Rory raised an eyebrow. "Are you headed there after this?"

"I think I will be, yes." Charlie stared into the fire, unsure why he'd equivocated. He knew where he would be headed after this. He didn't know what he would do once he got there. "If O'Malley had a good side to offset his evil, I didn't see it," he added after a moment's contemplation. "He was cruel and unfeeling even by my low standards. He did things I can neither forgive or forget. His death is a gift to the world. The person that killed him should be rewarded, not punished. But the same cannot be said about the girl who died, at least from what I have heard."

"If you think the man's death made the world a better place, I trust your opinion. I certainly won't miss him." Rory took another sip of his scotch. "As for the girl, I cannae speak to her character. But I do know she was sewed back together, neatly and carefully, and dressed in a decent gown. She was too long in the Thames for me to know for sure how she died. It might've been an accident, for all I know."

The usual unsettling feeling when Rory discussed his work came over Charlie. But he was surprised he did not feel the disgust he once had in the past. The thought of actually cutting into a dead body had always seemed unnatural to him. But as he contemplated Rory's words, he realized his feelings for Rory himself had coloured his feelings for the work Rory did, making the lines less rigid and the hues softer. He would never like the thought of Rory's livelihood. But he could accept it.

That it could have been an accident wasn't something Charlie had considered. But he had long since worked out that Miles' killer was likely one of the women who worked there. What Zoe said about the bodyguards had put him on the right track. Charlie knew how a gaming hell was run. The bodyguard would never have left O'Malley's side unless he was in on it or saw the killer as someone non-threatening. Charlie didn't think the bodyguard was capable of pulling it off alone—he had looked into the man's eyes, and he saw no mastermind within them. Charlie couldn't prove it, but he felt certain in his bones that someone else had to be there, whispering in the man's ear, making promises if he looked the other way. The most likely candidate in Charlie's mind was one of the women—someone who was underestimated every day, that no one looked twice at, just waiting for the right moment to strike.

Charlie had seen the women in his life be underestimated time and time again. And yet even a toff like Zoe was capable of killing if she had to. Men like Quinton had the luxury of seeing the world as they wanted it to be. If he was being honest, Charlie knew he was guilty of the same sin at times. But Charlie had also lived his life underestimated by many—it wasn't the same, but he understood that within that blind spot was also a quiet power to be had alongside the dismissal. No one ever saw them coming.

Downing the rest of his scotch, Charlie stood. "I appreciate your insights, Rory. I think it's time for me to take my leave." As he walked toward the door, Charlie could only hope that, right or wrong, he was making the best decision for all involved.

Chapter Thirty-Seven

"Hello there." Zoe smiled. "Is Lydia working today?"

The serving girl didn't return her smile but rather eyed her up and down suspiciously. Zoe couldn't blame her—it was a bit early in the day to be visiting a gambling hell. She'd had to bully her way into the building, and now no one was particularly thrilled at her and Mary's presence.

"We ain't open," the girl snapped.

"Yes, I'm aware." Zoe persisted. "Nevertheless, is Lydia here?"

"Look, lady, I don't know how else to say it. We ain't open. Now we don't make a habit of inviting constables 'round 'ere, but if you and yer friend don't get outta here, I'll send for that nice-lookin' runner to come back and escort ya out."

Mary snorted at that, clearly trying to choke back a laugh. She caught Zoe's gaze, an amused glint in her eye. They both knew who the girl was referring to.

"What was this nice-looking runner asking about then?" asked Zoe.

"My God, do ya not know how to listen?" The girl sighed, exasperated. "He wanted to know about Mr. O'Malley's bodyguard. But I told him we ain't seen him or the cash in the safe since the night the boss bit it. Now will ya please leave?"

Now that was quite interesting. But it wasn't why Zoe was there.

"I'm afraid not." Zoe reached in her pocket book and pulled out a five-pound note. "Now will you please go tell Lydia that Lady Demas and Miss Fletcher would like a word? I'm confident she'll want to speak with us."

The girl hesitated, but only for a moment. Snatching the note out of Zoe's hand, she turned on her heel and disappeared into the bowels of the back hallways.

As soon as she was out of earshot, Mary turned to Zoe. "You know I love stirring up a hornet's nest as much as the next girl, but are you sure this is wise? Especially considering what happened last time we went off on our own to confront a crazy woman?"

"Absolutely not." Zoe smiled at her friend. "But I won't give the Fairfaxes anymore. They took enough of us. We can't let fear stop us from doing what we can."

Though her words were glib, Zoe was internally more than a bit nervous. She was very aware of what had happened last time. But she also meant what she said—now that she and Mary had resolved some of their feelings from that night, she was done giving the Fairfaxes space in her life. That being said, she probably wouldn't be accepting any tea while they were here . . .

The girl finally returned. "Miss Lydia will see ya in the back." She led them back to the office where Zoe, Quinton, and Mary had met with Miles before. But where the man had once sat, now Lydia was behind the desk.

"Take a seat." Lydia gestured to the two chairs in front of the desk. "What can I do for ye, ladies?"

"I see you've wasted no time filling in for Mr. O'Malley . . . Lydia," said Zoe as she took the offered chair.

"Well, this is still a business, despite the tragedy of what happened to Mr. O'Malley." Lydia shrugged. "Someone has to keep things runnin'."

"Of course."

Zoe sized up the woman before her. She appeared a bit older than Zoe, but not by much. She was dressed in a plain day dress, her auburn hair styled in a simple low bun, and she wore no rouge on her cheeks or lips. She was the kind of woman that easily blended into a crowd, overlooked by the passive observer. But now that Zoe was no longer looking passively, she could see the intelligent grey eyes looking back at her, sizing Zoe up in the same way.

"I assume there's a reason ye wanted to speak with me," reiterated Lydia. "I don't mean ta be rude, but as ye can see, I am busy."

"Indeed. We won't take up too much of your time." Zoe glanced at Mary, who understood her cue.

Mary pulled out the slip of paper from her pocket and handed it to Lydia. "Do you recognize this stitch?"

Lydia glanced at it. "Of course, it's a herringbone stitch. Why are you askin'?"

"I assume you have some experience with it, being a former lady's maid?" asked Zoe, carefully skirting the question.

That got a reaction. Lydia's eyes narrowed. "What makes ye say that?"

"From what we've heard, you had a stellar reputation as a seamstress, despite favouring your left hand." Zoe again sidestepped the question. "It makes one wonder why you would give up a good position like that . . . unless it wasn't by choice?"

The paper in Lydia's hand—her left hand—crumpled as her grip tightened. The expression on her face was cold as she leaned back, contemplating them, her demeanour shifting. "So what is it that you want, my lady?" The accent had disappeared, but there was no mistaking the disdain in her tone when she said "my lady."

That was . . . actually a good question. Zoe couldn't arrest Lydia. She could only hope to keep her talking and that eventually she would talk herself into a confession.

"Well, it must be quite a tale how you ended up someplace like this." Zoe cocked her head. "I would like to hear it."

Lydia sniffed at that. She was silent for a few moments, as if contemplating her next words. Then she suddenly opened a desk drawer and pulled out a bottle of clear liquid, along with three glasses. She poured the liquid into each glass, in turn handing them to Zoe and Mary.

"Miles always kept whiskey in here." Lydia took a long sip. "I prefer gin."

Glancing over at Mary, Zoe could tell she was thinking the same thing. Accepting a drink from a strange woman was exactly how they had ended up in their previous predicament. But on the other hand, Lydia had drunk first . . . and Zoe didn't want to be rude and risk silencing her opponent.

Eventually she made her decision and took a sip, wincing at the bitter juniper taste. She hated to side with O'Malley on anything, but she really preferred whiskey to gin.

"You, Lady Demas, would not understand what it feels like to have your neck stepped on by the boot of someone with more power than yourself. To know that you are helpless against their will." Lydia turned her gaze to Mary. "But you, Miss Fletcher, have the look of someone who knows. Were you, by chance, ever a maid in a great house?"

Mary took a sip of her own drink. "I was."

Zoe knew the story, or at least the parts Mary spoke of. It was still a sore spot for her, so she did not speak of it often. But she knew Mary had been abused by the son of the house. Lydia was a perceptive one—and that made her manipulation so effective.

"I thought so." Shaking her head, Lydia took another long swig. "Then you know how it is. All it takes is a single suspicion— a single whisper of doubt—and your whole life is ruined."

"I do know what you're speaking about. But I have never been helpless." Mary looked over at Zoe. "I found my way when misfortune fell upon me."

Lydia snorted. "Yes, with the helping hand of one of the richest families in society. Quite the story of perseverance." She shook her head, her expression unimpressed. "Most are not so fortunate."

Mary inclined her head. "Perhaps not. But an injustice committed against you doesn't make it right to commit an injustice against someone weaker than yourself."

The tension in the room was thick as Lydia glared at Mary. "What are you insinuating, exactly, Miss Fletcher?" she finally said.

"I'm saying you may be able to justify scamming these lords out of their inheritance, or even killing O'Malley, but what about poor Katie Shorn?" Mary met her gaze evenly. "She wasn't in a position of power. She was just a girl trying to find her way."

Something flashed in Lydia's eyes—something harsh and violent and full of fire. She finished off the rest of her gin in a single shot, slamming the glass down on the desk. Zoe thought she was going to lose it, but when she spoke, her voice was soft. "I wouldn't know anything about that." Lydia gave a soft smile which chilled the blood in Zoe's veins. "We were just speaking hypothetically, of course. Now, if you'll excuse me, I'm actually quite busy today."

Zoe cursed inwardly. Lydia had seen them coming. There was little else for them to do.

As they walked to the door, Lydia said one last thing. "I fought, with blood and broken nails, for everything that I have." Her grey eyes were hard as ice. "I would be careful the next time you come to see me with nothing but roundabout accusations."

"The next time I see you, it will be at your trial," spat Zoe. "It's only a matter of time, Lydia. The vultures are circling. You won't be able to keep this up forever. Sooner or later, the truth will come out."

Lydia said nothing else, but as the door closed, Zoe could see her knuckles turning white as they gripped the edge of her desk.

Chapter Thirty-Eight

The afternoon was well begun by the time Alexander's valet rousted him from his bed. He awoke with a pounding headache and an ill temper.

His valet was used to it, dodging the slipper thrown at his head with ease. "You have a visitor, my lord," said Reed calmly as he retrieved the empty glass from next to Alexander's bed.

"What?" Alexander blinked and pushed himself up onto his left elbow, struggling to process this simple information. "Who is it?"

"A Mr. Quinton Huxley. He claims to be a friend of the family."

That sobered Alexander up quickly. What was the ogre doing in his house? None of the scenarios that ran through his mind as he hurried Reed to dress him were positive. Something must be terribly wrong.

Alexander rushed down the stairs, nearly oblivious to the echoing of his stomping through the house. By the time he reached the sitting room, his panic was full blown, his heartbeat rushing in his ear. "What has happened?" Alexander demanded as he threw open the doors. "Is someone hurt? Has something happened to Zoe?"

Quinton took a step back, clearly surprised at Alexander's explosive entrance, but he recovered quickly. "What is with your family and assuming the worst when I show up?"

"What are you talking about?"

"Nothing." Quinton sighed, his expression unreadable. "Zoe is fine. I'm here about O'Malley."

A surprising wave of relief washed over Alexander. He had never taken much of a liking to his stepcousin—she was too loud, too opinionated, too proud, *too French*—but he didn't wish her dead. Well, perhaps he had when they were children and she had stolen his favourite toy soldier . . . but that was beside the point.

The feeling of relief was quickly replaced by irritation. "What about O'Malley? Has he been arrested?"

"No. He's dead."

Now that was a shock. Alexander swallowed hard, thinking back to the last time he'd seen the unpleasant man just two days ago. He wasn't proud of some of the things he'd said—though honestly there was much he didn't remember of the encounter

Quinton continued. "His throat was slit two nights ago, the body discovered yesterday morning. A serving girl seems to remember you having a rather heated argument with him that same night as his death." He stopped speaking then, letting the statement hang in the air.

It took Alexander a few moments to register what he was implying. "Surely you can't think I had anything to do with it?" he hissed.

The stony expression on Quinton's face didn't change. "Did you?"

"No!" Alexander crossed his arms, his face flushed. "And I resent the implication."

The door to the sitting room suddenly burst open again, causing Alexander to jump. In his panic, he'd forgotten other members of the household were at home.

"What is going on here?" The question came from the Baron of Newark, Lord Baldwin Dovefield—Alexander's father.

"N-nothing." Alexander swallowed hard, his eyes darting between the two imposing men. "Father, this is one of my friends from the club, Mr. Huxley."

"Hmm." Baldwin raised his eyebrow. "I'm not familiar with the Huxleys."

Quinton met his icy gaze evenly, evidently uncowed by the lord's disapproval. "I doubt you would have run into any in society circles. Perhaps you've heard of my mother though—Annie Huxley? She was an actress at Covent Garden some twenty years ago."

Alexander winced at the words. He would hear about this later. He would probably hear about it in part now. "Er, did I say friend? I meant associate," said Alexander as he attempted to backpedal. "We just have a few things to discuss, if you wouldn't mind, Father."

Baldwin shook his head, the dissatisfaction which Alexander had become accustomed to evident in his expression. "Step into the hallway with me, Alexander."

His heart sunk at those words, but Alexander knew he didn't have much choice. He followed his father out the door, awaiting the scolding he knew was coming.

The door had hardly shut behind them before Baldwin began. "Alexander, you're far too old to still be keeping company with unsavoury characters such as this. The gambling, the drinking, the whoring—I understand a young man's need to sow his wild oats. But eventually they need to grow up and take responsibility for their duties. Yet here you are, at twenty-six years of age, having just risen, with your breath reeking of cheap alcohol." Baldwin pinched the bridge of his nose. "At the bare minimum, you can't bring these aspects of your life into our home. What would people say if they knew we were keeping company with an actress's son? Sitting down to tea with him in our sitting room?"

"We were hardly having tea," muttered Alexander under his breath.

"What was that?" snapped Baldwin.

"Nothing." Alexander was used to this speech—he knew it was in his best interest to let it go. But sometimes he just couldn't help himself. "I know I've made my fair share of mistakes, Father, but this isn't like that. Huxley isn't some unsavoury character—in fact, he's a friend of Uncle Hugh's—"

"Stop making excuses. Your uncle may lean toward the eccentric, but who he chooses to associate with is his business. I expect the members of my household to know better."

A familiar criticism. Alexander should have known better than to invoke his uncle's name as a defence. Hugh had made many unconventional choices in his life, much to Baldwin's chagrin. But by choosing to become a barrister, Hugh had been able to forge his own path, without having to take his title-holding older brother's opinions into account. Not every member of the gentry had such privilege. Alexander was acutely aware of how dependent on his father he was.

"I understand, Father." Alexander looked at the floor, taking notice of a knot in one of the wooden floorboards. This wasn't the first time he had spent time observing it. "I'll strive to do better."

"Somehow I doubt that." Baldwin sighed and shook his head again. "Sometimes, Alexander, I think you go out of your way to disappoint me."

There it was. Alexander was used to it, but somehow it still stung. A truth he had long since accepted was that he would never be able to live up to his father's standards, no matter how hard he tried. Eventually he had just stopped trying.

Baldwin jerked his head toward the sitting room door. "Get rid of him. We'll discuss this in more detail later."

With that Baldwin stalked off, leaving his son to absorb the impact of the conversation. Alexander took a deep breath, determined to get himself under control before he faced Quinton again.

Shoving the door open, Alexander forced his face into a neutral expression. "Pardon the interruption. I'm afraid I have some other appointments this afternoon, so let's wrap this up as quickly as possible. Where were we?"

"I believe you were telling me how you didn't kill O'Malley and resented the implication." Quinton's face hadn't changed—the man must be an excellent poker player—but the sharp edge of his tone had been lost. Enough to confirm Alexander's fear that Quinton had heard the conversation through the closed door. Baldwin had never learned how to moderate the volume of his voice.

"Right, of course." Heat crept up Alexander's neck. "Well, I didn't kill him."

"But you did fight with him?"

Alexander sighed—he didn't have the energy to do battle with Quinton anymore. "Yes, we fought. I was angry about Katie that night, and more than a few sheets to the wind. It felt like no progress was being made, and no matter which way you spin it, I had been made a fool."

It was the truth. If Alexander didn't tell Quinton how he would do anything to dull the memory of a laughing girl with a sparkle in her blue eyes and freckles splashed across her nose . . . to forget how she took him for a fool . . . to not picture her lying lifeless on a cold stone slab, those same eyes open but vacant of life . . . well, he didn't see how that was relevant.

"So you decided to go alone to gambling hell in a disreputable part of town and pick a fight with the owner, a man known for violence, whom you believe to be a murder?" asked Quinton.

"That's one way to put it . . ." muttered Alexander.

Quinton opened his mouth, clearly wanting to say more, but then abruptly snapped it shut again. He paused, as if turning something over in his mind before continuing. "So you went there that night and picked a fight. How'd it end?"

Running his fingers through his hair, Alexander thought back to that night. As he did, he couldn't help but contemplate the man standing in his sitting room—his father's sitting room. Quinton Huxley was a beast of a man, taller than Alexander by half a head and at least twice as wide at the shoulder. All it took was a cursory glance to deduce his size was not due to excess weight. Though not as expensive or rich as the clothes Alexander was accustomed to, Quinton's breeches and waistcoat suited him, well-tailored and classic in their look. His features were well formed, and his dark hair trimmed neatly. Even his dark brown eyes held an undeniable spark of intelligence. But worse than all of that was the way he carried himself. Alexander doubted Quinton had ever walked into a room and felt uncomfortable—had ever felt like maybe he didn't have the right to be there. He was just so confident, bordering on arrogant.

When their paths had first crossed, that's what Alexander had thought he disliked about him. What right did a man with such poor breeding have to be so comfortable in his own skin—to just walk through life, thumbing his nose at the rules, as if it was his right? But if he was really being honest with himself, Alexander had to admit that perhaps part of his ire had been inspired by . . . jealousy. Even now, within the walls of his own home, here Alexander was tripping over his own feet while Quinton watched and rolled his eyes.

"I don't remember everything," Alexander finally admitted. "We got into it in his office. We were both pretty worked up. The next thing I remember was that bodyguard of his dragging me down the street. He hailed a hackney for me."

"Hmm." Quinton's eyes narrowed, as if something had sparked in his mind. "So you don't remember if the argument got physical?"

"Well, not exactly. But I imagine slitting someone's throat is not a neat business. Fool though I may be, I think I'd remember if my hands were covered in blood." Alexander crossed his arms.

"I suppose that's a fair point." Quinton sighed. "You better hope when that bodyguard turns up that he corroborates your story. I still can't think what possessed you go there in the first place."

Something clicked together in Alexander's mind—a memory which up until then had been lost in the hazy fog of booze.

"Hold on, wait here for a moment," said Alexander as he rushed out of the parlour.

He ran back up the stairs and began rummaging through the drawers in his dressing room.

"May I ask what it is you're looking for, my lord?" asked his valet as he appeared at his elbow without so much as the sound of footfall.

"A note." Alexander continued his rummaging. "It came for me two days ago, in the late evening. I need to find it."

"Ah, yes." Reed pointed to the top of his bureau. "The maid found it in your trouser pocket. I returned it to the bureau for you."

Alexander spied it immediately with this direction and snatched it from the wooden surface. It was exactly what he'd been looking for.

"Good man, Reed." Alexander clapped him on the back as he left the room.

He only took a minute to return to the sitting room and hand the piece of paper to Quinton. The other man took it gingerly, unfolding it with a look of confusion on his face. The confusion evaporated quickly. "This is why you went to the gambling hell?" asked Quinton. "Why didn't you mention this earlier?"

"Well, I—you see—er—" Alexander sighed. "I forgot. But yes, I recall now that this note came in the evening, and that's what sparked the idea of going there."

A long pause filled the air as Quinton stared him down, clearly trying to decide how best to dress him down. Alexander braced himself for another scolding. "Very well. I'll look into it." The irritation in Quinton's voice was plain, but Alexander was surprised that was the only thing he had to say.

"Thank you." Alexander started to say more, but Quinton cut him off.

"Don't bother. You're still paying me, remember?"

Chapter Thirty-Nine

A s he strode along the street, hands buried in his pockets and hat firmly pulled down over his head, a single thought circled over and over again in Quinton's mind with every long stride.

Zoe and Mary were right.

Even though this discovery was a significant break in the case, the thought filled him with angst. As Quinton continued on his way, making his way through the crowds and across streets as he had done a thousand times before, he considered why it should bother him so much. He'd meant it when he told the ladies they had good ideas. He did not doubt their ability to reason out information and reach clear conclusions.

And yet he was peeved they had done just that.

If he was being honest, Quinton had to allow the possibility that the person he was really frustrated with was himself. He'd been apprehensive about the upcoming meeting with the Colevilles and taken his frayed nerves out on the ladies. He had seen the sparking anger in both their eyes as he turned to leave, but he had not missed the disappointment in Zoe's as well.

Blast. It. All.

The Black Dog came into view as Quinton quickened his

pace. The note he'd given Ezra had asked John to meet him there. And at this point, a decent ale sounded mighty good.

Entering the tavern felt good as a satisfying warmth rose up to meet him. He found a table and ordered two ales.

John slid into the stool opposite as the frothy beverages were placed on the table. His eyes looked equally unsettled. "Nothing new from Bow Street," he commented, taking a drink from the glass of beer. "I told them of Alexander's presence, but they are in no rush to arrest a peer. What about your chat with Lord Miscreant? A confession perhaps? He seems to be of little use on this earth."

The comments could have come from his own mouth, but Quinton found himself surprisingly annoyed by John's negative digs at Alexander. "There's no need to be cruel."

John looked at him incredulously. "Why are you defending him? You cannot stand the man. He's a spoiled ingrate and a wastrel."

"You're right that I have not been his biggest advocate." Quinton paused, considering his next words carefully. The conversation he'd overhead between Alexander and his father had been . . . revealing. Though he still considered the man irresponsible and obnoxious, Quinton had managed to dredge up an emotion he never thought he would feel for the young lord— pity. He had no desire to embarrass Alexander by revealing what he'd overheard, but he no longer despised him with same vigour as before.

"Let's just move on," said Quinton, unsure how to put his feelings into words. "No, he didn't confess. But he did give me something important."

"What is it?" asked John.

Quinton held the note Alexander had given him out to John. "I think Zoe and Mary might have been right. I think our killer is a woman."

John groaned aloud. "Not you too. We've been over this—I just can't believe a woman is capable of this kind of brutality."

"Just read the note," replied Quinton.

"Fine." John read the note to himself, but Quinton already knew what it said.

Katie's blood is on O'Malley's hands. Why have you not avenged her?

"So the wastrel was lured there." John set the note down on the table. "I'll grant that helps to rule Dovefield out, but it doesn't mean a woman sent it."

"Smell it."

It was an odd request, but John obliged him. His eyes flashed up at Quinton. "Is that . . . perfume?"

"It is." Quinton drank of his ale. "How many men do you know who scent their letters with perfume?"

Quinton heard Gwen's voice in his head as if she was standing next to him. *It's a mistake to put people in a box. If a lady needs to do something, she figures out how. Just like a man.* Even a young girl understood that. It was the men who were blind to it.

"I'll grant you, that's odd," admitted John. "But whoever wrote the note is not necessarily who killed O'Malley. Or Katie." Finishing his glass in a single long drink, John signalled the barmaid for another.

"Hmm." Quinton took the note back, slipping it into his breast pocket. "What did you discover about the bodyguard?"

"Very little of note." John sighed. "His disappearance might be considered more suspicious if everyone from patrons to fellow employees to his housekeeper did not say he was all muscle and no mind. There's debate over whether he can tie his own shoes, much less do any fancy needlework on the body. If it were just O'Malley on the slab, I'd say he may have killed him for the cash in the safe. But that doesn't account for Katie. No one has been able to recall even a single conversation between the two. He may be involved, but I don't see him as a mastermind."

"I agree." Quinton briefly laid out what Alexander had told him about the bodyguard escorting him outside and hailing a hackney.

"Very interesting." John leaned back, pensive. "Then that's likely our window for the killing."

Suddenly the door blew open, interrupting their conversation, and Zoe and Mary hastened in. As Mary closed the door, Zoe's blue eyes swept the room, coming to rest on their table.

"How on earth did you find us?" asked John as the women joined them at their table.

"Ezra found us." Zoe signalled the barmaid for two more ales as she sat. "He told us where you were."

"He told you?" Quinton raised an eyebrow. "How exactly did he convey this message to you, since he cannot speak?"

Zoe glared at him. "You are not the only one who can pay attention. I can understand him well enough to comprehend his point most of the time, and when that fails, the boy has a gift for mimicry. He does a very impressive impression of you drinking beer, complete with a stumbling fall."

Quinton wasn't sure whether he should be insulted or impressed. Probably both.

"Well, I'm glad we cleared that up." Quinton eyed the women suspiciously. "Which brings us to what you are doing here."

Mary and Zoe exchanged a glance. Whatever curtain had been hanging between them seemed to have disappeared.

"We know who did it," said Mary, her tone matter of fact. "And we know why *she* did it."

John sat up straighter at that. "Are you certain?"

"Well, aren't you going to argue there's no way a woman could be involved?" challenged Zoe.

"No." Quinton took the note back out and handed it to her. "I've come around to your way of thinking."

"I remain sceptical, but it's possible I could be convinced," grumbled John.

"Oh." Zoe appeared a bit deflated that no one had risen to the bait.

"And about earlier." It took a bit of doing, but Quinton

managed to swallow his pride. "I am sorry. I should have listened to you instead of disregarding your findings without consideration."

This was clearly not the confrontation both women had prepared for. Mary and Zoe sat in silence for a moment, as if they had to rethink what they were going to say next.

"Well, I appreciate that," said Zoe finally.

John sighed. "What have you've found that makes you so certain you know who the killer is?"

"And what motive have you discovered?" Quinton's brow furrowed. "We cannot reason out why someone would want both Katie and O'Malley dead."

"Well . . ." The women exchanged another glance, then Mary continued, "We know why she killed O'Malley at least."

"For the love of—will one of you just tell us what you know?" exclaimed John.

"John, please. You're being a bit hysterical, don't you think?" replied Mary, and Quinton could see from the gleam in her eye that she was enjoying the reversal. "Here's what happened . . ."

Chapter Forty

This wasn't the first time an unpleasant choice had been laid out before Charlie. His life had been one fork in the road after another, with no good options and only his own moral code to guide him. Often the decision came down to which one he would regret the least.

Despite this experience in the grey areas of life, Charlie still found himself wrestling with what choice he would make here. This woman he would soon find had killed twice. The world wouldn't miss O'Malley any more than Charlie would, but the girl was different. According to his moral code, tricking rich men into parting with their wealth didn't mean Katie Shorn deserved a death sentence.

Few would accuse Charlie of being a soft man. He understood that not every innocent could be saved and not everyone who deserved to would be punished. One would drive themselves mad trying to balance every scale. Charlie had made peace with taking accountability for his own little patch of London and the people under his care but leaving the rest be. Ordinarily in these situations Charlie preferred to stay out of it, letting John and Quinton mete out whatever the law deemed was justice.

But perhaps he was going soft as he got older. If it were him on the other side, Charlie would want one of his own to judge him by the codes of the street, rather than a judge who cared only for the letter of the law but not the spirit of justice. If nothing else, this woman had earned his respect by killing O'Malley, and for that, he would give her a fair hearing. There was also the matter of questions Charlie wanted answers to. Like how the woman got the upper hand with a man like O'Malley . . . that, he wanted to know. And what role did the girl play in all of this? Depending on those answers . . . Well, he'd made a single stop before he came to the gambling hell. He would know soon enough which fork in the road to take.

Charlie didn't enter the gambling hell by way of the front door—instead he slipped in the back, picking the lock to the back door, and walked along the maze of hallways until he found the room Miles had always used an office. Without knocking, he threw the door open and stepped in.

The woman sitting behind the desk started at his abrupt entrance but quickly recovered. "Who are you and what are you doing here?" she demanded.

"Lydia, I presume?"

She had gall, he would give her that. She watched him closely with wary eyes but didn't move, clearly determined not to give up an inch of power between them. It's what Charlie would do in her place.

"What do you want?" repeated Lydia.

Charlie sat in one of the chairs across from the desk. "I would like to have an honest conversation which may prove mutually beneficial."

Lydia's intense gaze didn't relent. "I know you. Miles used to speak of you. That eye is a bit distinctive. Charlie, isn't it?"

"That's me." Charlie resisted the urge to touch the scar that ran down his face. "I assume my reputation has proceeded me?"

She didn't reply, but the flash of expression across her face was enough to confirm Charlie was right. That was good—the next part would be easier if she didn't test him.

"Good." Charlie leaned forward. "Now I don't want to waste your time, so I'll get straight to the point. Let me make your position here very clear. I know you killed Miles and the girl called Katie Shorn. My associates are also aware of your involvement. They will not rest until they have the truth. They will see you hang if they have anything to do with it. You have very little leverage to use, and what little you do have is only currency with me. Do you understand?"

Lydia leaned back in her chair. "You can't prove anything."

"You have no idea what I can prove." Charlie smirked. "And it doesn't matter. I don't settle matters in courts of law. Whatever conclusion the two of us come to, it will end in this room."

A long pause hung in the air as she processed his words.

"I fought for this," she said finally. "I drew blood for this. I won't give it up on an empty threat."

Charlie didn't blame Lydia for wanting to hold onto what she'd gained. He wouldn't want to leave either. But he also knew one thing mattered more to her than the gambling hell.

"I don't make empty threats." Charlie said his next words without malice. "You're a survivor, Lydia. You've lost. If you want to survive this, I suggest you come to terms with that."

He watched her eyes as she pondered this. Charlie could picture what was going on behind them—scenario after scenario being run through and discarded as she tried to think her way out of this predicament. But Charlie was counting on her being rational and self-serving enough to make the smart move.

"Very well." Lydia still glared at him but seemed resigned. "What do you want to know?"

"Excellent," said Charlie. "I care about two things, the first of which is: what happened between you and Katie Shorn?"

At the mention of the girl's name, Lydia flexed her left hand, the one with the bandage. "Why do you care what happened with Katie?"

"Morbid curiosity." That was a lie, but Charlie didn't want her to try and soften the details to paint herself in a better light if she thought it would help her case.

"Fine. Katie was my friend, but she was also a business associate. I had a few girls working for me—I would pick a mark, and then they would clean him out with a sad story and some doe eyes. It was a lucrative scheme, and Katie had no objections . . . until she met that last one."

"What happened?"

Lydia shook her head. "She let herself get caught up in the usual lies of men. Even worse, she let herself believe she was in love with the fool. She wanted to tell him the truth, which would have ruined us all."

Charlie cocked his head. "So you killed her?"

"I was angry, but I didn't intend to kill her. I tried to grab her arms, to keep her from leaving. She pulled away and lost her balance. The next thing I knew, Katie was lying on the floor with blood pooling around her head."

"Hmm." There was a ring of truth to her story, and it matched up with what Charlie knew. "So then you dumped her in the Thames?"

Lydia shrugged. "Accident or not, her death would draw eyes toward the hell. And I didn't want Miles to have any leverage over me, so I took care of it—discreetly." Her grey eyes locked into his. "I'm sure you're familiar with how to lay someone to rest when the manner of death is unconventional."

She wasn't wrong about that, but Charlie wasn't going to give her the satisfaction. He matched her even gaze, but as he looked into her eyes, he was unsettled to see his own burning temper reflected back at him. "If that's how you treat your friends, I'd hate to see how you deal with your enemies," he said.

The anger in her eyes flared. "Katie was my friend. Her death was regrettable, but you know as well as I that the world is not kind to the weak. I laid her to rest with as much dignity as I could, but what's done is done."

The words were harsh, but Charlie thought he saw a glint of genuine grief behind the fire in her eyes. She continued, "And if you want to see how I deal with my enemies, you need not look further than the man who used to sit in this chair."

"Indeed." Charlie drummed his fingers against the arm his chair. "That brings me to the second thing I want to know. O'Malley didn't tolerate rivalry in his ranks, so the fact he allowed your scheming in his hell means he must not have had a choice." Charlie narrowed his eyes. "What did you have on him?"

She stared at him for a moment. "Leverage over someone he cared about."

Charlie shook his head. "If there was that kind of leverage out there, I would have used it myself. O'Malley cared about no one and no one cared about him."

"Perhaps you didn't know him as well as you thought you did," Lydia replied with a cunning smile.

Perhaps not. Charlie leaned back in his chair, appraising the woman before him. It was possible she was lying. But it was also possible she was telling the truth. If Miles O'Malley really did have someone out there he'd cared about, that turned Charlie's entire world view on its head.

"Tell me what you know." Charlie's tone was even, but he knew there was a dangerous edge alongside it.

She seemed to sense it too, shifting in her seat. "He had a son. Kept the boy hidden so no one could use him against him. Until I came along, that is. I think it's the closest thing to love O'Malley was capable of."

Charlie said nothing, not because he had nothing to say but because he was too stunned to speak. A son? He didn't know how to reconcile the man he knew with a loving father.

Lydia took his silence as an invitation to keep speaking. "I wanted to use the connections his gambling hell offered, but I needed a way to control him. It didn't take me long to sniff the lad out. O'Malley was ruthless but not terribly clever. It never crossed his mind a woman might be smarter than him until it was too late."

Slowly Charlie's senses came back to him. "Where is the boy now? Or was he a card you finally played?"

"I never got the chance to play the card," replied Lydia bitterly. "When Katie's body turned up, even Miles' limited intelligence was able to deduce that I'd lied when I said she quit. It gave him a leverage that cancelled out mine. But I had no intention of giving up my part of the business, so I did what was necessary to protect my own." She paused there, the anger still in her eyes. "I regretted Katie's death, but the truth is I would kill Miles again in a heartbeat."

Her logic was sound, he would give her that. Charlie stood at the fork in the road, turning her story over in his mind as he decided what to do next. Time seemed to stand still in the moment, both parties acutely aware of the heaviness of what happened next.

Finally after what seemed like an eternity, Charlie reached into the inner pocket of his coat and withdrew the envelope he'd fetched not an hour past.

"This is a one-way ticket on a ship bound for the colonies." He pushed it across the desk toward her but kept one finger on it. "It leaves tonight. It's yours, if you answer one last question. Where is the child?"

Glancing from the envelope, to him, and back again, Lydia seemed to weigh the options before here. After a about a minute of consideration, she reached for a piece of paper and a quill, quickly scrawling something out. "This is the address," she said, handing the piece of paper over. "He lives with a caretaker. No mother in the picture—died of cholera not long after the birth. Miles sent cash on the first of the month, so the boy has about a week before funds run out. That's all I know."

Charlie removed his hand from the envelope, allowing her to snatch it up. As he stood to leave, he said one last thing. "I'm giving you this opportunity out of respect, Lydia. You rid the world of a monster, so I am allowing you to leave. I suggest you make the most of your fresh start." He turned the full force of his gaze toward her. "But I will not be so generous should we meet again. If I hear of you gracing the shores of England again, the deal is off. Do you understand?"

"Yes." In her own eyes Charlie thought he saw something akin to respect. "I understand."

As he left, Charlie could only hope he was making the correct decision. Lydia was angry—so angry at the world, just like he was. Maybe a decade ago he would have taken the safer route and neutralized the threat for good. But Charlie didn't have it in him that day punish someone for something he'd do himself.

For now he found himself at another fork in the road.

Chapter Forty-One

Convincing his current superior had taken most of the day, but John knew it was worth it. The former magistrate had been his mentor as well as his friend, and John was still finding his way around this new man. But his carefully worded talk with the new magistrate had yielded an order to arrest "Lydia" for the murder of Miles O'Malley. John was confident they would get their man—in this case, woman.

John and the old magistrate had not parted ways on the best of terms, before the man's early demise. These days John couldn't even bring himself to say his name aloud. But despite John's best efforts to evict him from his memories, the man still kept house in his head.

The thing that stoked John's ire wasn't just that the old man had made a mistake. It was that he'd made a choice, deliberate and purposeful, to disregard the oath both he and John had sworn to uphold the law. He'd done it in the name of justice, but to John his choice to sacrifice one life to save others couldn't be justified. John didn't think the system was perfect—he knew there were injustices within it as well. But without law and order to guide their choices, life was just too slippery of a slope for one man to traverse on their own morals.

Of course, the matter with Rory had recently tested John's principles in the matter. He knew Charlie had skirted beyond the arms of the law to secure Rory's freedom—and just that one time, John had let him. But it hadn't been an easy decision for him. Only his absolute confidence in Rory's innocence had made John able to let Charlie's interference go unchallenged. But that one allowance had been exception, not the new norm. John wouldn't lose any sleep over Lydia's arrest and subsequent hanging.

His first stop was to Lydia's tenement, where her neighbour cheerfully steered John toward the gambling hell.

As the hell came into view, the winter sun had already dimmed, casting long shadows across the street. John hurried in, traversing the back hallways to the office, but the door was wide open and no one was inside.

John considered his next options, but as he stepped back out onto the street, he saw him—Charlie, contentedly eating a meat pie on the street corner.

At first he was pleased to see his friend, but as John's mind caught up with reality, he realized that something was off. What was Charlie doing over here? Could it be a coincidence that his friend was standing on this particular street corner when Lydia was nowhere to be found?

A growing sense of apprehension grew inside John as he stalked toward Charlie. "How did you even— Where is she?" he snapped once he was in earshot.

Charlie jumped at John's unexpected question, but relaxed once he laid eyes on him. "To whom are you referring?"

"You know who."

"I'm am not the woman's keeper." Charlie shrugged. "She could be anywhere."

An unusual heat filled John, from his toes to the crown of his head. It was a rare occurrence, but John was angry—properly angry. "I have been charged with arresting her for the murder of Miles O'Malley," John said stiffly. "If you know where she is, you need to tell me."

"I don't have to do anything," retorted Charlie. "Miles O'Malley had his untimely demise coming. I would suggest refocusing your effort on cases more deserving of your time."

"That's not your call to make, Charlie." John took a deep breath, trying to control his unusual temper. "You are not the Almighty who decides guilt and innocence. We have laws in civilized society—laws I'm sworn to uphold. I won't stand for this."

As soon as the words left his lips, John expected Charlie to throw the situation with Rory back in his face. That was the one time in his adult life John had not allowed the courts to decide the course of justice, and though he didn't regret the decision, it still weighed on him.

To his surprise, Charlie said nothing on the matter. "I won't apologize for the choices I've made just because they don't align with your view of right and wrong." Charlie took a step closer, his air dark. "Miles O'Malley deserved what he got, and I won't say otherwise."

John clenched his fists, trying to think of a way to reason with Charlie. "And what of Katie? Does she not matter at all in your equation of justice?"

Something flashed in Charlie's good eye, but it was gone too quickly to name. When he spoke, he was just as confident. "Of course she matters, but Katie's death was an accident." Charlie paused. "If I were in her place, I can't say I wouldn't have done the same."

"Is that what this is about?" scoffed John. "That you think you and Lydia are the same—both above the law. Do you have any more morals than a rat in the streets?"

Immediately John knew he had gone too far. Charlie's good eye darkened, a quiet anger rolling off him. John instinctively took a step back, bracing himself.

A long moment passed, and to his surprise, Charlie took a deep breath before speaking softly. "You are a brother to me,

John. But in my mind, this matter is finished. It is up to you to do as you please."

With that, Charlie shoved past him, leaving John with his mouth open and his temper flaring.

Chapter Forty-Two

The tea was carefully laid out, the tiny cakes and sandwiches beautifully displayed next to the scones and clotted cream. Alexander looked up anxiously when he saw Zoe enter the parlour. She approached almost warily, looking questioningly at Alexander.

He eagerly gestured toward a chair. "Please, sit."

"When I said I would be by around tea time, I wasn't hinting I expected a full spread, Alexander."

"I realize that." Alexander took the seat opposite hers. "But I wished to extend a peace offering of sorts."

After pouring the tea, Zoe picked up her cup, her expression still wary. "I don't think I have ever taken tea in your home."

Alexander knew for a fact she had not. He was still working out what kind of man he wanted to be after recent events, but he knew he didn't want to be the person Zoe thought him anymore.

"Oh." Zoe gasped, as if just remembering something of great importance. "I apologize for the other day when I sent you back to my house. I got caught up in everything else and I completely forgot Mabel was coming for tea. I hope the interaction wasn't too awkward. I've already sent her a letter of apology."

"Ah, that." Alexander felt a blush on his cheeks. "No, it was fine. Mabel—Miss Anderson—is very pleasant company." He quickly brushed past the topic, reaching for his own cup. "So your note said there were new details in regard to Katie's death?"

"Indeed." She proceeded to lay out what had happened since they last spoke, starting with Miles's death and ending with Lydia's disappearance.

"My God." Alexander shook his head. "I still can't believe that odious man is dead. And that I nearly took the blame for it. I also can't believe he was innocent."

"Well, innocence is relative. But in this case, yes, he was not responsible for Katie's death."

"And what of this Lydia? Is there no hope of bringing her to justice?"

Something flashed in Zoe's eyes but too quick for Alexander to properly identify. "For now . . . she has slipped through Bow Street's grasp. I would not get your hopes up too high that she will be captured in the near future."

His initial reaction was disappointment, but as Alexander reflected, he realized it didn't really matter. Katie was still dead, whether Lydia was in Newgate or not. He would have to grieve her and what she'd meant to him on his own, no matter what happened in a court of law.

Suddenly the door opened and Alexander's father strode in, looking equal parts annoyed and appalled. Alexander jumped up, surprised by Baldwin's intrusion.

"Alexander, I believe you've wasted enough of the day on useless pursuits." Turning to Zoe, his father made a gesture towards the door.

It was the rudest Alexander had ever seen his father behave toward her. Even Zoe appeared stunned. For the first time, he saw his family through his stepcousin's eyes, and Alexander was ashamed. "I will be available after my visit with my cousin, Father," snapped Alexander. "If you could excuse us, however, this is a private conversation."

To say Baldwin was shocked would be an understatement.

Alexander shared the sentiment. He had never stood up his imposing father like that before. But it was too late to apologize now, so he stood his ground, never breaking eye contact, and finally his father stepped back.

"We will address this later, Alexander," the older man said softly, and with that he was gone, the door closing softly behind him.

Alexander wasn't looking forward to it.

Turning, he saw Zoe staring at him, her expression having shifted from stunned to something more thoughtful. If he didn't know better, Alexander might have thought he saw respect in her eyes.

He took a deep breath. "I apologize for the intrusion. Would you like more tea?"

"No, thank you." Zoe hesitated. "There is one more thing. I do not know if it will give you peace or bring more harm, but I think you deserve to know. One of our companions learned that Katie's feelings for you were genuine. She planned to tell you the truth, which led to the fatal disagreement."

"Oh." Alexander had been wrestling with the truth over what had happened between them. On the one hand, if Katie did care for him, that meant he hadn't been taken completely for a fool. On the other hand, it meant that he was inadvertently responsible for her fate.

Still, the selfish part of him felt a wave of relief wash over him to know at least part of his relationship with Katie had been real.

"I cared about her too," he said quietly. Zoe was the last person he would have revealed these private things to a month ago, but everything was different now. Besides, it wasn't like Alexander had someone else to talk to. "You may find this hard to believe, but often when we were together, we just . . . talked. She was funny and insightful. She listened to my ideas. I know that there could be no future between us, but it changed me. Perhaps that sounds foolish, but my time spent with her . . . mattered. It made me a better man."

"I don't think that sounds foolish," she replied.

He helped himself to more tea and continued, "Soon I will be expected to choose a wife, and my thoughts have changed. There was a time not too long ago when an arrangement would have satisfied me. But now . . . I want more. I want a connection, one that brings happiness to both parties. Do you think I'm mad?"

"Yes." Zoe smiled at him. "But that's unrelated. I wish you every bit of luck as you search for that connection."

Alexander shifted in his seat—that was quite enough sentiment for one day. "So where is Mr. Huxley. Isn't he the one I was paying to investigate the matter? Shouldn't he be here to collect the last of what he's due?"

Zoe avoided his gaze. "Quinton had . . . other obligations to attend to. He sends his regards."

~

As Zoe walked toward the carriage, she thought of her cousin and wondered if the improvements to his personality would last. Her thoughts wandered back to a time not so long ago when she herself was the selfish one, before her own world had been turned upside down by tragedy.

Alexander reminded her of herself, on the cusp of that journey. She wished him well, something she never thought she would feel towards him.

Perhaps the two of them would become friends. At the very least, she should give him back that toy soldier she stole all those years ago. Zoe wondered if he ever missed it.

Chapter Forty-Three

The sound of the horses' hooves had a strangely calming effect on Hugh, the rhythmic clopping noise grounding him in the moment. But as he glanced over at the young man sitting next to him, he could see that Quinton was not experiencing the same effect.

Quinton stared straight ahead, his shoulders stiff and his expression stony. Hugh had seen men bound for the gallows who were more relaxed than him.

"They may not like it, but you have the weight of the law on your side," offered Hugh by way of comfort. "There is nothing they can do."

His words were acknowledged with a quick nod, but Quinton didn't speak. Hugh sighed, leaning back against the carriage. It was hard to blame Quinton for his discomfort. Not every day did one reunite with a family who didn't want anything to do with you. Hugh couldn't begin to imagine the mix of emotions swirling within Quinton. Was he fearful of rejection? Anxious to make a good impression? Angry at their unwillingness to acknowledge him years ago? Did a small part of him crave their acceptance? Perhaps even Quinton was unsure of his feelings.

There was no way to know how the meeting with the

viscount would go. If Quinton's accounting of the last meeting was anything to go by, the younger Coleville had at least accepted the reality of Quinton's standing, even if he wasn't happy about it. Hugh himself hadn't been thrilled to hear of Quinton's standalone exploits, but he would admit the meeting didn't seem to have gone as poorly as it could have. Now they would just have to wait and see what the viscount would say.

Hugh had been correct when he said the law was on Quinton's side, but that didn't mean his family had to like it. If the reputation that proceeded the viscount was to be believed, Hugh feared the man would not be welcoming. But on the other hand, people did sometimes mellow with age. This was an opportunity to meet his grandson—the son of his long-dead heir. Perhaps the viscount would surprise them all. The fact he had requested this meeting at all showed at least some interest in Quinton . . . or perhaps that was just wishful thinking on Hugh's part.

The horses pulled the carriage up the half-moon drive and stopped in front of imposing doors. The coachman leapt down and pulled out the step with the efficiency that came with regular practice, and both Hugh and Quinton stepped out of the carriage. Hugh nodded to his man, and the horses and carriage soon disappeared around the back of the house while a footman escorted the two men inside.

The butler took their coats and led them to the back of the house. The room they entered boasted a ceiling as high as Hugh had ever seen, advertising the Coleville wealth to any who entered. Hugh couldn't imagine how much it cost to heat.

Lord Philip Coleville, Viscount of Hereford, and his son Montgomery stood side by side, neither appearing very happy to be present. Nevertheless, good manners were too ingrained in the gentry to be set aside, even for something of this magnitude. The younger lord greeted them politely, gesturing for Hugh and Quinton to take a seat in the chairs next to the fire.

The viscount took his time, measuring Quinton in his gaze.

Quinton for his part met his eyes and did not move until finally the older man looked away.

"What kind of man brings legal counsel to introduce himself to his family?" asked the viscount after a long pause.

The words were directed at Hugh, but Quinton answered. "A smart man," replied Quinton. "I speak for myself, Lord Coleville, but I have no intention of being bullied by the likes of you."

"By the likes of me?" The viscount's eyes flashed with anger. "I am a gentleman, with a bloodline going back to the conqueror. I've travelled the continent, studied at university, and been privy to the counsel of kings and queens. Who are you to speak to me this way?"

Quinton's expression didn't waver. "Your grandson."

The heavy silence which fell over the room at those words could have crushed a plough horse. Hugh waited with bated breath to see what the viscount would say in response. He wouldn't be surprised if they were escorted out immediately.

"I can't deny my eldest son was your father, though I wish I could." Lord Coleville's tone could have cut through steel. "But I do object to any legal right you have in my life. Graham's poor choices should not be able to derail his family's life from beyond the grave. Now, I am not an unfair man. I am willing to offer you a sizable settlement. But it is conditional on you never attempting to exercise this claim again."

The younger Lord Coleville's expression was strained as his father spoke, but he stayed silent. Hugh wondered if he'd always been a coward or if his father's domineering personality had smothered whatever individuality he might have once had.

If the viscount had thought this speech would put the young man in his place, he would soon find out how wrong he was. Quinton's eyes narrowed as he glared at his grandfather. "I am not some bastard you can sweep under the rug," he growled. "Though the fact you would seek to do so speaks to your own character, sir. My father and my mother were legally wed. I am your blood, and the home we sit in is my birthright. I will have what's mine. If I have to wait until your corpse grows cold in the ground to do so, so be it."

Well, Quinton certainly wasn't holding back. Hugh wasn't sure if this was the approach he had been preparing in the carriage, or if he was mirroring the older lord's aggressive disposition. Either way, tensions were rising.

"Now you listen here, you insolent wh—"

"Pardon me, Lord Coleville." Hugh cleared his throat, deciding this might be a good moment to step in. "I mean no offense, but you must understand how these things work. An eldest son will always have the right to the title, and with the entailment in place in your case, the title comes with everything. You may not like it. You may not think it's fair. But Quinton's claim isn't dependent on his choosing to pursue it. It is fact at this point. I suggest you come to terms with it."

The heavy silence fell over them again, each man sizing the other up, considering their next words. After a moment, the younger Lord Coleville stood abruptly. He grabbed a decanter from the side table, and poured the golden liquid into four glasses.

"Father, I understand this isn't what you wanted," said the younger lord as he distributed the liquor. "It's come as a shock to me as well. But let's be realistic. I have four daughters, whom I love, but Deborah is past her prime child-bearing years. Is it possible we could produce an heir? Yes. Is it likely? No. Which means when you die, everything will go to Cousin Gerald, whom I know for a fact you despise. Perhaps this whole thing is a blessing we didn't recognize at first. Wouldn't you rather your legacy was secure in Graham's own bloodline?"

Perhaps not quite the coward Hugh had judged him to be.

The viscount was silent for several moments, as if shocked by Montgomery's defiance. "What I would prefer . . ." he finally said. "Is if my son were still alive to claim his inheritance himself."

The younger Coleville sighed, swirling the whiskey in his glass. "I don't think you would."

"What?"

Hugh, too, was shocked by Montgomery's admission. He glanced at Quinton and he could see they both understood that this wasn't a fight that involved them.

"You say you want Graham back." The younger lord suddenly slammed his glass down on the table. "But when he was alive, all you did was try to change him. The two of you fought every chance you got. You blamed him for his rash, modern ideas, but it was you and your constant criticism that drove him into the arms of the actress."

"You have no idea what you're talking about." The viscount's voice grew louder with each word. "Graham made his own choices, and he brought the consequences down on his own head."

"So did you." The younger Coleville didn't shout the words, but they landed with as much force.

The viscount stood. "I don't have to sit here and be insulted in my own home."

"Yes, you do," snapped his son. "You owe it to Graham to sit here and do right by his son. *We* owe Graham that, at the very least."

It was ugly to watch, but Hugh suspected this was a fight long overdue between father and son. Old resentments, bottled up for far too long, were rising to the surface, and once they broke free there was no stopping the tidal wave.

Hugh glanced at Quinton, noticing him holding his pocket watch in his hand and running his thumb over the worn engraving. It was a familiar motion which Hugh had come to recognize as Quinton's way of calming himself. As Hugh looked back toward the tense scene unfolding before them, he realized the Viscount's gaze had also drifted to the golden watch. For a moment the old man's eyes softened, and Hugh wondered if he was perhaps picturing it in his firstborn's grasp.

The shock was still clear on the older man's face, but after a moment's hesitation, he returned to his seat.

Montgomery took a deep breath. "I know you loved Graham. But you made mistakes with him you can never take back." Montgomery glanced at Quinton. "And now you have a second chance to do the right thing. If you squander it, I know you'll regret it for the rest of your life."

There was a long moment of silence. Hugh didn't know which way the old codger would go.

"Give the boy a tour of the estate." With those final words, the viscount left the room, a black cloud following in his wake.

Hugh and Quinton exchanged a glance.

The younger lord let out a deep sigh and took a swallow of his whiskey. "With my father, that is the closest you'll receive to his blessing . . . for now." He leaned back, the fight with his father having clearly taken a toll. Hugh said nothing, letting the man take a breath as Hugh collected his thoughts.

To his surprise, Quinton spoke up. "Actually, Lord Coleville, it's a better start than I expected." Quinton raised his glass. "To reconciliation, wherever we may find it."

There was a brief moment of hesitation before Hugh and Montgomery both joined Quinton in his toast. As he downed the last of his whiskey, Hugh found himself strangely proud of the man Quinton was becoming.

Chapter Forty-Four

This whole thing is exceedingly odd.

That was the dominant thought in Zoe's mind as she entered the tea house. The small establishment was hardly the Twinings she was used to, but it was respectable and charming enough. The place was surprisingly busy, with patrons sat at tables pushed too close together, partaking of piles of little sandwiches and scones with clotted cream and carrying on lively conversations which all blended together into an indecipherable chattering.

Unable to keep her hands still, she smoothed the light muslin of her dress underneath the heavy cloak, suppressing a shiver. When dressing, Zoe had chosen the day gown impulsively. It was far too cold this time of year to be wearing such a light dress, even if it was long sleeved. Not to mention it was two seasons old, but she knew the cut was particularly flattering on her, and the dark blue jewel tone complimented her eyes. The choice had been driven both by vanity and sentimentality. This is what she had been wearing when she'd first met Quinton—though she doubted he would remember.

This morning he had sent Ezra with a note, inviting Zoe to take tea with him that afternoon. The note was not in itself odd, but what was strange was that the invitation didn't extend to Mary, or any other member of the household. Whatever he wanted to discuss, he wanted to do so in private.

As her gaze roamed over the room, she finally located him on the far side. He had secured a table apart from the others in a window alcove—as close to a private area as one could achieve in a public area. Quinton hadn't spotted her yet; he was sitting exceptionally still, his pensive gaze fixed straight ahead as if one of the cucumber sandwiches had personally offended him. Clearly whatever was on his mind was occupying a great deal of space. Would she, perhaps, finally be told what that was?

As she made her way over to the table, he caught sight of her. Rising quickly to his feet, Quinton took her cloak and hung it on a nearby hook. As his knuckles lightly brushed against her shoulders, Zoe swallowed hard and stepped away.

"Thank you," she muttered as Quinton pulled a chair out for her.

After he sat back down, a girl came over to pour their tea. The wait was agonizing to Zoe as the dark liquid slowly filled each cup.

"Do ye need anythin' else?" the girl asked.

"No." It came out a little louder and harsher than Zoe had intended. She swallowed again, and attempted to moderate her tone. "No, thank you. That will be all for now."

Once the hovering pretence departed, Zoe expectantly turned her attention back to Quinton. She wanted to blurt out her questions, demanding an explanation for his behaviour, but she resisted her natural inclination, instead waiting for him to initiate the conversation. Surely he would not have invited her here unless he had something important to discuss.

After a long pause—during which Zoe wanted to peel the skin from off her bones—he finally spoke. "Do you ever think about your father?"

It seemed she was wrong.

"My father?" said Zoe, stalling for time while she backpedalled in her mind. This wasn't where she had been expecting this conversation to go, and the mention of her father set her back on her heels. "I suppose I think about him occasionally," she said, unsure of what Quinton was looking for exactly.

Quinton pursed his lips, his gaze still avoiding her own. "What do you remember about him?"

"Well, I was quite young the last time I saw him. I remember his laugh, and the feel of his hand in mine as we walked through the garden. But the few memories I have are clouded by the innocence of youth and the passage of time. In my mind he was a larger-than-life presence that brought comfort and joy, but I can no longer picture his face at all. Besides which, as an adult I have come to terms with the reality that he was not a perfect man. He was as good a father as he was able, but he had many flaws as well." Zoe paused in her rambling, fearing she had overshared. "Why do you ask?"

Sitting back with a sigh, Quinton seemed to gather his thoughts as he looked out the window. The light streaming through caught the angles of his features, illuminating his face as if he was one of the angels they spoke about in church. He really had no right to be as blasted handsome as he was.

"I've been thinking about fathers quite a bit lately," he began. "Mine, to be specific."

He paused, and Zoe thought she might scream. *Get to the point already!* He also had no right to be as infuriating as he was.

"I don't remember anything about him." Quinton shook his head slightly. "Not a scent, or a feeling, or even a hazy image. He's just a blank spot in my life. I know what my mother told me—that he was a wonderful and kind man, and she had loved him and he loved her, but I've never been able to corroborate her version of events myself. I just accepted it as what she needed to believe, and whether it was true or not, it didn't really affect my life very much."

Zoe said nothing, waiting for him to continue. Quinton wasn't one to share very much about his past—this was the most she'd ever heard him speak about his father. She still wasn't sure where he was going with it, but she didn't want to interrupt.

After a brief pause he continued, "The only fact I have ever been completely certain about in regard to my father is that the relationship he carried on with my mother was not sanctioned by the church."

She had heard this part before. When Theo had offered to help him find out about his heritage a little over a year ago, Quinton had given a similar speech. He was a bastard by birth. It was an immovable fact, regardless of his parents' feelings for each other. There was only so far an illegitimate child could reach, and he had chosen not to learn anything further. Zoe would not have chosen the same in his place, but she did understand his reasoning. He had felt there was little to gain by the knowledge other than resentment, and she couldn't say he was entirely wrong.

"In my world, being a bastard didn't really affect me much. Bloodlines don't matter so much for actresses' sons. I didn't give it much thought . . . until recently." Quinton's gaze finally met hers, an indecipherable emotion smouldering in his dark brown eyes. "Until I met you."

Zoe's breath caught in her throat, her chest suddenly tight. Was he saying what she thought he was saying? Her mind flashed back to her conversation with Mary. Her response could dictate the rest of her life. What should she say?

"Quinton, I—"

He held up a hand. "Let me finish, please."

Ah. So there was more. Zoe didn't take well to being interrupted, but in this case she would allow it. She needed a few moments to gather her own thoughts.

"I'm a practical man. I may brush shoulders with those in social circles higher than my own, but I've always understood the reality that belonging in those circles was beyond my grasp. Like it or not, that is the way world works." Quinton paused, taking a deep breath. "You're a part of those higher circles. It's where you and your family belong."

Wait . . . this wasn't going in the direction Zoe had thought.

"Whatever my personal feelings, I would never put you in a position where you'd have to choose. I would never betray your stepfather's trust in me by compromising your place in society." He took another breath, his gaze once again drifting out the window. "A lady and a bastard could never have a future together."

It felt as though he had punched her in the stomach, knocking what little air was left from her lungs. Zoe gripped the arms of her chair as the room appeared to spin around her. The wound on her wrist ached from the pressure, but she couldn't let go. If she let go, she feared the spinning would swallow her alive.

"What are you saying?" she managed to grit out.

"I just want you to understand my position. My feelings—"

"Oh, I think you've made your feelings and your position clear." Zoe blinked back tears—she wouldn't give him the satisfaction. She put her napkin on the table and stood, the realization dawning on her that she hadn't drunk any of the tea.

"Wait, Zoe—"

"I don't need to hear anymore." This time it was she who raised her hand, cutting him off. "My stepfather's trust? Really, Quinton? What about my trust—what about my right to choose my own life?" Zoe shook her head. "I do appreciate you taking the time to tell me to my face. And maybe you're right—maybe you and I couldn't have a future together. I guess we'll never know. But just so you're aware, I would have chosen you, bastard or not." With those words she snatched her cloak from the hook, turning on her heel and striding toward the door, leaving the most infuriating man she'd ever met sitting alone.

It wasn't until the door had closed behind her that Zoe allowed the tears she'd been holding back to fall.

Chapter Forty-Five

Zoe cried herself to sleep that night and moped around the house in a foul mood for the next two days. It wasn't until the morning of the third that she felt the full humiliation of her interaction with Quinton. That was when Simone finally informed her about the ball Theo had arranged that night—and its purpose, which was to introduce Quinton as a titled member of society.

After hearing the full story, Zoe had at first refused to attend, furious that everyone else had been in on the truth except for her, and that she had made a fool of herself in front of Quinton without knowing all the facts that everyone else had been privy to. But eventually Hugh had convinced her to come along, after a great deal of grovelling and negotiating.

As Zoe stood in Theo's grand ballroom, she felt the energy of the room, abuzz with anticipation. It wasn't every day that a long-lost member of the nobility was introduced to society, and even more tantalizing an eligible bachelor with a title and a fortune in his future. Zoe herself felt little other than burning fury towards the man.

If she was being truthful with herself, that wasn't entirely true. She was angry—at Quinton, at her family, but mostly at herself. Zoe had meant what she said. She would have taken Quinton as he was without a title or estate. But at the root of that anger was uncertainty. Now she wasn't sure if he would take her after her outburst. Suddenly he had all the options in the world, and Zoe didn't know where his heart lay.

Suddenly the ballroom went silent, and Zoe turned to see the focus of the event enter. As loathe as she was to admit it, he did look impeccable. His suit was from Weston, and it fit him perfectly, showing off his excellent physique and broad shoulders.

The mothers and daughters of society immediately began to circle, sensing fresh blood in the hunt. If only they knew Quinton as Zoe did—the bad-tempered version who drank too much and lacked basic communication skills on any subject of depth. And yet, as Quinton smiled charmingly at a petite blond girl whom Zoe recognized as his newfound cousin, Ivy, Zoe felt something ugly rising within her.

Was she actually . . . jealous? What a childish reaction. Quinton could speak and smile at whomever he wished. Zoe blinked back tears, turning away so quickly she nearly ran smack into Mary.

Her friend eyed her with that innate knowledge they had always shared. "I believe your hair could use attention, my lady? Care to come upstairs so it can be addressed?"

Zoe knew her hair was, in fact, absolutely artful, but she appreciated the reprieve. Her lady's maid, Camille, had learned from the best. The girl had recently begun adding her own touch, allowing the curls a bit of freedom on top of Zoe's head, lending a whimsical and pleasing look. A few tendrils carefully framed Zoe's face, cleverly contrived to look as if they had escaped but in fact part of the overall plan.

As she turned to follow Mary, Zoe caught the eye of a familiar figure. Mabel Anderson smiled at her, raising her glass in acknowledgment. Zoe cursed inwardly—she had sent a letter of apology to her friend, but she still needed to make amends in person. She made a mental note to seek her out again later in the evening.

Mabel did look exceptionally pretty that night. She still wore the lavender colour of half mourning, but the cut favoured her lack of curves, and her green eyes glinted with a lightness Zoe hadn't seen in her before. While she would never be the most beautiful girl in the room, Zoe had to admit her friend was not as plain as she had once thought.

Mary led the way upstairs to Zoe's room as Zoe mused on what could be the reason for Mabel's newfound lightness. Yet another reason to re-invite her friend to tea.

Theo's large manor hosted a great many bedrooms, and this one was always set up for Zoe. As they entered, Zoe collapsed dramatically on the sofa.

"Feeling a bit out of sorts?" asked Mary, her tone unsympathetic.

"It's been all of a day since his parentage was presented to the ton, and already there's rumours of an engagement between Quinton and Ivy." Zoe's eyes flew open. "You don't think Quinton is really considering a future with his cousin, do you?"

Mary shrugged. "It makes sense when it comes to keeping the Coleville fortunes intact."

Zoe glared. "Since when do you care about the Coleville fortune? You're supposed to be on my side."

"I pay attention." Mary sat down next to her. "And I am always on your side. But perhaps, if you had told him of your feelings as I suggested days ago, this awkward situation could have been avoided."

"As it happens, I did tell Quinton that I would be willing to throw my lot in with his, but he was too busy telling me we had no future to listen," retorted Zoe, her chin held high.

"You did?" Mary's tone was sceptical. "And Quinton told you he had no feelings for you? Surely not."

"Well . . ." Zoe squirmed, her chin lowering. "He didn't

exactly say he had no feelings. He just went on and on about his honour, and how a bastard and a lady had no future."

Mary's eyes narrowed.

"When was this?"

"Three days ago. I met him privately at a tea shop, at his request."

Taking a deep breath, Mary's eyes narrowed more. "So you're saying Quinton asked to have a conversation with you in private that he did not wish to share with me, or John, or your father. And that conversation centred on the fact that he could not pursue a relationship with you if he was not born to wedded parents. Is that about right?"

A flush crept up Zoe's neck to her face. Could she have gotten things so completely wrong? Saying nothing, she risked a glance at Mary.

Shaking her head, Mary muttered under her breathe. "You may not have known Quinton was a Coleville, but Quinton has known for some weeks. If he was going on and on about how being a bastard would prevent him from pursuing you romantically, it must have been to tell you that was no longer a barrier. How did you leave it?"

Groaning, Zoe closed her eyes and let her head fall back against the sofa.

"Well that explains why you've been in such a foul mood." Mary tried unsuccessfully to smother a laugh. "You're an absolute ninny sometimes, you know that, right?"

"Yes, I am aware." Zoe had seldom felt more embarrassed. "Oh Mary, what do I do now? I believe I have made a complete shambles of this whole thing."

Wiping a tear from her eye, Mary's laughter slowed. "Oh, there's no need for dramatics. Quinton still only has eyes for you. I'm sure you'll find the words to make things right."

Zoe was less confident, but she knew Mary was correct about one thing—she needed to talk to Quinton.

As they stood and moved toward the door, Mary changed the subject. "Did you notice your friend Mabel downstairs?"

"I did. Did she do something different with her hair? She looks uncommonly pretty tonight." Zoe glanced at her friend. "Why do you ask?"

"Because I saw her engaged in a rather lively discussion with none other than your dear cousin, Alexander."

"No," Zoe gasped. "Really?"

Mary nodded conspiratorially, and Zoe thought back to the last conversation she had had with Alexander. He was definitely still Alexander. But there was a thoughtfulness that Zoe had never seen before. He said he wanted a connection. Perhaps he had already found one.

If anyone could understand the transformative effects of tragedy, it was Mabel Anderson.

Alexander could certainly do worse. Mabel on the other hand . . . well, she was a grown woman and Zoe would let her be the judge of her cousin's character.

Chapter Forty-Six

T he ballroom was an amazing sight to behold. In addition to the high ceilings and dazzling chandelier, the entire floor was covered in a beautiful chalk drawing, complete with a whimsical sun, moon, two comets, and multiple shooting stars. Quinton could not hide his amazement—and horror—as he realized the drawing would be scuffed and unrecognizable as soon as the dancing began.

"It's really a practical matter, young man," said a voice at his elbow. He turned to see the dowager Theo regarding the floor. "I can see in your face you think it's terrible waste, but the floor is quite slippery. My last ball, Lady August's daughter took quite a spill, head over ballroom slippers. It was scandalous. I personally hoped it would knock some sense into her, but the match she secured with Lord Burrows put that idea to rest."

It took Quinton longer than it should have to understand her meaning. "Ah. The chalk offers traction so the floors are less slippery." He nodded as comprehension dawned on him. "But, my lady, the entire celestial heavens? Practical?"

Dowager Dovefield smiled. "If one is going to present a lily, my boy, one should always gild it. And from now on, address me as Your Grace. It's more befitting your new station."

Quinton took the correction with good humour. If he wanted to learn to live in this world, a few stumbles were to be expected.

His smile faded as he turned towards the parlour, where the guests awaited his arrival. Lady Dovefield's home had movable walls that could allow for smaller rooms to be combined to a large ball room, and she had arranged entrance through her formal parlour.

"We arranged this ball as an introduction of sorts, of you to society," said the dowager, perhaps sensing his unease. "You will be the subject of many stares and much whispering, but it is to be expected. It's no reflection upon yourself. Stand tall, hold yourself proud, and walk in like you belong. And for heaven's sake, smile. It's a ball, not a funeral."

It was good advice. Quinton took a deep breath, squared his shoulders, and walked in, announced by Theo's butler. As the conversation died and every eye turned towards him, Quinton agreed on one thing—it didn't feel like a funeral. It felt more like he was walking into battle.

Within a few moments, the veneer of politeness came back into effect for the nobles, and conversation continued among themselves. Quinton glanced around, searching for Zoe. He needed to speak with her. Their last interaction had haunted him in the days since. He had considered many times sending a note, or simply going to her house to explain himself, but each time cowardice had won out. Thinking of his bungling of the conversation at the tea house brought a warm blush of shame to his cheeks. If only he had gotten to the point sooner—and if only Zoe had less of a quick temper. But her spirit was one of the things Quinton found most attractive about her, and he would not change it. He would just have to hope that she would accept his delayed explanation.

But that explanation would have to wait. For now he smiled at each girl who was introduced to him, and soon a petite girl with golden blonde hair stood before him, Lady Coleville at her side.

"May I present my daughter, Lady Ivy Coleville."

"My lady, it's a pleasure to make your acquaintance." Quinton bowed respectfully.

"The pleasure is mine . . . Lord Coleville," replied the girl.

Suppressing a wince at the use of his new name, Quinton returned her smile. It was going to take a while before he was used to being addressed that way.

As he glanced up, he just missed catching Zoe's eye as she turned to meet Mary, and both of them turned to leave. *Blast it all.* Quinton hoped he had not missed his opportunity to speak with her in private.

"Would you care to add to my dance card?" asked his cousin, bringing Quinton back to the moment in front of him.

"Ah, of course." Quinton hoped Ivy hadn't said anything else of import while he was distracted.

He quickly scanned the card attached to her wrist and added his name to one at random. His mother had made sure he was proficient in all the ballroom dances, and while at the time it had seemed utterly pointless, Quinton was grateful she had insisted. He was equally grateful for the refresher Simone had offered him.

"Thank you, my lord." Ivy batted her thick eyelashes. "I still have one more waltz free, if you'd care for a second dance?"

"Certainly."

Quinton allowed she was a pretty thing, with her petite frame and hazel eyes and golden locks styled in the latest fashion. The youthfulness about her didn't appeal to him. But he also didn't want to hurt her feelings, so Quinton scanned the card and absentmindedly added his name to the waltz as well.

There was no missing the speculation in her eyes. Clearly her parents had instructed her to make a good impression on him. Quinton sighed as his cousin floated past the queue of other girls waiting to speak with him. Letting her down gently wasn't a discussion he was looking forward to having, but fortunately for him, it was one that could wait. He already had one serious conversation on his mind for that evening. Quinton turned his attention to the next girl in line, while mentally rehearsing what he wanted to say to Zoe.

An hour passed in much the same way, with Quinton greeting women and then dancing and then greeting more women. Both his dances with his cousin came and went uneventfully, despite her best efforts to make conversation. All the while, Quinton scanned the crowd, searching for the dark-haired, maddening woman he wanted to find.

At the end of his second dance with Ivy Coleville, she leaned in and suggested going out to the balcony to get some air. Quinton hadn't yet looked for Zoe on the balconies, so he agreed.

They were halfway to the outside doors when Lady Dovefield appeared at his shoulder.

"Quinton, might I have a word in private?" Simone smiled at Ivy. "Pardon us, my dear."

As Simone guided him to the side of the room, she spoke softly. "For a man of the streets, Quinton, you are stunningly naive."

"What?" Quinton quickly thought back over the evening's events, wondering where he'd gone wrong. "What did I do?"

"To begin with, you danced with the Coleville girl twice."

"I did." Quinton was still trying to catch up. "She asked me to fill out two lines of her card. It seemed rude to refuse."

Lady Dovefield pinched the bridge of her nose. "Quinton, a gentleman never dances with a lady twice in the same ball unless he has intentions towards her."

Quinton's cheeks turned red. "I didn't know."

"It's not your fault; one of us should have warned you." Simone tilted her head, taking in Ivy through her side eye. "You may not have understood this, but I can tell you for certain Deborah Coleville is more than aware. Whose idea was it to leave the house?"

"Lady Ivy Coleville suggested we get some air."

"It's freezing outside, Quinton. Hardly the weather to be taking air in the pitch black." Simone shook her head. "I would guess that even now a convenient witness is lurking in the shadows, waiting for the young Lady Coleville to put herself in a compromising position with you."

"Why?" Quinton frowned. "I thought such things were scandalous in society and that a young woman could be ruined by even a whisper of such a thing?"

"Only if you refuse to marry her," countered Simone. "And being a man of honour, you would likely feel compelled. It's a dirty trick, but an old one."

Across the ballroom his cousin was quickly joined by her mother, the two of them engaged in their own hushed discussion. When the mother, Deborah, glanced up, she was met with Simone's icy glare. With the sharp turn of her heel, she grabbed her daughter's wrist and quickly departed the ballroom.

"Thank you for your assistance, Lady Dovefield." Quinton felt himself shaken, realizing he had just barely missed an entanglement that could have changed his future. His previous premonition of battle had not been far off.

"You may call me Simone." She smiled at him. "And there is no need for thanks. You are a friend of the family."

Though the words themselves were ordinary enough, Quinton knew enough about the lady to understand the weight behind them. He felt honoured that she thought so highly of him.

He cleared his throat, knowing Simone wouldn't want to dwell on the moment. "I cannot fathom that a girl like Ivy would be willing to shackle herself to someone she entrapped in marriage. How could any such union bring happiness?"

"That is because you are a man." Simone took two glasses of claret from a passing tray, handing one to him. "For someone in Ivy Coleville's situation, it's preferable to marry a man who does not want her than lose her position and her allowance. And without the backing of wealth and connections, who else would want her? She's a pretty enough girl, but not that pretty."

Quinton felt an unexpected pang of sympathy for the girl

who had so nearly ruined his life. For all he had gained, she had lost a great deal in the trade.

"I will speak with Deborah," said Simone. "This won't happen again."

"Your assistance is most appreciated, La—Simone."

As Quinton turned to go, he looked across the ball room, feeling his heart skip a beat. Zoe had finally returned. She was wearing a gown the colour of her eyes, and like her eyes, the colour of the gown rippled as she walked, bringing to his mind the sea, as her presence often did. Her dark curly hair was piled high, emphasizing her cheekbones and determined chin. She caught his eye and began to move through the crowd towards him.

The dowager was wrong. A true lily needed no gilding.

As Quinton met her on the edge of the ballroom, Zoe immediately saw a change in his demeanour. An easy assurance she had not seen before filled him. He took her by the arm, guiding her to a private enclave. The room around them was full of colour and motion, but Zoe felt as though none of it existed. They were the only two who mattered.

Zoe took a breath, having rehearsed what she wanted to say. But just as she was about to speak, Quinton took a step closer, closing the already small gap between them. His brown eyes met hers with an intensity that made Zoe lightheaded, and as he leaned in toward her, she was overwhelmed by the surprising scent of red wine on his breath. Time seemed to speed up and stand still at the same moment, and Zoe's mind felt for the first time in her life completely blank.

Suddenly a shout from across the ballroom broke the spell between them. Both took a step back, faces flushed, as they look in the direction of the commotion.

Several footmen were rushing to the parlour adjacent to the far edge of the ballroom, and most concernedly, she saw her mother standing stock still. Zoe followed her gaze, a deep sense of dread coming over her when she saw what had so shocked her mother.

Lady Theodosia Bexley was lying motionless on the floor of the parlour.

Zoe immediately raced across the floor, but the guests blocked her path as they began to crowd around. "Get out of my way!" she snapped, icy fingers of terror wrapped around her heart.

A few tried to move, but her demands were lost in the rising volume of panicked voices. Suddenly she felt a presence by her side. Quinton took her arm firmly and began to push his way through the crowd, using his size to his advantage to forge a path. After what seemed like an eternity, Theo came back into view.

Hugh was already there, murmuring Theo's name as he knelt next to her, and Alexander appeared beside him, face ashen. Theo had always had a soft spot for her nephew, and he for her.

Zoe sank to her knees beside her aunt, searching for signs of life and terrified she would find none. How old was Theo? Zoe wasn't sure, just somewhere in her sixties. Did people drop dead for no reason after a certain age? Zoe knew her thoughts made no sense, but she didn't know how to think rationally in that moment.

Finally Theo's eyes fluttered slightly, and relief washed over Zoe in a wave strong enough to drown her. Hugh drew his sister up into his arms, lifting her from the ground. The crowd moved out of his way, and he quickly whisked her up the stairs, Alexander following close behind.

The guests glanced at each other, unsure of what to do next.

"Ladies and gentlemen, we apologize for the abrupt ending to tonight's festivities." The voice of authority belonged to her mother. Simone still appeared shaken, but she had recovered enough to take over Theo's duties as host. "Unfortunately, this is now a time for family. Please take your leave at the earliest convenience."

The crowd started to shift, though there was no great exodus.

Quinton still stood at Zoe's side. She found his presence more comforting than she could express.

Not long after, Simone made her way over to them. The elegance with which she always carried herself was still there, but Zoe could see her hands were shaking, just slightly.

"You and your mother should go up with Theo," said Quinton suddenly. "I'll make sure the guests are seen out."

A deep gratefulness shone in Simone's eyes as she nodded. "Thank you, Quinton. Could you please ask the cook to send up broth and tea to the bedchamber, as well as a repast for Lady Bexley's sitting room? This may be a very long night for all of us. Oh, and have her butler send for the doctor, if he hasn't already done so."

Quinton inclined his head. "Of course. And there's no need for thanks. You are friends of my family as well."

An understanding seemed to pass between the two of them, and Simone gave him a slight smile. Zoe wondered what that was about, but it wasn't a prudent time to ask. As Simone headed toward the stairs, Zoe followed, although she spared a parting glance over her shoulder at Quinton, who was already busying himself with the task at hand.

As if out of the mist, Mary popped beside her. "I have never met anyone as ready to face what comes as Lady Theo. Let's not find ourselves looking down paths that won't need to be walked. She wouldn't hold to it."

Zoe nodded numbly, knowing in her heart that Mary was right. She also felt a bit guilty, because as terrified as she was for Theo, there was also a part of her that was still thinking about a certain interrupted kiss.

Chapter Forty-Seven

Despite having requested the repast, her mother appeared to have no interest in the food. Zoe did not blame her. Quinton and Mary, however, had no such trouble reducing the chunks of cheese and meat, crusty bread, fruit, and cake to nothing but crumbs within the hour. Likely realizing Zoe hadn't eaten at all during the ball, Mary tried to get her to nibble on a piece of cheese, but Zoe couldn't seem to force it down her throat. Her mother, though clearly just as distressed, was a more practical creature and so did manage to choke down a few bits of fruit and some sweetened tea.

As her tea grew tepid, Zoe found herself reflecting on Simone's relationship with Aunt Theo.

During the early days in their inclusion into the Dovefield family, the only solace Zoe had found from her childish anger was in the company of Aunt Theo. But now, as Zoe reflected back on those times with the clear eyes of hindsight, she remembered the look of warmth on the elder woman's face as she greeted Simone. When Zoe would stay at Theo's for a few days, revelling in the welcome she felt there, Simone was the one who would drop her off and take tea in the library with Theo, visiting while Zoe raced off to settle into her room.

As her young self had wandered back, hoping her mother was gone, Zoe remembered often hearing peals of merriment coming from the sitting room, more than once entering to see her mother wiping away tears of laughter, brought about by some story Theo had told. Now, for the first time, she thought about how relaxed Simone had been there, at Theo's house. Clearly amid what must have been a tumultuous time for Simone as well, her mother had found a friend. That friendship had simply deepened over the years, though Zoe had not noticed its growth.

Simone didn't have many in the way of friends. Certain women of society she associated with, but she was a private woman, having survived all these years by building the walls around her heart high. Few had been able to scale them, with one of the exceptions being Theo. The fear in Simone's eyes at the possibilities before them made Zoe's own blood run cold.

What would become of either of them if they did not have Theo Bexley to lean on?

Attempting to offer some comfort, Zoe took her mother's hand in her own—at least they were not alone in their fear. But as the minutes continued to tick by at a shockingly slow rate, Zoe found herself nodding off, which was not surprising as it was now the wee hours of the morning.

She awakened sharply when the door suddenly opened. Alexander entered the room, exhaustion clinging to his body and weighing down his shoulders. Zoe could not tell from his demeanour if the news was good or bad.

"Well?" she demanded.

"The doctor has done a thorough exam. It seems Aunt Theo suffered an apoplexy." Alexander made his way slowly to the chair near Zoe and sat carefully, as if he had aged three decades in the span of the night. He continued carefully, no doubt repeating what Hugh had told him to say. "Dr. Carlton has treated Aunt Theo with bloodletting, and she has recovered enough to speak briefly. At this time she is having trouble forming her words and has some drooping on her left side. It remains to be seen if she can walk, although she was able to raise both her arms."

He paused to take a deep breath. "Dr. Carlton says a full recovery is possible, but he cannot say it is probable at her age. Some people do regain full movement and speech, others remain compromised. Only time will tell us which of these is Aunt Theo. But her life does not seem in danger for now."

A collective sigh filled the room as Alexander closed his eyes.

"Thank the Lord," Zoe said softly, her body finally relaxing. As long as Theo had breath left in her body, she would fight. That was all that mattered to Zoe.

"Thank you, Lord Dovefield, for letting us know." Quinton's authoritative tone was unmistakable. "Please make sure Lady Bexley is aware of each of our concerns and hopes for a full recovery."

Alexander opened his eyes and a smile touched his lips. "Are you dismissing me, *Lord Coleville?*"

"Don't be ridiculous," huffed Quinton.

"Well you do outrank me now, so it's within your prerogative—"

"I meant no disrespect—"

"Relax, Huxley." Alexander's use of Quinton's mother's name had a soft note to it. "I am only having a bit of fun with you."

Quinton's brow furrowed. Zoe wondered if he would snap at her cousin or put him in his place. But after a moment, he relaxed back into his own chair. "Quinton. You might as well start using my first name."

"Alexander."

If someone had told Zoe the two men would be on peaceful —if not friendly terms—a week ago, she would have laughed in their face. She shook her head, not quite believing it herself. Her cousin glanced at her, and Alexander's next words stunned her. "I expect we shall all be family soon enough."

Startled for a moment, Quinton then laughed. He turned to her and drew her to her feet. "Speaking of which."

He led her to the opposite side of the room, escaping the amused whispers of the room's other occupants, and Zoe opened her mouth to speak.

"Just this once, Lady Demas, hear me out."

Staring into his soulful brown eyes, all else seemed to fade away, and Zoe smiled. "Just this once."

Taking both her hands in his, Quinton took a deep breath before speaking. "I am not perfect by any means, but I do feel I am a man of honour. I have been in love with you since the day you tackled a large man with a club to save a particularly ugly dog, though I did not know it then. I have never known any woman with the fire and conviction and downright stubbornness that lives within you. You surprise me every time we are together, equal parts enchanting and maddening. But before now, I had nothing to offer a lady, and I refused to bring you down to my level."

Sensing the words on the tip of her tongue, Quinton held up a finger.

"I know you were willing to throw your lot in with mine, and for that I love you all the more. And you are right—class and status should not matter in affairs of the heart. But they do. In the world in which we live, they do. Maybe it was my own pride as much as my regard for your well-being, but I had resigned myself to a life apart from you. But, as I tried to tell you at the tea shop, things have changed now. We are equals in the eyes of the ton. I now have the means to offer you what I have always wanted to offer. You have always held my heart, Zoe. I want you to hold my name as well, and a place next to me for the remainder of my days."

After a slight pause, Quinton spoke his final words, seeming as lost in her eyes as she was in his. "I want you as my wife."

As Quinton had been speaking, a warmth had bloomed in Zoe's chest. These were the words she had longed to hear. Freedom wasn't free, and if the price for hers was to be bound to

Quinton for the rest of her days, then it was a price she would gladly pay.

"Then you shall have me."

Dropping one of her hands, Quinton placed his hand at the back of her neck, his fingers intertwining with her hair as he pulled her closer. When his lips touched hers, Zoe closed her eyes and leaned into the kiss, both lost in the moment and desperately trying to remember every detail.

The sound of applause and a bawdy cheer from Mary interrupted the magic, and they broke apart. Blushing, Zoe turned back to the small audience she had forgotten were watching. Silent tears streamed down Simone's face, but Mary just grinned, her demeanour infuriatingly self-satisfied. Once the couple had made their way back over to them, Mary enveloped her in a hug tight enough to cause a person to lose consciousness, before moving on to Quinton. Alexander hugged her as well, before clapping Quinton on the back.

Simone moved to her side and gently touched her shoulder, the smile upon her face letting Zoe know her tears were not from sadness. "Quinton asked for permission from Hugh and I days ago. You have our blessing."

Those words meant almost as much to Zoe as Quinton's had. Zoe wrapped her own arms around her mother, so happy in the moment she thought she might burst.

Her hot temper had gotten the best of her that day at the tea house, and probably would again. But as Zoe turned and caught Quinton's eye, she saw only love and warmth within them. No one was more aware of her nature than Quinton. They would find a way.

Love always found a way.

Epilogue

TWO MONTHS LATER

Quinton allowed his coat and scarf to be taken and reflected upon how the house was beginning to feel familiar. As he was announced in the large sitting room upstairs, his eyes sought out Zoe's first, as always, but then quickly found Theo Bexley. She was seated near the fire with a blanket over her legs and looked years older. But when she raised her eyes they still were still sharp, with her usual glint of humour.

"Still around to make trouble, I assure you, Lord Coleville." Theo said with a smile as he approached her and greeted her formally. The left side of her mouth still drooped, making her smile seem strangely off centre, but her words were clear.

This was the first time he had seen her since her apoplexy two months previous, but he'd had regular updates from both Zoe and Hugh—and occasionally Alexander. Quinton's membership at White's was his own now, rather than a gift from a guilty uncle, and the difference was evident in the level of service he received. It surprised no one more than Quinton when Alexander had begun to seek him out, but as he got to know him, he found he formed a certain friendship of sorts with the young man. Alexander had curtailed his more questionable behaviours, though the young lord did enjoy the whiskey and gaming tables at White's, still often staying until the wee hours of the morning. After a few whiskeys, the young Lord Dovefield was very talkative, particularly about his new attachment to a certain Mabel Anderson. A chance encounter at Zoe's and a conversation about loss had sparked an interest in both of them.

Those late evenings speaking with Alexander at White's were a welcome break from the planning of his own wedding. He and Zoe had agreed to postpone the event until Theo was able to attend, and Lady Bexley had wasted no time in doing so. She was now able to walk with assistance, and her speech was improved to almost indiscernible from before the event.

Joining Zoe on the settee, Quinton felt satisfaction at the warmth of her body next to his. He did not believe he could possibly be happier, though he did long to hold her in his arms without the eyes of their friends and family upon them. Only three more weeks and she would be his wife and they could finally be alone together. He glanced at her, wondering if the twinkle in her eyes meant her mind was wandering down similar paths.

His most pleasant reverie was interrupted by the arrival of John and Savita. Although he never truly doubted a resolution would be reached, Quinton had been relieved when John confided in him that the couple had found a compromise and made amends. Shortly afterwards they announced wedding plans, both eager to start the next chapter of their lives. Quinton had never seen Charlie prouder than when he walked his sister down the aisle, while Quinton had been equally pleased to stand by John as the couple exchanged vows. The couple had also reached another compromise on a blend of traditional British and Hindu wedding customs. The red and gold sari Katy had loving crafted looked beautiful on her daughter, suiting Savita perfectly. It had been a joyous occasion, and Quinton couldn't be more pleased for the two of them. They had been married almost a month now, and both glowed with joy. It was a good match, as the nobles would say. They found their seats on the sofa, sitting pleasantly close to each other, chatting intelligently with Theo before turning their attention to Quinton and Zoe.

"We have finished the inner wall separating a portion of the room off," said John. "Savi is making it into a proper bedroom, with a door to the rest of the house. She plans to add to the kitchen next since we have no use for the office space."

Savi smiled. "The home suits us perfectly. And Ezra has been such a help with his knowledge of plastering. He has repaired several holes and also helped with the added wall."

Having moved into a secondary Coleville property near the Dovefields, Quinton had gifted his old residence to John and Savita as a wedding present. Though he had the right to the larger manor Montgomery and his family currently occupied, he had decided to allow them to continue their residence. Their lives had been put into enough turmoil without losing their home as well.

As for Quinton, the smaller property was still huge by his standards, and close enough for both Zoe and himself to easily spend time with Hugh and Simone. Even Oscar had settled into her new life and was enjoying being spoiled by the cook he'd hired.

"How is Ezra adapting to life at his new school?" asked John.

Quinton laughed. "He is adapting. I visited him last week and though he had some complaints, he was overall in good spirits. I think he has enjoyed being around others like himself."

When Quinton had brought up Braidwood Academy—a school which specialized in teaching deaf children—to Ezra, he hadn't seen the boy again for three days. But eventually he had convinced Ezra to visit, and Quinton had immediately seen how engaged the boy was with the other young people. Although it went against his independent nature, Ezra agreed to allow Quinton to pay for one year of schooling. It was a boarding school, so he lived on site, but Quinton popped in regularly to check on him, and Ezra was allowed to visit on holidays.

"Gwen misses him, but she's looking forward to the holiday when he will visit." Zoe took a bite from a dainty cucumber sandwich. "I am interviewing tutors for her this week. They must be skilled in mathematics, as Gwen has a head for numbers."

Quinton could not agree more. He glanced over at the girl, who was sitting on the floor across the room with Brutus by her side, absentmindedly petting his massive head. Zoe's younger siblings—who up until that point Quinton had forgotten existed—were also there. Normally children wouldn't be allowed at a social gathering, but since this was a family affair, Hugh and Simone must have decided to make an exception. Pheobe sat on the other side of the beast, chatting away enthusiastically about something, Walter stood a few feet away—Quinton suspected the fourteen-year-old thought sitting on the floor was beneath his dignity as he neared adulthood—but close enough to still overhear. When Pheobe finally stopped speaking and Gwen opened her mouth to reply, Walter took a step closer, clearly very intent on hearing her response. Quinton had to wonder if there was something more there.

A commotion at the door of the sitting room drew the group's attention, and moments later Charlie and Katy came through.

"It is the custom to let the butler take your coat. Do you really think the man would steal it? He works for Lady Bexley." Katy all but cuffed Charlie across his head, but Charlie would have none of it.

"No one takes my coat from me, *maa*. No one," snapped Charlie, clearly already sweating in the heavy overcoat. "He should have stepped back after his first attempt."

Rory came last, dressed impeccably, with his tailored waistcoat fitting perfectly again and his beard neatly trimmed. More important was the subtle shift in the way Rory stood. His confidence was back, and when he smiled it reached his eyes. After greeting Theo warmly, Rory stopped to chat privately to Charlie, their heads together. To Quinton's surprise Charlie laughed out loud and Rory looked pleased. Looking around, Quinton noticed Mary also watching the two men and looking equally pleased.

Whatever had transpired between them, it seemed to be to everyone's satisfaction.

Looking around at the group of people, Quinton felt content. Finding out truths in his own life this past year had not set him free, as truths were want to do. If anything, knowing his heritage and unearthing old secrets had tethered him more than freed him. But it was like a boat adrift in a storm finally finding refuge in port, tethered to the landing. The bonds of his life had anchored him to a path he was excited to explore.

Quinton suddenly felt compelled to raise his glass. "A toast, to Lady Bexley, and to many years ahead with her by our side."

The others raised their glasses as well, and murmurs of agreement could be heard about the room. The lady herself scoffed. "Oh enough of that. I am truly tired of all the fuss over me."

Light laughter filled the room, but any who knew her couldn't be surprised. The group returned to mingling, taking the offered drink and small bites.

The only awkward air in the room was between John and Charlie. It had lessened in the two months since Lydia's disappearance, but there was no mistaking the lingering discomfort between the two men.

Quinton knew Charlie was not one to live with regrets and had remained unapologetic for whatever part he had played in Lydia's escape. On the other side, John was a man of principle. He wasn't one to hold a grudge, but he also wasn't one to easily forgive once his trust had been broken. Quinton could understand both points of view and had stayed carefully neutral. He suspected they would soon repair their friendship—if not for their own sake, then for Savita's.

As people naturally paired off into smaller groups to converse, Quinton found himself with Zoe, Charlie, John, Savita, and Rory. The conversation naturally drifted toward the events of two months previous.

"I do wonder at Lydia's past," murmured Rory. "What tragedies influenced her fall into darkness?"

"According to the lady's maids we talked to, Lydia was accused of stealing and let go without references. Worse yet, it was rumoured the lady of the house had sold the jewellery herself and then dismissed Lydia," answered Zoe.

"An injustice to be sure, but enough to push her into the kind of woman who would steal and cheat and kill to earn her bread?" Quinton shook his head. "I doubt it."

"Perhaps." Rory took a sip of his scotch which Theo kept on hand for him. "But the same injustice can befall two people and affect each of them very differently. In Lydia's case, this injustice may have broken her thread of morality, allowing her to do whatever was needed to rise above."

"She need not have starved." John stared into his whiskey, his expression unreadable. "With her needlework skill, she could have found employment with a tailor or seamstress. It was her choice to do what she did, and no one else's. And we will never know how far her reach was. We caught up to the bodyguard, drunk in a pub. It didn't take much for him to corroborate what we already knew, as well as fill in a few blanks. He confirmed it was indeed her doing to have Alexander scared stiff in White's, in the hopes that he'd break things off with Katie before she told him the truth. The man who did that was long gone by the time we tracked him, but it was a friend of one of Lydia's serving girls who worked at the club."

"We cannot know what her life would have looked like if she had taken a different path," countered Charlie. "We do not know her whole history, or what other tragedies she suffered."

Silence fell as the two men eyed each other, but after a moment, Savita caught John's eye and he seemed to relax, taking her hand in his own with a soft smile. A good sign for things to come.

"How has Finn been settling in?" asked Savita, clearly attempting to change the subject.

"He is doing well." Charlie nodded toward his mother, who was across the room deep in conversation with Simone. "Mother's been teaching him his letters and numbers, and he's a quick one for being only eight years old."

The boy was an unexpected addition to Charlie's home. Shortly after the situation with Lydia had been settled—at least to Charlie's satisfaction—he had appeared with young Finn in tow. His friend had offered little in the way of explanation, but Quinton had noted the obvious resemblance between the boy and a certain deceased Irishman. It seemed the boy's mother had had an influence as well, as Finn's hair was dark and he could reasonably be described as handsome.

The timing worked out well, as once Savi was married, Katy had decided to cut back on her midwife work. She would still pop in from time to time if Simone needed her at the Haven, but she was now content to leave most of the midwife services to her well-trained daughter. After decades of providing for her family, Katy was ready to step back and assist Charlie in caring for the child.

"He is a sharp lad," said Rory. "I've taken it upon myself to introduce him to the important things in life. As Julius Caesar said, 'A friend should bear his friend's infirmities.' Charlie can offer much, but the boy's literary sense shall have to come from me."

The group laughed, but Quinton found himself wondering what the boy's future did hold. When he had asked Charlie about his plans for Finn, all Charlie had said was that the future had a way of taking care of itself. And Quinton knew that the boy had a tribe to guide him, not just Charlie. The boy would love Shakespeare and spicy curry to be sure.

As the conversation played itself out, each of them drifted back off to join others. Rory and Theo started an animated conversation about a recently opened play that neither had seen but both somehow still had strong opinions on. As they cheerfully argued, the three younger women started to discuss yet another wedding detail that made Quinton's head ache just thinking about. He rose to replenish his glass, finding Hugh had beaten him to the table.

"Your life has changed dramatically, but you seem to have found your way through to the other side." Hugh gestured at the room. "Family intact."

"With no small thanks to you, sir," said Quinton sincerely. "I could never have managed this alone."

"I have every confidence you would have, but it was my pleasure to help." Hugh took a sip from his glass. "It will be good, once you have returned from your honeymoon and everything is settled. I think you will find the life of a nobleman will suit you."

Quinton wasn't so sure. He knew he was expected to leave his days as an agent behind, since it was considered crass for a gentleman to earn a living. But Quinton feared that without purpose, he would lose his mind with boredom.

"Do you think there's any room for compromise in the life of a gentleman?" asked Quinton.

"In what way?"

"Well, you seem to have found a balance, between your passion as a barrister and your duties as a member of the gentry." Quinton paused. "Do you think it will be possible for me to find such a balance?"

Hugh eyed him from the side, his expression amused. "I was going to wait until you had returned to broach the subject, but as a matter of fact, I have been approached discreetly by more than one person within your new social circle to inquire if your services would be available." Hugh patted him on the back. "It seems your reputation has preceded you. And we both know Zoe is impossible when she finds herself bored. When you and she return, let me know your thoughts."

Hugh turned away with a smile to join in Rory and Theo's increasingly animated debate, leaving Quinton to consider what his future held. He found his eyes wandering over to where his wife-to-be sat. As she looked up to meet his gaze, Quinton reflected that Charlie was right about one thing.

The future would take care of itself.

About the Authors

Sandra and Taylor Preisler share a love of reading and writing, an obsession with foster kittens, and of course, DNA. *The Truths That Tether* is the mother daughter duo's third novel in their Q&Z Regency Mystery series. While both are from Casper, Wyoming, Taylor now lives in Phoenix, Arizona with her sister, roommate, a Pit Bull, and probably some of those pesky fosters. Sandra and her husband Ken split their time between beautiful Wyoming and equally beautiful Arizona. Their two cats love the change every time and have never complained.

f facebook.com/sandraandtaylorpreisler

⊙ instagram.com/taylor_and_sandra_preisler

Other Books in the Q&Z Regency Mystery Series

www.ingramcontent.com/pod-product-compliance
Lightning Source LLC
Chambersburg PA
CBHW020126120726
47903CB00007B/2119